Mine

Susan Curran was born in Aylesbury and read English at the University of Sussex before working in insurance and computing. She published her first book in 1979, and has written and co-written sixteen books on computing and new technology, plus numerous reviews, articles and a couple of word processor manuals. In 1987 she fulfilled a lifelong ambition by turning to fiction, since when she has published romances, historical novels (*The Mouse God* and *The Heron's Catch*) a contemporary novel (*Mrs Forster*) and a guidebook for aspiring writers, *How to Write a Book and Get it Published.*

She lives in Norwich with her sons Rufus and Evan, and is a Labour member of Norwich City Council.

Mine

Susan Curran

RAMPANT HORSE

First published in Great Britain in 1994
by Rampant Horse Limited
140 Whitehall Road Norwich Norfolk NR2 3EW

Set in 11 pt Times Roman
Cover concept: Tim Bartlett/The Advertising Works
Cover design: Susan Curran; photography Julian Swainson/Susan Curran

A CIP catalogue record for this book is available from the British Library
ISBN 1-898839-50-6 hard cover
1-898839-00-X soft cover

Printed and Bound by Bookcraft Ltd, Midsomer Norton, Avon.

Acknowledgements

I could not have written this book without the detailed advice provided to me by Stephen Hague of the City Engineer's Department, Norwich City Council. I'm also grateful for help and advice from Inspector Chris Warren of Norfolk Constabulary, Alan Brown, Ron Manwaring, Brenda Ferris, Kate Morgan, Robert Short and Eamonn Burgess. Any factual mistakes are, however, down to my own failings or to dramatic requirements.

Those familiar with my home city will recognize similarities between it and Costhorpe; but Costhorpe is fictional, as are all the characters and incidents in this book.

Susan Curran
Norwich, 1994

1

THERE'S nothing like waking to the phone after a late night. The room was stale and chill, my mouth stale and hot. Grey light filtered through my bedroom blind from a grey morning. As I rolled over to fumble for the receiver, I peered at the radio alarm: just past eight o'clock.

'Erica Massen,' I murmured.

'Asleep? Get stirring.'

Nick Halton: no great surprise.

'I have an alarm clock, thanks. I set it for —'

Nick paid no attention. 'I haven't called a pre-meeting, but I'm worried about the Courdon House renovation report. Judith reckons the Tories are going to leak it. Get there early, and cling onto Canning. Make sure he doesn't get a chance to talk to Patty Fowler.'

'How am I supposed to do that?'

'Use your charm, darling.'

'On Rex? Anyway, if he doesn't leak it during the meeting he can always call —'

'Just try, eh? Sit him next to you. I'll see you at nine-thirty, darling.'

'And I'm not your —'

Darling any more, I finished, but silently, to the dialling tone. With an inward curse I swung my legs out of bed and stretched them, my arms, my back and neck. All of me was stiff from a too-short sleep after a too-long day.

Nick probably thought I'd got to bed at eleven, but habits change as partners change – or rather, go. He was the early-to-bedder, not I: and it was a small compensation for sleeping alone that I could stay up till two when I chose, and have no one nag me.

Actually it had been nearer three. Me, a slowly-emptying electric coffee pot, and a report on the Belgian car industry to translate from Dutch to English. I had a new client, the promise of good pay, and a tight deadline. Work was as hard to come by as honest statements from members of the Cabinet, so I needed to turn in a decent job on time.

I'd also needed an extra half-hour's sleep. Damn Nick for robbing me of it. It had been thoughtless too to call me darling. Okay, I hadn't been heartbroken when he'd moved on to my best friend Jenny, but that had happened barely three months ago, and it took time to adjust.

We'd sold the house we'd shared for the previous three years, split the money, and I'd bought this smaller one, with two rooms downstairs and two and a half (one led off another) up. There was no hall, you walked straight into the living room, but that was like half the houses in Costhorpe.

The bathroom was downstairs, beyond the kitchen – a drag on a February morning. I grabbed my dressing gown, slid on Turkish slippers, and headed past the elm dining table Nick and I had once chosen together. Mao-mao rubbed against my ankles, so I stopped in the kitchen to feed her.

I thought about Courdon House under the shower.

Costhorpe was a honeycomb, dripping with old buildings, many of which the City Council owned. Our beautiful headaches included the five-hundred-year-old merchant's house. It housed an arts centre which laid on fringe theatre, a comedy club, a photographic studio and modern jazz evenings. None of them made much money, and the trust that ran the place was always broke. Whatever the lease said we'd have to pay up ourselves for the urgent repairs, or we'd drive them out of business. Then Costhorpe would lose its alternative comedians, and we'd be unlikely to find another tenant.

This was nothing to apologise for, and the report coming to the Planning Committee was only confidential because it gave details of the trust's finances. Okay the repairs, and we'd issue a press statement which left out those details. However that wasn't likely to stop Rex Canning leaking the report, or Patty Fowler trying to make a scandal out of it.

We hadn't had to deal before with a reporter like Patty, who didn't care how she got her stories so long as they made the front page. Or an opposition councillor like Rex, who treated information as a corporate raider treats company assets. Insider trading was his forte. Put those two side by side at the end of a committee table, and you could watch them faxing silent messages to each other.

How could I put some static on their line?

Not with a yawn like that one. I leaned out of the spray, shower curtain clinging damply to the small of my back, and peered in the mirror over the basin. There were black circles under my eyes. I was thirty-two, and looked every day of thirty-three.

There was time to wash my hair, which always helps to wake me. I ducked back under, felt the warm water flatten it down to my skull – it's a fair frizz, which I wear long – and through the drumming in my ears, heard the phone ring again.

What did Nick want now? It was too late to change his mind about the pre-meeting, and anything else could surely wait till he saw me. I didn't want to answer him, I wanted to luxuriate in my shower. I took my head out of the jet and counted his determination, ring by ring.

Eight, and it hadn't stopped. He might have guessed why I wasn't replying. If I went to answer it, of course he'd ring off the moment I got there.

Fifteen. The stubborn idiot. I switched off the water, grabbed a towel and padded to the living room, drips from my hair running down my face, drips from my legs making a trail on the carpet.

'What is it now?'

'That the Council?'

It wasn't Nick after all, but a strange male with an accusing tone that even twenty rings and a sharp question didn't justify. I might be an elected councillor, but I wasn't a twenty-four hour emergency service.

I counted to three, and managed to pretend to be even-tempered.

'You caught me at an awkward moment. I'm Erica Massen, councillor for Hillside ward. What can I do for you?'

'There's an'ole in our kitchen.'

'What sort of a hole?'

'An 'ole in the ground. The wall's fallen down.'

HOLES in the ground are a regular problem in Costhorpe. This might be a hoax, but I couldn't risk it. I spent five minutes dialling every emergency number I could think of, and another ten scrunching my damp but unshampooed hair dry, tying it back, and putting on red tights, a grey jersey skirt, a grey jersey tunic top and a red jersey cardigan. A kagoul went over the top. Cycling's faster than a car in Costhorpe's rush-hour, but it still took me twenty minutes of drizzle and traffic fumes to get across the city to Flint Hill.

I swung off the inner ring road as the staff were arriving at the parade of shops and began, panting, to climb the hill. My shoulders were hunched against what was becoming lightly-driven rain. The paths held a thin drift of late commuters and mothers taking their kids to school.

On my left was a row of post-war council-built semis, and on my right an older terrace of larger square-bayed houses, built of a deeper red brick with white detailing. Graham Bunting had told me number thirty-three, which turned out to be a right-hand semi with a police car parked outside. The lawn was ragged-edged, splotched with bare muddy patches, and the flowerbeds looked as if nothing but weeds ever grew in them. The front door was powder blue with chrome numerals, a sign of tenants who hadn't bought their house.

A multicoloured object festooned the wrought-iron gate. I parked my bike inside the garden wall, hunched my shoulders higher and bent to look.

'Morning, councillor.'

It wasn't Mr Accusing, but the pleasant face and yellow-and-blue striped sweater of Bill Baxter that greeted me as I straightened and turned. Behind him, a policeman was emerging from the house, followed by a stocky man with brushed-back greasy hair, wearing a once-black t-shirt advertising Black Sabbath's 1988 Tour.

Bill was the Council's chalk-mine expert – I knew him because he occasionally reported to the Planning Committee.

'I suppose,' I said, 'she pulls it tight when she shuts the gate, to keep the kids in.'

'That thing for fixing suitcases onto roof-racks? Suppose so.'

'An octopus, I've always called it. Quite irrelevant – have you see the hole?'

The policeman cut in, 'Are you from Social Services?'

'No, I'm a city councillor.'

He scowled as if politician was a synonym for useless. 'Can't have you here, miss. We're evacuating the area.'

2

PROS never ask what they can do to help, they pick an congenial job and get on with it. Half-asleep amateurs like me end up humping furniture.

Not that I minded; it was useful work, it kept me busy. With a thin-faced constable I dragged Formica tables with flowered plastic cloths and red plastic three-piece cruets from left to right of Flint Hill Methodist Church Hall, which was Thirties red-brick gothic, matching the Victorian red-brick-gothic church. We set out jumble-sale trestles in the space we'd cleared. Doris Hughes, organiser of the pensioners' lunch club, pursued us from side to side, tight-mouthed, asking what we imagined her ladies would think.

They'd think it a disaster, I supposed, which was what it was.

The refugees began trickling in before we had half finished. Pensioners in drab tweed coats, harassed mothers with whining toddlers, yawning shift-workers, listless unemployed youths with sleep-bleared faces and unbrushed hair, bustling middle-aged women and gaggles of students, treating it as a lark. A few risked the Formica tables, but Mrs Hughes swept them off again; the rest settled uncomplainingly around the trestles.

The constable dropped his end of the last table onto its trestle with a thump. I let go of mine, brushed the dust off my hands and searched the room for familiar faces. Apart from Louise Hoggett from the Housing Department there was nobody I'd known more than an hour.

The atmosphere held no panic, just resignation and cigarette smoke. The urn in the kitchen was beginning to steam, and a couple of women were setting out white china cups. Two students sitting knee-to-knee in a corner had spread out their books. A tall black dreadlocked youth leaned against the wall, headphones clamped to each ear, nodding to a private rhythm.

The emergency team was fully functioning, and there were plenty of willing tea-brewers. Planning Committee would have started. I decided to check that Louise would be able to fix accommodation for anyone who wasn't allowed back by the evening, then go on to City Hall. I was heading her way when a substantial beer-belly with a Black Sabbath t-shirt strained over it moved into my path.

'Everything okay, Mr Bunting?' I asked.

Bunting was two inches shorter than I in my low-heeled black pumps. He gave me a half-uneasy, half-contemptuous upwards look, then said, 'Bloody awful, innit? Mandy's over there.'

He waved vaguely at the middle trestle, and headed towards it. I followed. Bunting stopped behind a woman with shaggily-cut streaked-blonde hair, wearing a scoop-necked black sweater which was almost submerged beneath gold chains and bangles. She had angled her plastic chair to face a tousle-haired young man in a blue blazer, who had a biro in his hand and a spiral notebook on his knee. An elbow kept the baby on her lap out of range of her cigarette, while her other hand held onto a toddler in yellow dungarees.

'This is the councillor,' Bunting said.

'Counsellor?' asked Blue-blazer, half-standing.

'With a ci. City Council,' I explained.

Mandy half-turned to me. 'I was talkin', if you don't mind.'

I forced a smile. 'I'm happy to listen.'

Bunting moved so I could stand at Mandy's shoulder. There were no free chairs. Mandy bent over to take a drag on her cigarette, and flicked the ash onto the floor.

'Like I was sayin', we didn't know nothin' till about two o'clock. I heard these noises —'

'Like what?' Blue-blazer interrupted.

'A thump, like, and a sort of tinkle. What I thought was, it was bloody burglars. So I gave Gray a shake and said, there's someone downstairs, an' 'e said what the 'ell, there wasn't nothin' to steal downstairs an' 'e wasn't bloody goin' after 'em.'

'That ain't —' Bunting began, but Mandy ignored him.

'I was tired, I'll tell you mate, I was so bloody tired. Jade wakes me five or six times some nights. So I lies there and listens for a while, but there ain't no more to hear. Then I guess I fell asleep again.'

'And?'

'Ben woke me in the morning like he does, early, and I told 'im to shut up and went down to get 'im a drink and do Jade's bottle. 'Alf the bloody kitchen 'ad disappeared. There was a bleedin' great 'ole in the wall and a bleedin' great 'ole in the floor. So I ran back up screamin', and Gray got up and saw me out and the kids, knocked up Mrs D over the road and talked her into takin' us in, then 'e rang the police an' all them.'

'He rang me,' I put in.

Blue-blazer scrawled a couple more lines of shorthand. 'Who's Mrs D?' he asked.

'Dunbury. I do some jobs for 'er 'usband,' Bunting said. Mandy kicked his leg with a stiletto-clad foot, jerking the baby, and he added, 'Nothin' paid, just favours. That's 'er, over by the window.'

He flicked his head, and I turned to look. Did he mean the middle-aged woman with the pinched face, sitting at the end of the next trestle, handbag clutched on her lap? I couldn't imagine her giving a gushing welcome to Mandy and her kids at seven am. Still, if Bunting was —

Behind me the baby gave out a high whine, followed by an unmistakable splat. 'Sod it,' Mandy said. 'I got no Pampers wiv me.'

'I'll see if I can find you one,' I offered.

'You'd better take 'er. I'm stuck 'ere wiv Ben.' She dropped her fag-end on the floor, ground it out under her sole, loosed Ben, and grabbing the baby under the arms, humped her up and over to me.

I've changed my sister Alice's kids when I've babysat, but even so... I reminded myself Mandy was being admirably stoical in the face of disaster and tried to keep clear of Jade's rear end. Jade began to grizzle, and waved plump arms towards her mother. I backed to the wall, alternating it's-all-right noises to Jade with apologies sprayed left and right.

'Miss Massen, this isn't fair. There's always been a no-smoking rule in this hall.'

'Mrs Hughes,' I said through gritted teeth, 'if you want to tell these people they can't have a cigarette to calm them down...'

'It's not my job to tell them.'

'Nor mine. I don't suppose you have any nappies?'

'That baby smells.'

'So she does. Excuse me.'

I disposed of Jade to a social worker who tut-tutted at my baby-holding technique, checked with Louise, who seemed in control, and side-stepped the dreadlocked youth, catching a few bars of a squeaky drumbeat. It was too much to hope I'd get to the street door without being accosted – but I was surprised it was by the faded blonde who had taken Mandy in earlier.

'You're the councillor?'

Warily, I agreed. Mrs Dunbury was fifty-five at a guess, stylelessly dressed in a gored tweed skirt and cabbage-green Courtelle jumper. Her jewellery – boss-shaped jet earrings and a matching carved oval brooch – was classier than her clothes. Pink lipstick outlined a discontented mouth. She eyed my still-damp hair and unmade-up face as if they were a personal affront.

'They're saying we'll have to stay away from home overnight at least.'

'I imagine so,' I said. 'I'm sure it'll be a terrible inconvenience, but it's important to make sure your house is safe. The police and Social Services are doing a marvellous job, aren't they?'

'They expect us to leave our houses unguarded.'

'They'll keep a careful eye on everything.'

Mrs Dunbury moved a step closer, enveloping me in White Linen, and lowered her voice. 'Some of the people in this area – you only have to look around you. I want a twenty-four hour guard. If we don't get one, and anything's taken, I'll hold the Council responsible.'

I counted to ten. 'That's a police decision. It's their responsibility, not the City Council's. The Council don't control the police, Mrs Dunbury. If you're not satisfied, I suggest you talk to the officer in charge.'

'You know he's got a record.'

'Who?'

'Him, of course.' A pink-fingernailed hand, rapidly extended and even more rapidly pulled back, indicated the dreadlocked youth with his Walkman.

Did she know that, or was it pure prejudice? Whichever, I didn't want to listen. 'If he does,' I said, 'the police will know. Now if you'll excuse me, I'm late for a meeting.'

'There's another thing. This is going to affect the value of our house. I want the Council to compensate us.'

'I can't promise that.'

'We've got to have compensation. My husband'll be onto you. I don't see why we ought to suffer because other people —'

'I don't see why the Council ought to suffer either,' I retorted. 'Anyway, we don't even know what caused the hole yet. I'll be back this afternoon, but now I have to go. Excuse me.'

A litany of 'It's not good enough. It's negligence, clear negligence, and if you don't take up our case I'll make sure you —' followed me to the door.

Don't get my vote again, I finished for myself as I put a solid inch of painted oak between me and her, me and the cigarette smoke. It wasn't the strongest of threats, since I couldn't imagine I'd ever had it. She had probably only approached me because Rex Canning wasn't around.

Even so, I shouldn't have snapped back. Phlegm's thicker than panic in North Anglia, but anyone's justified in going spare if there's a chance their house will fall down.

I glanced at my watch: just past eleven. I'd get to City Hall in time to catch the tail-end of Planning.

3

Bill Baxter joined me as I was unlocking my bike, which I'd relocated to the railings outside the church hall. 'Okay?' he asked.

'You're asking me?'

'All right, it's obviously not.' Bill grinned. 'I mean, is there anything I can tell you before you go?'

I grinned back: Bill was likeable, especially after Mrs D. 'There's plenty I want to know, but I don't expect you to have all the answers yet. I assume it's a chalk mine?' It was a safe bet, since Costhorpe's shallow hills have been mined extensively: sometimes in quarries, but often by tunnelling. They've been left like worm-eaten wood.

'I can't even guarantee that till I've looked down the hole, but it's odd's-on, yes.'

'Then I'm reasonably up on general information. I guess everyone in Costhorpe knows a bit about tunnels, and I know a bit more, because I read your report, and I've heard Judith lecture on the chalk and flint industries.' Judith Armitage, leader of the Council, is an amateur industrial archaeologist. 'I didn't realise Flint Hill was high-risk, though. Isn't it the fifty-foot contour you go by?'

'That's just where the vein of chalk and flint hits the surface,' Bill said. 'Of course there was mining round here, hence the name, and there's actually a quarry behind Flint Avenue. But we didn't know there were tunnels leading off it in this direction, and of course we didn't have much joy finding a method of locating them.'

Bill's report had been a hefty effort, covering every aspect of tunnel-investigation. Most of the tunnel entrances were filled in centuries ago, and records of their location are few and incomplete. The fifty-foot contour isn't much help either, because there are miles of it, tracing each meander of Costhorpe's intersecting river valleys, so for generations the city's residents have learned where the tunnels are only when they collapse.

A broken sewer, a badly-placed soakaway: water triggers it, usually. The chalk of the tunnel roof dissolves, sending the glacial gravel and mud that tops our chalk layer cascading into the tunnel void, and creating sudden chasms in backyards, pavements and for the really unlucky, under houses.

Inconvenient, that, which was why Bill's team had tried to find a way of locating tunnels and predicting collapses. But they'd discovered only that geophysical techniques don't work well in cities like Costhorpe, so it wasn't through incompetence that they'd failed to predict the collapse in Flint Hill.

Bill's job now would be to stabilise it. I asked what his schedule was, and discovered he might have some more information if I came back that afternoon. I told him I'd aim to, and with that, mounted my bike and rode off, ruminating.

Costhorpe's residents live amid the debris of a thousand years. The street pattern, the remnants of the medieval city walls, the buildings of ten centuries, the tunnels beneath our feet all shape our lives, maybe more than we care to admit. Jonathan Sayer, whom I once unwisely married, still claims it's impossible to be a radical here.

That's a thesis I won't buy, but I've always liked the overused metaphor for guidebook writers: get to know flint, and you'll understand the North Anglians.

Flint's cussed stuff, only used to build half Costhorpe because there's no good building rock in North Anglia. Thick veins of it run through the chalk, which is itself so hard it will hold a tunnel without shoring. Great knobby lumps with white-crusted outsides. Fault-ridden sheets like unopenable black books. Shiny-grey, coal-black, occasionally almost blue. It's sometimes chipped into sharp-edged square blocks, sometimes piled-up anyhow with dabs of lime mortar. Although uningratiating, it can be lovely. Cut it on the right angle and it shines.

Same's true of Bill Baxter, of Judith, of many of my North Anglian acquaintance. Even, in a sense, of...

Yuck. Rex Canning.

I'd enjoyed romanticising, but even a glancing thought of Rex brought me back to the nastier aspects of the Flint Hill disaster. I trusted Bill to handle it as well as possible, but even so it would affect almost every department of the Council, every resident of Costhorpe. Housing problems, traffic problems, extra money on the tax bills: unpleasant ripples spread out from number thirty-three Flint Hill like a stone thrown into water.

When they hit Rex he'd jerk into glassy-edged action. He'd try to fix blame on the Council – specifically, the ruling Labour Group – and Mrs Dunbury wasn't the only person who'd be inclined to believe him. So I thought, glumly, as I negotiated the final inner-ring-road roundabout and freewheeled down St Nicholas Street.

City Hall car-park was crammed, so it was just as well I had a bike which needed only a stretch of railing. I locked and stripped it, shook off the drips and dumped my carrier and kagoul in the Members' Room upstairs. The committee rooms are on the same – first – floor. I checked the list, discovered Planning was in the Chorley Room, and stopped to catch my breath before slipping through the door.

The Chief Planning Officer was presenting a report. He paused as I slid onto the empty chair to the left of Nick, and I said, 'Sorry I'm late.'

Nick, a bearlike figure with ponytailed black hair, barely glanced at me. 'Had a puncture?' he asked. 'Or is it just that your private plans are more exciting than Planning? Harry, had you finished? Wilf, you had a question?'

Thanks Nick, I thought irritably, as I noticed the sly grins on the councillors' side of the table. He's a bloodhound, trained to sniff out point-scoring opportunities: preferably from the opposition, but he doesn't worry about his aim so long as he raises a laugh. It's called a sense of humour, apparently.

All right, I hadn't come in early as he'd asked, but I'm normally reliable, so he should have known I had a good reason; and it shouldn't have caused him any serious problems since nine other Labour members were there. Against five of the combined opposition we'd hardly have been pushed to win every vote.

Nick had claimed he wanted me to keep Rex Canning away from Patty Fowler, but any of the others could have done that. However they hadn't: Rex was sitting at the far end of the table, right next to her. We almost deserved to have the Courdon House report leaked.

Grey-suited, blue-tied, Rex was leaning back with legs crossed – body angled towards Patty – and one arm across the back of his leather-seated chair, looking arrogant and slightly bored, as usual. He gave me a quizzical look. I stared back into his baby-blue eyes across the expanse of blotter-and-agenda-strewn mahogany, then realised too late what point he was making. My eyes had been on him for the best part of a minute, and I hadn't even got out my agenda.

I quickly looked away, and rummaged through my briefcase. From the corner of my eye I saw Nick scribbling, so it was no surprise that as I put the agenda on my blotter, he slid across a note.

'1. An explanation would be nice.

2. Canning???

3. You lead off on the nature reserves?'

He'd signed it, too. *'NH'*: real affection in that.

It takes two to be juvenile, and I wasn't playing. I wouldn't make a face at him in front of Rex and Patty. I wouldn't criticise his trousers, which were filthy, or his sweater, which was unravelling at the wrist. I'd rarely noticed his scruffiness when we'd been together. Had he got worse, or was the change in me? Jenny's as immaculate as a synchronised swimmer, so I couldn't believe it was her influence. Maybe he was unconsciously emphasising the gulf between him and Rex.

I turned the page upside down and wrote, *'House collapsed in Flint Hill. Chalk mine?? Big story – Patty could maybe give me a mention. Shall I break it now?'* I slid it back, went for a cup of stewed black coffee from the hotplate in the corner, and returned to find another note waiting for me.

'No. RC would use it. Okay to 3?'

I didn't reply.

Nature reserves apart, there wasn't a lot I wanted to contribute to the morning's business. Over the next hour I drank several cups of coffee, half-listened to the debate, made the odd comment, thought about Nick's attitude and brewed yeasty resentment.

True, Rex would use Flint Hill if he could, but he wouldn't find it easy. If we gave the Costhorpe Argus a political story they always asked the Tories for comments, but the fact that I'd been at Flint Hill wasn't political. I couldn't see why Patty should ask Rex to comment on that, and even if she did, how could he match it?

Blue-blazer's story on Flint Hill would keep Courdon House off the front page even if Rex did leak the renovation report, but I still wanted a mention that I'd been on the scene. Okay, I was hardly Princess Di, but I felt sure that if I told Patty, she and her editor would oblige. It was never easy to upstage Rex, so why should I waste this opportunity?

Patty had pulled her chair back and set her computer in her lap. Her glossy brown hair swung about her shoulders as she tapped in her copy.

I couldn't plead with Nick in the middle of a committee meeting, and I wouldn't convince him in a note. Should I simply disobey him? He'd grumble, and if he was feeling mean might report me to the whip, but giving the press a story wasn't a treasonable offence.

Combine the darlings that morning with his jibe when I'd come in, add my private conviction I was right, and the outcome was indisputable. I stood and made my way down the room. Eyes averted from Nick, I leaned over Patty on the side Rex wasn't, and told her I'd like a private word.

Patty, being a good pro, had watched me coming. She had shut down her document before I reached her, and followed me out of the room without a word, ignoring – as I did – Rex's raised brows.

We only went as far as the screens of the Home Safety Exhibition in the lobby, where I filled her in, telling her I reckoned she could cover the political angle.

It was a bit weak, I could see now. I should have kept cool at the church hall, taken Blue-blazer to one side and told him what to write. Patty was a grabber and wouldn't complain, but she would see the inconsistency: my 'political angle' wasn't actually one at all.

She eyed me coolly when I finished, then said, 'You've nothing else to tell me?'

'Not for now. Just, the police and engineers were doing a great job, and I've been doing my bit too.'

'Frankly, Erica, I'd have thought you —' She broke off in mid-sentence, because the door to the Chorley Room had opened.

Rex emerged and set off across the lobby as if he was going to the Members' Room. He gave us a careless glance, hesitated, and amended his route. We were his only audience, and we both knew he wasn't exactly astonished to see us talking, but he mimed it meticulously.

'Rex,' Patty said, with an innocence as fake as his surprise, 'you represent Hillside, don't you?'

'I sure do. Why do you ask?'

She told him.

He listened to her, but watched me. I was livid, and didn't hide it. Elegant charade or not, he had no right to gatecrash my briefing. He'd have been furious enough if a Labour councillor had crept up behind him when he was giving the press the confidential report on Courdon House.

As he was most likely planning to do. Thinking of that, I glared even harder. Rex's blue eyes locked onto mine. I acquired the unpleasant impression he was enjoying my annoyance, and swung back to Patty.

'Erica says,' Patty finished, 'she's confident the engineers have handled it perfectly.' She half-smiled, expectantly, and Rex duly set about contradicting me.

'I wouldn't take that for granted. I'll certainly be asking some questions – like, why didn't the engineers foresee this? Did they miss warning signs? Was Flint Hill a known danger zone? From the sound of it, people could have been killed. It should never have been allowed to happen, and —'

'Rex,' I cut in, 'is this the new Tory tactic, accusing our staff of negligence before you find out the facts? You've no possible justification for those accusations.'

'They are not accusations. I'm simply saying I want to know —'

'And I'm saying you should find out first, and talk to the press afterwards. Bill's report last month told us he couldn't predict mine collapses. For you to slander our staff when they're only —'

'They're doing their job, but we don't yet know how well they're doing it. You're the one making assumptions, not I.'

'Not at all – I was there. Unlike some people, I know what's going on in my ward.'

I wouldn't come up with a better exit line, and wouldn't gain by staying longer. I'd given Patty some reasonable quotes – and alas, proved Nick right. Now Rex would make the Late Final.

I slammed the door as I came back into the committee room. The officers, who sat with their backs to it, jumped. Nick gave me a poisonous look, and whispered 'Where's Rex?' as I retook my seat.

'With —' Galloping gorillas. Still with Patty, and most likely now filling her in on Courdon House.

4

I DIDN'T linger in the Chorley Room after the meeting finished, so as not to give Nick any opportunity to tackle me. Rex had returned ten minutes after me, with Patty, both looking smug. Most likely Courdon House would be the next day's headline.

We'd debated the pros and cons of repairing the arts centre's building, but with the press and public excluded, so they wouldn't know we'd had the better of the arguments. And it was Nick whom Patty would ask for Labour comments, so that was no reason for me to hang around.

I was feeling low as I made my way down to the car-park – there had been too many days recently when my good intentions had led to dubious results – but a brisk bike-ride home, followed by black coffee and a ham sandwich, returned me to something like normality. I did a short afternoon's work and set off for Flint Hill at just after three, so I'd get there in daylight.

The rain had eased, and the morning crowd in the church hall had thinned down to stragglers. There was no sign of Graham Bunting and Mandy, which was a small relief. No Mrs Dunbury: a bigger relief. I even got a smile and a friendly hello, from Dennis Thorndon, a Party member and regular letter-writer to the Argus who lived, I discovered, at the top end of the road.

No Rex. I'd guessed that with his publicity already lined up he wouldn't take extra time off from his work – as an accountant – to wave his Tory flag, but still that was confirmation my luck had changed.

Through the haze of stale smoke I made out Louise Hoggett sitting behind the trestle farthest from the door, pen in hand, forms spread out in front of her, dealing with a middle-aged couple. When they moved off I asked her how things were going.

Louise is cheerful and efficient, not the type to whine even when told to do the impossible. 'Not bad from this end,' she said. 'We've found temporary accommodation for all the council tenants, and most of the other residents have relatives or friends to stay with. I wish the engineers could tell me how long it'll be for, though.'

'I'll ask them,' I promised. 'Is Bill Baxter still around?'

'Erica...?' someone put in from behind my back.

I knew the voice, and while turning round I set a name to it.

'Allie! What are you doing here?'

'I live here, Erica.'

I'd sometimes pushed French translations Allie Sotherton's way when I had more than I could handle myself. She lectured in French at the university. We'd often shared a coffee and chatted for half an hour about books or films, but she had never offered any information about her private life, and her self-contained manner had kept me from asking. Even admitting where she lived seemed to embarrass her; not that I judge people by their addresses, or that Flint Hill was a disreputable one.

Mind, I was surprised to discover she was a resident. The university was on my side of the city, and most of the faculty lived close by. Allie's style – long skirts, trailing chiffon scarves and Oxfam-oriental jewellery – wouldn't have looked odd down London Road, but it was exotic over here.

'Ah well,' I said. 'I've never canvassed this road, so I wouldn't have known. Have you lived here long?'

'Only a few months. I used to have a flat in Suffolk Place, but when Phil and I decided to move in together – Phil Murray, he lectures in engineering – he was determined it'd be to his place. It's roomy enough, but... not me. I'd like us to buy something jointly, nearer the university, and he's put the house on the market, but there haven't been any takers yet. And now this has happened...'

'Which number are you?'

'Thirty-five.'

Then there would be no takers ever. If Phil owned the place, he'd be in an even worse fix than the Buntings. I supposed the insurance would cough up eventually, but that was thin consolation. I said how sorry I was, but I had the impression Allie was barely listening. She interrupted before I'd finished.

'Someone said the Council don't even investigate? They go under their own houses but stop dead as soon as it gets to private land?'

I didn't know, and promised to find out. Allie paid little attention to my answer, glancing distractedly round the room. I followed her gaze, but I didn't see anyone pick it up.

‘Raze told me,’ she said, without looking at me. ‘Phoned me at lunchtime. Apparently it was on Radio Costhorpe, but I don’t listen at the uni.’

I doubted she was in a frame of mind to explain who Raze was. A gesture from Louise caught my attention. Behind Allie’s back she shook her head and pointed at the files on the trestle, then at Allie, with a questioning look. I made out her message, and mouthed an assurance that I’d do what I could.

‘Have you found somewhere to stay?’

It took Allie a moment to turn to me, and even then she didn’t quite focus. Her face melted into misery, like stringy mozzarella.

‘It’s not that I expect the Council to fix us up. I just don’t... Jeez, this is ridiculous. We haven’t any relatives around here, none at all. We’ve friends, of course, but not many of them have a spare room, and I’m no good at...’

Asking favours, I completed. I wouldn’t have been crazy about it myself. But I didn’t mind doing them, and after three months living alone it’d make a change to have someone else about.

Allie had more sense than to protest when offered my spare room. Instead she promised me they wouldn’t impose, and would start to look immediately for a flat to rent. I didn’t doubt they would.

‘Do you need to get anything from your house?’ I asked.

‘I’m not allowed to,’ she told me. ‘It’s too dangerous, apparently. The firemen packed us a case each, and we have to manage with that.’

‘I haven’t yet talked to our engineer, or seen the damage. Can you stand to wait while I take a look?’

‘I’ll come with you,’ Allie said.

I did wonder if it was asking too much of her, but I was reluctant to leave without seeing all I could. I hate sitting in the back row with heads between me and the screen, and I didn’t fancy going to my Labour Party Branch meeting that evening and saying, yeah, well, I spent three hours on Flint Hill but I can’t tell you what the collapse looks like.

Allie had already put her and Phil’s cases in her car, so we had only to ask Louise to let Phil know where to go, should he leave the university before Allie could phone him. Then we set off down the hill.

There were barriers midway down and at the bottom, with policemen stationed by each. Bill Baxter was also at the upper barrier, involved in a heated argument with an apple-cheeked young man in a snappy light-grey suit – at least, the man was heated. Bill wasn't.

Apple-cheeks looked vaguely familiar, but I couldn't recall where I'd met him. Bill clearly needed rescuing, though, and Allie and I needed an escort past the policeman, so I went over and said, 'Anything I can help with?'

The man scowled at me. 'If you don't mind...'

'Erica Massen,' I went on, holding out a hand. 'I'm one of your city councillors, assuming you live round here. I know it's a mess, but the emergency services are doing all they can.'

'Forget it, Baxter,' Apple-cheeks said to Bill. Ignoring me and my hand he stalked off, stiff-legged. Bill and I watched him go. 'Number thirty-one?' I hazarded.

'Uh?' Bill turned to me, amiably unruffled as ever. 'No, that's Miles Keylock. He lives farther down the road.'

'The estate agent, of course.' Nick and I had talked to Keylocks when we were selling our house, although they hadn't got our business. I'd met Miles in their office. 'It doesn't seem much of an advert,' I added, 'for a pro to own a house round here.'

Bill shrugged. 'Stranger things have happened. Come and meet the team.'

We went on down to number thirty-three, which was now the focus of an irregular semicircle of low metal posts and red tape. I introduced Allie, and Bill introduced the supervisor from City Works and two colleagues from the structures section of the City Engineer's Department, Sheila Brennan and Gary Temperley.

Sheila looked to be about my age, an attractive woman with dark curly hair, wearing a covetable green suede jacket. Gary was younger, newly out of university I guessed, with a big body which was all bones and joints, and an acne-scarred face.

'Are you waiting for something?' I asked Sheila.

'Not really. We've done most of what we can do today.'

She seemed a little condescending, but I persisted. 'Will you shore up the house, or will you have to demolish it?'

Bill answered for her. 'We've already demolished the bit that was hanging over the hole, because we can't have bricks falling on our heads when we go down to investigate. Some of it came down by itself. The rest's shored-up, and that's how it'll stay, at least until we've investigated the hole properly.'

'Can you confirm now that it's a mine?'

'Not for certain. There's a chance it's a well or a natural cavity.'

'I know your type, Bill. The only place you leap to rash conclusions is in the sweater shop.'

Gary Temperley let out a bark of nervous laughter, and Bill smiled, but Sheila Brennan frowned. She said sharply, 'Bill can hardly be blamed for being cautious, councillor. We won't know if it's a mine until we go down the hole, and nobody's going down today, not even Bill and I.'

Maybe not, but she didn't have to be so aggressive. I hadn't shoved my way in with demands, and nor was I about to make any: if anyone was going to swing down into the dark on a rope ladder, I didn't mean it to be me.

I supposed she was one of those officers who resented all councillors. Every department has some people who can't stand having to explain everything to us, then bite their tongues when we make decisions they disagree with: but that's local democracy, and nobody has yet worked out a better system. If Sheila couldn't live with it, she was in the wrong job.

However I wasn't looking for aggro, so I turned back to Bill again, and asked him if Allie and I could take a quick surface look. Bill agreed that although it wouldn't be safe to go through the Buntings' house, it would be okay for us to circle round and look from the back.

He asked Sheila if she wanted to come, but she said curtly that she had too much to do, and Gary also declined, so it was just Bill, I and Allie. We went up the side of number thirty-seven, over their lawn, and legged it across the low picket fence that divided their garden from Allie and Phil's.

'Please be careful,' Allie begged. 'Phil's awfully fussy about his garden.'

I could see why: as February goes, it was a great garden. The ground rose up steeply from the backs of the houses, and Phil had handled the rise in a series of little curving terraces held up by low brick walls. The paths were mellow brick, and the beds were filled with evergreen shrubs and the spiky tips of tulips, daffodils and crocuses. The highest terrace was arched over by a trellis, with a gap in the middle to show off a sundial surrounded by concentric brick circles.

Bill plunged up the centre, rounded the sundial and headed along the trellissed terrace. 'Not through the raspberry canes,' Allie groaned.

Definitely through them, since they filled a three-foot gap between the side fence and rear fence. I followed a little guiltily; but Phil's garden was likely to suffer worse before he moved back, if he ever did, and they were last year's canes.

Once through the gap, I could see why Mandy kept her front gate secure so Ben could play out there. The Buntings' back garden was a hummocky wasteland of rubble, rusting pushbikes and old tyres, spread over mud, and overgrown with the slimy remains of last year's nettles and the yellow-white corpses of last year's long grass.

The house at the far end looked normal enough, except for the corner. It had been opened up like a d-i-y textbook illustration. The back door was there, but nothing on our side of it. I stared straight into a kitchen with yellow-painted cupboards, marigold-patterned walls and work surfaces still crammed with cornflake packets, an open bottle of milk, a bread bin and unwashed plates. A square of scaffolding held up the floor of the room above, but the wall had gone from this too, revealing a child's bed and balloon-patterned wallpaper.

5

SUBDUED'S the word for how I felt, cycling back home. I could imagine, and not imagine. Say, that morning: Nick's phonecall waking me, padding down to the shower, still sleepy, stopping on the edge of... nothing. The bricks and mortar of my life suspended over emptiness. Everything I took for granted sliding into a black hole.

I and my bike wobbled down the side-alley as if I had sea-legs. I went through the back door, and just got to the front as Allie's car drew up. I let her in, and drew back to allow her to orient herself.

When one woman enters another's house, whatever the circumstances, she has to praise the decor. I'd only lived in Morton Street for six weeks, and the tweedy wallpaper and carpet weren't my choice. The Liberty sofa was, bought after a run of EEC work a couple of years before: she'd like that, I guessed, and like the Victorian fireplace more, with its marble surround and cast-iron grate surrounded by green and yellow lily-pattern tiles.

She did. 'How lovely,' she said, dropping her case and crossing the room. She traced the outline of a lily with a stubby finger, straightened and picked up the sculpture I kept on the mantel, a bronze cast of a goose about to fly off from choppy water. A friend of Jonathan's had made it, years before.

Allie was a strong-looking woman. She had a high-cheekboned, rather Slavic face and a sturdy peasant's body: square torso, thick legs, short neck. I'd always thought her attractive, but it was a triumph of style over unpromising raw material. I didn't feel alienated from her, but I was conscious of an essential foreignness. I value my space, just as she had always seemed to me to value hers, and although I was happy to lend her my spare bedroom, I didn't intend us to stray too far from our undemanding acquaintance.

'Glad you think so. I'll put the kettle on,' I said, and heard the sharp edge on my own voice. 'There's a phone down here, or there's another upstairs in my office if you'd prefer.'

'Oh... yes. I'll call Phil now.'

PHIL was a little younger than I'd expected – late twenties, I guessed – and had a blunt physique like Allie's, topped with a square freckled face. He looked a capable man, and I suspected he'd have preferred to fix his own temporary accommodation, but he thanked me for my offer without embarrassment, and didn't say so.

He'd arrived with lists of people to contact and things to do, and two bottles of Rioja. We drank the first (one glass for me) while watching North Anglia Round-up, which featured police constables redirecting traffic, Mandy Bunting repeating her story, and Bill Baxter telling the cameras about chalk mines.

I'd asked myself whether I should skip that evening's Party branch meeting, but councillors are expected to turn up, and I doubted Allie and Phil would really be grateful if I stayed at home. I dished up ham omelettes, then made my apologies and left them drinking the rest of the wine and going over the first of Phil's lists.

After dark, I drive: and for once it was a pleasure to have glass and steel between me and the darkness and bright lights. I slotted highlights of Don Giovanni into the car cassette player, and when I got to Hillside Community Centre I stayed in my Renault, engine off, listening to Samuel Ramey and Kathleen Battle finishing *'La ci darem la mano'*. It was so lovely I rewound the tape and played it again. Danger and lust, overlaid by an awesome sense of calm. I needed that.

Branch meetings no-one needs, but the system does; and there's a calming effect too in begging letters from the Third World Centre, arguments about unpaid subscriptions and plans for the next jumble sale.

It was Mike's – Mike Soley, the other Hillside ward Labour councillor – turn to give the councillor's report, but I added what I could about Flint Hill. Ernie Harding grumbled about the traffic, and wanted a promise the road would be reopened within a week, which I couldn't give him; otherwise the reaction was apathetic, except for the Souths, who buttonholed me in the bar afterwards and repeated a story they'd told me before about selling their last house. One mention of subsidence and they'd panicked, flogging the place to a builder for ten thousand less than they'd originally hoped to get.

Reasonable perhaps if there had been a mine underneath, but it didn't often happen. I wasn't convinced Harry and Molly had acted as sensibly as they seemed to think. Hell, the first estate agent Nick and I had gone to had spouted the same kind of doomy warnings, and we'd afterwards discovered he'd had no real justification. Still, Harry wouldn't have appreciated my pointing that out to him.

The Souths are the biggest bores I know, and I dreaded getting Harry onto the fine print of his buildings policy. Maybe he was right. Phil would probably be thrilled if the Flint Hill business only cost him ten thousand. I pleaded fatigue and visitors, and left after a single orange juice.

It was strange to come home to find the lights on. As I was getting out my key I could hear the television faintly through the window, and see the flicker of the fire. It was even stranger to have Allie jump up and offer to make me cocoa. Nobody had done that since I'd lived with my parents.

We spent a pleasant half-hour talking about the university, the translation business and how I should decorate my front room. I didn't mention Flint Hill, and neither did Allie or Phil. They went to bed at eleven, and I stayed up for another half-hour, flicking through the Argus. There wasn't much on the Planning Committee: most of the coverage would come next day. Flint Hill was the lead, but it was a pedestrian piece with an uninspiring photo taken from the road, enlivened only by some ripe quotes from Mandy. Rex got a little mention on page two, but I didn't.

Who cared? Not me, right then.

As I undressed I couldn't help being aware of Allie and Phil cuddled up in my tiny spare room. I had the big room, and a half-empty bed. I wouldn't have wanted Nick to fill it, mind. Really I liked freedom, and the sense of unimagined opportunities ahead.

Only I woke around four am, and thought for a moment I'd cried out loud. My nightmare had ended with me falling down a well, and my body was still tensed, waiting for the crash.

WHEN I got home the following afternoon from a Museums meeting there was a message from Bill Baxter on my answering machine.

He and Sheila Brennan had sent a video camera down the Buntings' hole, he reported, and confirmed that there was a tunnel at the bottom. It appeared to run north-west to south-east, like many in Costhorpe, and sliced diagonally across the road, but there might be other tunnels running off it so he couldn't yet say which other houses were endangered.

I phoned Bill back, but he was out of his office, so was Sheila, and

Gary Temperley couldn't add much. I asked him to keep the Housing Department in the picture, and told him that when Bill went down the tunnel I wanted to be there.

'I don't know if that's allowed,' Gary said.

'Oh yes it is,' I informed him. What was this with the City Engineer's Department? First Sheila had been abrasive, now Gary was prickling.

There were no other messages, so I was able to get in a good afternoon's work before Allie and Phil returned from the university. Phil offered to go for a Chinese takeaway, Allie made jasmine tea, and I flopped on the sofa and read that evening's Argus.

This wasn't entirely pleasurable, since most of the front page was taken up with a photo of Rex Canning and an article by Patty Fowler about Courdon House Arts Centre, spelling out all the confidential details and harping on how much the repairs would cost local taxpayers.

'You look like you've just read your best friend's obituary,' Allie commented, depositing a tray on the floor and settling down next to it.

'Men.' I folded the paper in four and flung it at the far wall.

'One in particular?'

'Several. Arguably all.'

'You're divorced, aren't you?'

Yes, but... Oh, what the hell? Allie wasn't expecting a two-hour analysis of my lovelife (or lack of one), just making casual conversation.

'True, but I was only married briefly, years ago. When that broke up I lived alone for a long time, then I lived with another councillor for three years. That ended recently, and I'm not heartbroken, but it's left a gap. I still see him at meetings, and tonight he'll be spoiling for row.'

'You don't relish the prospect?'

'No.'

'I thought all politicians had an insatiable appetite for arguments,' Allie said calmly, pouring the tea. 'I went to the House of Commons once, and I've never forgotten the insults they yelled.'

'At the opposition,' I pointed out.

'Is that so very different?'

I paused on the brink of retorting 'Obviously': Allie isn't naive.

She looked up at me, a dumpy figure swathed in maroon. 'What I don't like about politics, Erica,' she said, 'is the cruelty. I don't believe you're insincere, not on the left at least, but I think the habit of knocking and sniping tends to corrupt. Sorry, that's a hard word, but it's the only one that fits. It makes you seem hard – no, not only that, it makes you *be* hard. Don't get me wrong, I know you have a social conscience and I'm deeply grateful to you for helping me and Phil, but I reckon all politicians eventually become ruthless. Of course they argue that everything they do is in the interest of their party, but...'

It's an old argument and I've never liked it. 'Let's get this straight, Allie,' I said. 'It's a Tory councillor who got me mad enough to hurl the paper at the wall.'

'Your boyfriend was a Tory?'

'No, of course not – that's a different man. And all right, Nick's not being angelic either. But when my non-political friends have split with their partners, I can't say any of them have been in line for sainthood.'

Allie's round strong-featured face creased into a frown. 'I suppose I shouldn't have said anything. I'm tactless, I know – everyone tells me. But it worries me that you come across as so formidable.'

'Too aggressive to get another man? I thought that line died out about nineteen-seventy.'

'Well... maybe a little aggressive to get a nice man.'

'I don't know I value niceness that highly.' I wasn't surprised Allie tended to avoid personal conversations, if this was her usual manner of conducting them. 'I like doers, not bleeding-heart ineffectual types; and if you think politicians are tough you ought to see businessmen, Allie. It's academics who are out of line with the rest of the world, not us. Anyway I won't argue with you, because this is my half-hour for collapsing – with Mao-mao, who knows I'm a pussycat really.' Mao-mao climbed up and draped herself round my neck as if to prove it, and Allie mercifully shut up.

So, more surprisingly, did Nick, at the Council's Labour Group meeting that evening. He and his new partner Jenny sat on the opposite side of the room from me, and made no attempt to come closer. But on Saturday I had my regular squash date with Jenny, and she launched in as we were changing afterwards.

As I'd expected, the Courdon House leak had caused Nick a lot of aggro. As I'd feared, he reckoned I'd intentionally contributed to it by ignoring his advice. Why?

I'd assumed Jenny knew why. In fact I knew she knew why, because over the years we'd talked plenty about Nick. She knew I didn't think Nick as brilliant as Nick thought Nick, and that I'd objected to his ordering me around. For months before we'd split up I'd regularly gone against his so-called invaluable advice on principle.

The trouble was, after years of agreeing what a pain he was, Jenny had fallen in love with the man.

'Honestly I didn't mean to cause him hassle. I doubt I could have prevented Rex leaking that report whatever I did,' I said, and shrugged a smile.

'Erica, you're not sulking about Nick and me, are you? I honestly thought you didn't mind when we —'

'I didn't,' I said hastily. 'I don't. I'll apologise when I next see him, and you can tell him I'm furious with Rex Canning.'

'I will.' Jenny dragged a pink sweatshirt over her reddish-brown curls, and gave me a concerned look. 'Erica, are you happy at the moment?'

'Sure. Why not?'

'I wonder sometimes. Nick and I are so blissful together, and you're alone. I know it's awkward. If you'd rather not keep on playing squash with me...'

'Don't be ridiculous,' I said.

I ARRIVED back home to find Allie and Phil hugging each other and a bottle of champagne in my front room. They were celebrating having found an ideal flat in Hunter Court, three roads from my house. The only problem was, it would be a week before they could move in. Awfully sorry, Erica, could I bear to have them stay with me that long?

For a nasty moment I felt I couldn't. Suddenly the world seemed full of happy lovers and people criticising my mental state. But I couldn't have refused, and I surely wasn't at such a low ebb that a week of Allie and Phil would drive me to distraction. I told them they were welcome, and Phil offered to make supper as a thank-you.

Fine, I said, and retreated to my office, where I checked over the final five pages of Dutch into English, then fished Bill Baxter's report on chalk mines out of my filing cabinet.

I read about lime kilns. Costhorpe's last one shut down in the sixties, but the ruins are still to be found if you know where to look. Double-skinned beehives built into the quarry sides, their entrances are usually bricked-up and overgrown with nettles.

I read about vaulted cellars in the city centre, and underground passages linking the castle and the Shirehall, the castle and Courdon House. Bill repeated the rumours of tunnels between the river, the cathedral and the old jail, although these had never been found. He quoted letters to the Argus, old men who recalled stumbling on the tunnels as children and standing under the streets with a stub of candle, listening to the trams overhead.

The tunnels had been used as wine cellars, beer cellars and general dumps. Mushrooms had been grown in them, and in both world wars they had acted as air raid shelters. Bats roosted in those that had open entrances. Back in the nineteenth century one network had been turned into a tourist attraction. The promoters had hung up coloured lights, and led *'the most distinguished families of this city'* down Discovery Street to banquets in Bacchus Street, under the road near the Catholic Cathedral.

It was a weird idea: the tunnel as asset. People bought houses for their wine cellars, so why not go for a house with a tunnel under the garden? I thought of trying that line on Mrs Dunbury.

I jotted down a list of questions to ask Bill, and was just finishing when Phil called me for supper.

He'd made onion soup, the creamy English kind, with garlic bread, and followed by spare ribs, peppery rice and mixed-leaf salad. As finishing touches he'd provided a bunch of purple grapes, a large hunk of perfect dolcelatte, and two bottles of Koonunga Hill Cabernet Sauvignon.

Two bottles, and Phil and Allie had tossed back the fizz that afternoon. This wasn't to calm their nerves, they downed it like a Saturday night routine. So did I, although it wasn't a routine for me. I hadn't eaten and drunk so well since...

Since my last dinner party with Nick. Everything seemed to be conspiring to remind me I was alone.

'You won't let us mess up your weekend plans, will you, Erica?' Phil said. 'If you normally go out on a Saturday night...'

'I don't always,' I told him. 'I was out at meetings yesterday and the day before, so I'm not complaining at being home tonight.'

'No boyfriend to take you to the flicks?'

'Phil,' Allie warned; but he'd already asked it. And it was only a day since she'd called me aggressive, so I bit on my annoyance and said, 'Lots of friends, but none I'd want to wake up next to. Shall I make some coffee?'

'Aren't you looking for someone?'

'Not at the moment. Look, I'm sorry if I'm crowding you, but this is my house, and —'

'I didn't —' Phil was protesting, when the phone rang.

Just as well: as soon as I'd said it, I'd known it was mean. Sexual frustration, or practice in the council chamber – whatever, I was getting dangerously quick with the barbed retort.

'Erica Massen,' I said as usual, and a man answered, 'Hope I haven't disturbed your supper,' which left me trying to place a voice he seemed to expect me to recognise.

It was deepish, cultured but not quite plummy. Attractive, especially after four glasses of strong Cabernet. I couldn't fit a face to it, but at least he'd provide reassurance to Phil and Allie that men did call me. Nor had he launched into an argument or complaint. Rather more equably I said, 'As if I'd mind. No, only the cheese.'

'Brie?'

'Dolcelatte.' I rolled the word round my mouth.

He laughed: pleasantly, not critically. 'Erica, you've been drinking.'

'An excellent Australian red.' I still hadn't placed him, and it wasn't bothering me.

'You've company. Can you spare a minute?'

'Ask him over,' Phil said, loud enough to carry to the receiver – the phone's in the living room, but I was close to the open door.

'What a tempting suggestion,' the voice said.

'Is it?' He'd implied it was an unexpected one. Apprehension prickled me, like gravel under bare feet.

'Don't worry, I won't take up the offer. I'm about to head off to a party, but I wanted to fix this with you first. Are you free next Friday?'

'It depends what for.'

'Say it like that, and I'll wish it was something more exciting. I'm afraid it's only a public meeting on Flint Hill. Half past seven at the Methodist Church Hall.'

Voice and face clicked together in my head, and sent chill

comprehension trickling down my spine.

'A Tory Party meeting?'

'A public meeting – interested parties, me included. It won't compromise you.'

'I'll think about it.'

'What is there to think about? People have a right to be kept informed.'

'Yes, but that's not the only way of informing them. The thing is, Rex, you'll get a roomful of residents wanting the Council to spend a fortune investigating the mine and filling it in – and you know as well as I that although we'll have to investigate, we can't afford to fill in the whole thing.'

'It's a question of priorities.'

'It's not. It's a question of not being able to afford it.' His smugness irritated me. The Tories always pretended there was plenty of slush in our budgets, but ask them to pinpoint some and they hedged and mumbled. 'And it not being our responsibility either, except under roads or our own houses. You remember what it cost last time we had to fill in a section of mine. What if this one goes under a dozen private houses? All we'll be able to say is, hard cheese, folks – and you'll get a riot.'

'I hardly think so,' Rex said condescendingly. 'It's a respectable area, and I'll be taking the chair. I'll get an engineer to explain what's happening, and a police spokesman to handle questions about the traffic flow while the road's closed. There won't be anything contentious, it's simply a public relations exercise.'

I wasn't so sure – I've seen public meetings get out of hand before. But if this did turn out to be a genteel occasion, and no one from the Labour Group turned up, it would look bad for us. 'I'll talk to the Leader,' I hedged. 'Although Friday won't please her: that's the night of the pre-Council Labour Group meeting. Any chance you could make it a different evening?'

'No. I've already invited several people.'

There was me imagining I was first on your list, I thought wryly. 'Oh well,' I said. 'I'll see what I can do, and get back to you by Monday.'

Rex thanked me rather shortly, and rang off. I supposed I'd miffed him by questioning his wonderful idea, but I couldn't see why he should have expected me to love it. If it went badly, the Council would get shoved down the helter-skelter; if it went well, it'd be the headline in the next Tory newsletter.

Damn him. When Rex had first been elected Mike and I had assured each other he'd be nothing more than a paper councillor, but in fact he was all too active.

I stepped back through to the dining room to find two pairs of eyes fixed hopefully on me. 'Fellow councillor,' I said, to cut off the questions.

'Male. Single?' Phil asked.

'Tory.'

'Is that important?' asked Allie.

'Definitely important.'

6

NEXT day Phil cooked a Sunday lunch good enough to smooth tempers all round, and over it, told me he'd like to watch Bill Baxter investigate the mine. I passed on the request when I phoned Bill Monday, and learned that assuming the Environmental Health Committee granted the funding, he would go down that Thursday.

He agreed Phil and I could come along, so long as we settled for watching from the surface. We should phone Thursday morning to check that they were going ahead, in case there had been a hiccup in committee, or the weather was forecast suddenly to turn bad.

Strange: I'd thought of Bill as the type who'd not notice a little mud when he was enjoying himself.

'Erica, you dummy,' Phil said when I told him. 'It's not the wet he'll be worried about, it's the gas. High pressure falling fast provides the ideal conditions for a concentration of carbon dioxide underground, and no sane engineer would go down in those circumstances.'

'I didn't think carbon dioxide was poisonous.'

'It's not, just unbreathable,' Phil cheerfully assured me. 'It kills, love. You can walk into a concentration of odourless and tasteless gas, pass out and die without ever knowing what did it to you. The most frightening thing is, CO_2 makes you feel euphoric, and puts you in just the mood to go in deeper. Even in good conditions I expect they'll carry oxygen meters.'

'Might there be any other nasty surprises lurking under your house? Underground lakes? Rats?'

'Erica.' Phil put on an expression of comic regret. 'Even a scientific illiterate like you must know that chalk's porous. Those tunnels will be dry and dead, like a moonscape. Utterly lifeless.'

THURSDAY morning, Flint Hill was entombed in silence. A carless expanse of tarmac, a childless row of gardens. No open windows, no washing on the lines. Instead Phil and I encountered a battalion of diversion signs, a couple of City Works vans, and a yellow-painted skip by the kerb.

Remembering the state of the Buntings' back garden, we'd both donned jeans and wellingtons. The orange arm of a crane loomed from behind the rooftops, tracing an arrogant slant across a well-laundered blue sky. The barometer was rising, Environmental Health had approved the funding: now it was all up to Bill and Sheila.

A man in overalls stopped us at the barrier, found us hard hats identical to his, and directed us round the side of number thirty-one. The crane had been brought this way, saving Phil's garden – more because of the little brick walls than out of concern for his feelings, I suspected.

He had reason to be grateful. The remnants of number thirty-one's wooden fence were stacked in an unsteady pile, and a muddy curve of caterpillar tracks crossed the lawn before ploughing into the wasteland beyond the boundary.

Heaps of earth and chalk rubble shrouded most of the dead nettles on the Buntings' side. An orange canvas roadmen's shelter had been erected at the bottom of the garden, and a dozen workmen were spread out around it, the crane, and the perimeter of the hole. I had to look twice at the orange overalls and white hats before I made out Sheila Brennan's dark hair curling from under one of them.

'You're dawdling, Erica.'

I glanced at Phil, surprised at his snippiness, only to realise I should have taken in several signs of it earlier. Normally phlegmatic, he'd sworn when he'd splashed coffee on his shirt that morning, and driven carelessly when we were crossing the city.

The pressure was clearly getting to him, and no wonder, when his house was peering into a chasm. 'Coming,' I said, and followed him across the caterpillar tracks.

Sheila had seen us, and was heading over. She frowned at me, but produced a smile for Phil when I introduced him, and expressed her sympathy. Bill joined us a moment later, relaxed, even enthusiastic, and the shadow of the other two's edginess faded.

I left Phil to ask the questions. He raised all those I'd have asked myself, plus a few I wouldn't have thought of. He'd told me structural engineering wasn't his field, but the set-up clearly made a lot more sense to him than it did to me.

Bill let Sheila give most of the answers. We were later than we'd intended, but we hadn't missed anything worth watching, apparently.

The engineers had merely knocked more loose material off the sides of the shaft, scooped the debris out of the tunnel and dumped it on the nettles. Bill explained that if they went down repeatedly they would line the shaft with corrugated steel, but this first time the crane's safety-cage would serve as protection.

'Are you ready to go down now?' I asked.

'We will be in an hour, maybe,' Sheila said.

Phil promptly said he'd like to go into his house to fill another suitcase, since Allie had been grumbling all week about the firemen's idea of emergency packing. Bill agreed he could, so long as he kept his hard hat on and appreciated that it was at his own risk, and off he went, jingling his keys. Sheila went off too, and Bill gave me a vaguely apologetic smile. A vee of sweater, electric-blue zigzags on a grey background, peeped out from behind the zip of his overalls.

'You know this'll be pretty tedious.'

'My boredom threshold's high,' I assured him. 'Bill, is Sheila nervous about going down the mine?'

He seemed surprised. 'I shouldn't think so. She's been down mines before. What made you ask?'

'Her attitude. She acts as if she's annoyed that I'm here, and I thought maybe that was the reason. Displaced tension.'

Bill shook his hard-hatted head. 'Can't see it,' he said. 'I'm sorry if she was rude to you, though.'

'It wasn't as strong as that.' I didn't want to get Sheila into trouble, just to know what lay behind her attitude. But I guessed she wasn't a woman who would confide worries to her boss.

TIME passed. The sun disappeared behind clouds. An icy wind whipped across the garden. Phil returned, cheered by his success in finding everything on Allie's list, and we waited some more. Eventually Sheila and Bill got into the crane safety cage and were lowered down the mine. It was, as Bill had warned, undramatic.

We wouldn't learn much until they came out. Gary Temperley was stationed at the top of the shaft, Sheila would apparently wait at the bottom, and Bill would go off exploring. I'd assumed they would use radios to keep in contact, but Gary pointed out contemptuously that radios wouldn't work underground. Sound travelled well in the tunnels, so shouted time-checks would do the job. Gary yelled 'Okay Sheila?' at regular intervals, and we all heard the loud but indistinct reply.

Imagination had to supply the rest. I'd seen Bill's photos of other chalk tunnels, and knew most were eight or nine feet high, tall enough for a man to stand clear of the roof, and shaped like a pyramid with the top cut off. The sides and roofs were of white chalk streaked with yellow impurities, studded with broken seams of shiny black flint. They looked light on the photos, but that effect was produced by arc lamps: without them, the tunnels would be pitch dark.

I thought about Bill and Sheila, under the earth. Bill heading under our feet, under the road, under the Victorian bay-fronted houses on the other side of the road. A wedge of light from the beams on his helmet ahead, and blackness behind. Cold. Watching an oxygen meter for signs of the gas which couldn't be seen, couldn't be smelled, which could kill in one deadly minute.

7

Bill shouted to Sheila, Sheila shouted to Gary, Gary shouted to Sheila, Sheila shouted to Bill. All the checks worked, the oxygen meter barely flickered, and up on the surface we stamped our feet and rubbed our hands together.

Eventually Gary told the crane driver to get moving again, and Sheila and Bill were brought up from the depths. Both looked filthy but euphoric.

But Bill, steady as ever, said, 'Tea first,' so we had to wait some more while Frank from City Works, who was in charge of the primus, brewed two fresh mugs. Sheila took off her hard hat and wiped the back of a grubby hand across her forehead. She and Bill exchanged a smile, in which I sensed real affection.

I'd got it wrong before, I decided. She hadn't been scared, and there was no aloofness in her attitude to her boss. It made me wonder if Sheila's problem with me was simply an unattached woman's instinctive rivalry with other similar women. I looked for wedding rings, and couldn't see one on either of them – but Bill was married, surely. He smelled of it.

Half his tea downed, Bill began on a methodical account. He had explored as much of the mine as was accessible, which amounted to a long length of the main tunnel and a spur. As he had anticipated, the main tunnel went north-west to south-east, diagonally across Flint Hill, towards the old quarry behind Flint Avenue. He'd reached infill in that direction, while the other two ended in 'sandpots' – solution pipes in the chalk, whatever they were. From what Bill said, they would have been a logical place for the miners to stop digging.

He reckoned the spur came off beyond the east side of the road, and angled back towards the row of houses. It would be necessary to map the tunnels properly before it was apparent how many houses they ran under. The spur too came to a dead end.

'So this shaft's now the only way in,' Phil said.

'Now that's the intriguing bit. There ought to be two other

ways in.'

'How do you mean?'

'I mean I found two doors.'

'Doors?' I exclaimed.

'You heard me.' Bill grinned. 'Ordinary wooden doors. It's an interesting feature, but not unique: some of Costhorpe's other tunnel systems have entrances from cellars or down flights of steps. If you want to make an entrance secure, you put in a door. Anyone got some paper?'

Sheila produced a spiral-bound pad and a biro, and Bill squatted, resting the pad on his knee as he sketched the layout. It was simple enough: the y of tunnel and spur, and a brick-vaulted section about half-way along the spur, with two brick-vaulted flights of steps leading off it. He'd tried the doors – although maybe he shouldn't have, he acknowledged, since they were probably on private property – but neither had opened.

'Do you think they could be opened?' Gary asked him.

'I don't see why not. The brick tunnels are in good condition, and the doorframes aren't distorted. I expect they're locked or bolted on the other side.'

'Where would that be?' I asked.

'At a guess, in a cellar, or possibly in a garden, down steps. It'll be below ground: they're down the hill from here, but the slope's not particularly steep.'

Phil said, 'Let's have this clear. Most likely these doors lead to the cellars of houses over the road, farther down the hill?'

'I should think so,' Bill agreed.

'So the owners of those cellars would have known about the mine?'

'That's a reasonable conclusion.'

'And they didn't let on about it.'

'Apparently not. Of course that's assuming the doors do lead to cellars, which isn't proven. Do you know if those houses have cellars?'

Phil frowned. 'I've only been into Raze and Steve's – number six. It's the sort of house that could have a cellar, but I can't say I've been down to one.'

'You don't know, councillor?' Sheila asked me.

'I've never been in any of those houses.'

'Well,' said Bill, 'the doors must be on someone's property, and we'll have to find out whose. Mapping the tunnels would tell us eventually, but it'd be easier and faster to locate them on the surface. We'll have to ask around – carefully, though, because I don't want any idiots to wander off into the tunnels unsupervised.'

I said, 'How about Rex's public meeting? Are you going to it?' I'd been told by Judith to go myself.

'I'm speaking, yes. I'll think about sending out an appeal from the platform.'

PHIL had taken Bill's news calmly, but on the way home I watched him absorbing it, and tapping a good deep vein of anger. A couple of times he had to stand on the brakes at red lights, and he swore at a jaywalker in Southern Road.

I was relieved to get back home in one piece, and didn't say anything when he stalked off to his and Allie's room without a word. I gave him twenty minutes, then made two mugs of coffee and carried them up. My office was only a door away, so I could easily go back to my word processor if he snapped at me.

My knock earned a 'come in', and I did, to find him lying on the bed, hands behind his head, his eyes closed. It made him look like a tousle-headed, square-chinned boy.

'Coffee,' I said. 'I'll leave it on the bookshelves.'

There was a half-minute's silence, then he opened his eyes and said, 'Thanks. I'm sorry. We're being lousy guests.'

'Anyone would be upset, Phil. D'you want to discuss it?'

'Uh... yes, Erica. Thanks.' He sighed out loud. 'What rats me's the thought of people knowing. All right, a blocked-off mine can't easily be traced or a collapse foreseen, and I don't blame Bill Baxter and his lot; but how could you have a door in your cellar that led to a mine, and not tell anyone about it? Especially after a major incident. Even Raze and Steve... they're flaky, they're not keen on the authorities, but I wouldn't have believed they'd simply keep mum about knowing where the tunnel went and how to get into it. Christ, someone nearly got killed.'

'Maybe they hadn't had reason to tell anyone earlier, but they should have done after the collapse,' I agreed. 'Assuming their house does have a door.' I settled myself against the door-jamb. 'Tell me about them.'

Phil considered for a moment, then sat up, propped himself on an elbow and reached out for his coffee mug. The bookshelf was only eighteen inches from the bed. He drank, then said, 'Raze is a Rasta. You've maybe seen him around. He's tall, medium build, mid-twenties or so.'

'So I have.'

'He's okay when you get to know him. He works on and off for Butterworth Housing, the trust that deals with homeless youngsters. Allie really likes him. He's the only neighbour she does like, come to think.'

'And Steve's his... flatmate?'

'Partner. A straight-looking guy who works in a garage. He's bright, he read philosophy at the uni.'

'Which garage?'

'Big Nick's, on North Road. I could phone him there and ask him if he knows anything.'

'Maybe it's better to leave it to Bill.'

'I don't know. I've been trying to think of ways they'd react to the collapse, reasons they might not... I don't know.'

'It might not be them,' I pointed out.

'I don't know who else lives over there.'

'I'll dig out the electoral roll from my filing cabinet.'

'Do it this evening. I'd better get back to work now.'

PHIL told Allie what had happened while I was stuffing baked potatoes for supper. He was his normal phlegmatic self by then, and she took the news calmly too.

But they both wanted to know more, so when we'd eaten I fetched down the electoral roll for Hillside ward. We discovered number two Flint Hill was empty, or had been when the roll was drawn up. Keylock, Miles Frederick, was listed at number four.

'That little squirt,' Phil said, and grimaced.

'Not your type?' I wasn't surprised.

'Hardly. He's the sort who has a black and grey living room, and hangs out in the discos on Saturday night.'

'Phil, you don't know that,' Allie protested.

'I can guess,' Phil said. 'Carry on, Erica.'

Number six gave us Black, Stephen John, and Garron, Robert, and at number eight were the Dunburys, James Alexander and Norice Mary. Not a heaven-sent combination.

From what Bill had said, the doors probably belonged to

neighbouring houses. Raze and Steve, and Miles Keylock? It was hard to believe an estate agent would buy a house with a door onto a chalk mine. Raze and Steve, and the Dunburys? Neither Allie nor Phil knew the Dunburys, and my speculations about them didn't get us far.

We might have been on the wrong stretch of road. Nobody was listed for number ten. Allie read out the names for numbers twelve to twenty, but they meant nothing to us.

'Let's go back to Raze and Steve,' I said. 'Do they own their house? How long have they lived there?'

Allie thought they owned the place, Phil reckoned they rented it privately. Both agreed the pair had lived there longer than the three years Phil had lived across the road.

'How did you come to know them?'

I didn't expect my question to be contentious, but it silenced them amazingly. Allie looked at Phil, Phil looked at the tabletop. I went to put Mozart's Fortieth Symphony on the stereo.

When I sat down again they still hadn't decided whether to answer me. I picked up my coffee mug, leaned back, balancing my chair on its rear legs, and asked myself why.

I'm not a prize listmaker like Phil, and I didn't try to be methodical. I watched Allie, now staring down at her clasped hands like a Rembrandt model. She wasn't a fidgeter by nature, but she wasn't at ease. She kept looking up at Phil, and when he looked up too I saw them give each other a 'You decide' look.

Couples. Couples with secrets. I thought fleetingly of Nick telling me about himself and Jenny, then concentrated. How do people like Allie get matey with their neighbours? They had the university in common with Steve, but not subjects of study, and I wasn't aware that either Allie or Phil belonged to any societies there. Bisexual entanglements? They didn't seem the type. Squabbles with other neighbours? No, they barely knew them. Hillside bridge club? Cheery chats at the garden centre?

Allie said, 'I'll tell her, shall I?'

'Have to, really,' Phil replied.

She turned to me. 'This is in confidence, Erica.'

'Cross my heart.'

'Steve's our dealer – nothing hard, just hash. He only deals in a small way, you know, supplies his friends.'

Now I knew, it seemed obvious. I was a little surprised they'd thought I might be shocked: there weren't many people of our generation who'd never passed a joint. Maybe they thought politicians were above such things? Maybe they were right. I hadn't smoked dope for years, hadn't missed it, and the law was the second or third thought that passed through my mind.

I could hear a disapproving voice whispering, *he's got a record.* I soon placed it: Mrs Dunbury, at the church hall.

'That's your business,' I told Allie. 'It won't keep me awake at night. Do me a favour, though: think up another answer in case someone else asks the same question.'

'Who ever would?' Phil asked.

I repeated to him my conversation with Mrs Dunbury. 'Rumours spread,' I pointed out, 'and Mrs D's uptight enough to manure them. She'll most likely tell Rex Canning, my favourite Tory councillor, what she told me.'

'I don't think Raze does have a record,' Allie said.

'Maybe not, but Steve does,' Phil told her. 'He once mentioned to me being had up and getting a fine. I suppose Erica's right, the moral majority could have fun with rumours of stashes in the cellars. You can tell your Rex we got to know Steve at the uni, which is more or less true.'

I was tempted to say, he's not my Rex, but I decided to let it pass.

8

NOBODY over the age of ten would expect generosity from Rex Canning. If he'd asked me to his meeting, he had a reason. I had no paid work on now the Belgian report was finished, so it was worth taking half an empty morning to fathom it out.

Maybe it was as simple as, he hoped to show me up for an ill-informed fool. Not a hope, Canning, I thought grimly. I made a list, Phil-style, of questions the Flint Hill residents might ask. Then I made a list of answers, or people who might provide them.

I rang Louise Hoggett, and learned she would be at the meeting. I rang the police station, and discovered their spokesman would be Superintendant Ransome, commander of the Costhorpe North subdivision. I rang Bill Baxter, and asked if Rex had talked to him. He had, that morning. 'I'm afraid he wasn't too happy, councillor,' Bill told me. 'My fault, really – I let slip that you'd been there when we went down the mine yesterday, and he seemed to think he should have been invited too. I told him it wasn't political bias, just that you'd asked to come and he hadn't.'

I'll admit, I felt smug at that. I asked if Bill had had any further thoughts on the doors, and learned he'd done some rough calculations, and decided they had to be located around numbers two to twelve. 'There's one other thing,' he added.

'What's that?'

Bill hesitated, then said, 'Just something I'm not happy about. I think it might be a good idea to pass it by someone. I'm starting to wonder if I'm seeing things that aren't there, and...'

'Your very own obsession?'

'You maybe could call it that.'

'Tell me. I won't laugh.'

He hesitated again. 'It's not easy to explain on the phone. Is there any chance you could come into the office?'

I was going into City Hall for a lunchtime meeting, so I agreed to call in on him afterwards. But when I got to the City Engineer's

Department – they're in a separate building to City Hall, on the other side of St Nicholas Street – Bill wasn't there.

The receptionist thought he'd come back after lunch, and if he'd gone out since he should have booked out properly, she said; but he hadn't. He never left the office without booking out. It was against the health and safety regulations. She couldn't believe he would have overlooked the system.

Bill's colleagues surely knew where he was. I asked for Gary Temperley, but it was Sheila Brennan who came to the reception desk. She was looking smart in a charcoal suit with a black velvet collar, and as before, not at all pleased to see me.

'Was there something special you wanted to know, councillor?' she asked in a chilly voice.

'It's not so much that I wanted to know something, as that Bill wanted me to,' I explained.

'Of course: he did some calculations on the Flint Hill mine this morning.'

'It's not that, because he told me about those over the phone. There's something else.'

'Honestly, it's barely a day since we —'

'I wasn't criticising,' I said hastily. 'I'm just curious to know what he wanted. When he comes back, will you ask him to call me?'

'If you like,' Sheila said. But I had no call from Bill that afternoon.

NEON lighting didn't improve the off-cream walls and fake-aged beams of Flint Hill Methodist Church Hall. When Allie, Phil and I arrived at seven-fifteen the Formica-topped tables were stacked along the walls, and half a dozen rows of plastic chairs had been set out in the centre of the hall, facing a long trestle covered in Tory-blue cloth. Most of the chairs were already taken.

Allie and Phil went to join Raze and Steve, a slightly-built man with fair hair and a buttoned-down shirt. I said hello to half a dozen acquaintances, caught up on old and new problems – Flint Hill apart – and when I'd done my ward-councillor duty, headed for the area round the trestle.

Louise Hoggett was there, looking pained, and no wonder: a plump red-faced man was standing too close and grilling her. Patty Fowler, notebook in hand, was interviewing Superintendant Ransome. Rex, grey-suited, was bending over to huddle with the Tory Group Leader

Jack Wells, an elderly estate agent, and a very short woman of fortyish in a sharply-tailored blue coat. I recognised her as Dilys Drake, Tory MP for Costhorpe North, and silently groaned.

'This is what I call disproportionate representation.'

Tony March, a bearded Liberal backbencher, had spoken in my ear. I gave him a rueful smile. It was obvious now that Rex had planned the meeting as a propaganda coup for Dilys, and that I, like Tony, had only been asked along because the Council's officers wouldn't have agreed to attend otherwise.

It was a mistake to have come; but it was too late to withdraw. I'd just have to do what I could, and hope the meeting rebounded on the Tories. Also, I could find some answers for Phil and Allie. I went to Louise's rescue, saw off Red-face, and asked her to fit names to faces.

Wonderful Louise first pointed out the couple from number ten – three rows back, a dark-haired man and a woman in a blue and white checked jacket, both thirtyish, and rather chic. 'There wasn't anyone down for number ten on the electoral roll,' I said.

'They're French, that's why – Daniel and Marie Duchêne.'

'They look it. Who are the Uttings from number twelve?'

'I didn't deal with them, they talked to Mrs Gold from Social Services and went off quickly. Then there's the Dunburys...'

'I know her. Is that her husband in the brown leather bomber jacket, over by the window?'

Louise squinted across the hall. The tall man in the bomber jacket was standing next to Mrs Dunbury, but he didn't look as I'd imagined her husband would. She was drab in a black coat and sludge-green silk scarf; he was flash, with blow-dried grey hair, a heavy tan, and expensively casual slacks and sweater.

'I think he must be,' Louise said dubiously.

'Any idea what he does for a living?'

'None. I'll ask if you like.'

'It's not your job, Louise: I'll ask myself later. Miles Keylock I know.' He was sitting in the front row.

'And you'll know his father too.'

'Only by reputation.' The older coterie of city estate agents were cronies of Jack Wells, Tories when they admitted to any politics, and I never encountered them as a rule. Nor had I met Fred when I'd been to his office, but he was easily identifiable because he was a shiny-red-and-black sort of man like his son, except his hair was sparser and more slicked-back.

'Who else...?' Louise thought out loud.

'Erica,' Rex interrupted, 'where's Baxter?'

Why was I supposed to know? Watching him go down the mine didn't make me Bill's best friend. 'On his way, probably,' I said. 'Don't panic, Rex. He's only five minutes late.'

'That's enough, for a do like this. Have you talked to him today?'

'Is it any of your business?'

Rex scowled, as if it wasn't normal for women to mind his interrupting their conversations, let alone to answer him back. 'I didn't ask you what you said,' he retorted.

No, but... I swallowed my ire, conscious of the public's eyes on us, and said more moderately, 'And I won't tell you,but you may as well know that I spoke to him on the phone this morning. I arranged to see him this afternoon, but he'd gone off somewhere. I expect something urgent came up.'

'If it did, he could have detailed someone to take his place.'

'So he could. Don't glare at me, Rex. I'm not responsible for Bill's shortcomings.'

'I wouldn't put it past you to have —' Rex cut himself short, and swallowed. 'Sorry, I take that back. I'm not prepared to hold up the meeting, so we'll have to start without him. Maybe someone could phone...'

'One of your many Tories?'

Rex's face went blank, as if he was shocked by such combativeness. 'Why don't I?' Louise suggested. She seemed amused by our bickering. 'You won't need me at the start, will you? Do you have his home phone number?'

Rex and I both gratefully accepted her offer, and admitted we had no idea of it. We left Louise to the unenviable job of working through the Baxters in the phone book, and took our places behind the top table.

Rex organised us. He put himself in the middle, with Superintendant Ransome on his left, and Jack Wells and Dilys Drake flanking them. Tony March was placed at one end, I at the other, and empty chairs were left next to us for Louise and Bill respectively. Patty Fowler took a seat in the front row, and a photographer from the Argus snapped Dilys Drake standing while we all sat.

The hall was now crammed. Rex called for silence, briefly introduced us all, then asked Dilys to speak.

Dilys was a pro, and it was too much to hope she'd make a mess of it. She did her usual solid job on the predictable lines of Your Caring Conservative Party, Working Hard for You. Apparently the incompetent Labour council had been doing their best to frustrate the intrepid investigators of the opposition. Questions would be asked in the House. She twice mentioned that an expert from the City Engineer's Department had been invited to speak but had failed to come. Mean of her, I thought, considering we didn't know why Bill was absent, but Dilys always acted as if it was a personal insult that her constituents should have helped vote in a Labour city council.

As soon as she sat down, Allie stuck her hand up to ask a question; and I signalled too, although I doubted whether Rex would allow me to speak yet.

He didn't. He said there would be questions later, and moved straight on to Superintendant Ransome. A dark, thin-faced man, Ransome too spoke effectively, explaining the police role in handling emergencies, emphasising that they were keeping a close watch on the area, and describing the diversions which had been set up.

All this was sensible, if rather tedious. The audience were shifting on their hard seats, doubtless wondering whether we'd tell them when they could go back to their houses. Next Rex called on Jack Wells.

I'd never had much time for Wells, whom I'd found to be pompous and slow-witted, and I reckoned Rex had made a mistake. The audience didn't want to hear another Tory knocking the City Council, they wanted hard information. Wells rambled on about committee schedules and funding priorities, the shuffles and mutters increased, and I watched the door. It was too much to hope Rex would give me a good chance to contradict Dilys and Wells, but if Bill appeared he would do the job convincingly.

The door opened: but it was only Louise, who turned empty palms towards us.

Rex himself took over from Wells, amid a few shouts of 'When we can go home?' He silenced them by saying he'd spoken to the Council's engineers that morning, and had some good news: they had found no tunnels under the northern end of Flint Hill, and people living in numbers forty-five and upwards, and at the top end of Flint Avenue, could return home the next morning.

Half the hall cheered, while the rest looked glum. Rex added that the engineers were continuing their investigations, and he hoped some more houses would be cleared very soon.

'Where's the engineer?' someone yelled.

'He's been held up, I'm afraid,' Rex said, 'but I've told you exactly what he'd have told you himself if he'd been here. We can't allow anyone to go home until it's safe, and the engineers aren't yet confident about the houses towards the bottom of the hill.'

'They're taking long enough about it. What the hell've they been doing this past week?'

'Investigating,' Rex said. 'And they're continuing to investigate, as I just told you.'

'Wasn't nobody around today,' another man shouted. 'I came up here to see, and the whole damn place was deserted.'

'That's right,' someone else yelled. 'They ought to get a move on.'

'It's only been just over a week, and —'

'A week? You know how long a week is when you can't get into your own house? I'll give you a bloody week, mate!'

'Please calm down. We're doing all we can, and —'

'Are you hell! Your friends just told us they're a bloody shower at City Hall. We don't want no working to rule, we want them out there every bloody minute until they've finished the job. We want those tunnels filled in and us let back into our houses, and we want it done fast!'

A dozen people were yelling at once, and several were on their feet. One man came up to the trestle and shook his fist in Rex's face. 'Don't you treat us like idiots, mate!' he shouted. 'Doing their bloody best indeed!'

Phil was standing and waving his hand, but even if Rex had called on him, the audience wasn't in a mood for sober reason. Tony March leaned over Wells to Superintendant Ransome and gestured to the man in front of Rex. Ransome got to his feet and unobtrusively left the room. I hoped he was going for police reinforcements: I'd have preferred to see Rex drown in disaster some time when we weren't sharing a platform.

I'd thought things might turn nasty when we explained what work the Council would and wouldn't pay for, but we hadn't got to that.

'Order!' Rex yelled. 'Order! If this goes on I'll have to adjourn the meeting, and I'm sure that's not what you want. You want answers, and we've got some to give you. Now can I have some quiet, please, and I'll take questions.'

The fist-waver retreated, and the volume fell. Rex didn't wait for silence: as soon as the last person was sitting he announced, 'Mr Utting, you had a question.'

A thin bespectacled man in the fourth row stood up. He was, I supposed, the Mr Utting from number twelve. I hadn't seen him waving his hand earlier, so he was probably a Tory plant. I only hoped Rex hadn't primed him to criticise the Council.

Utting looked nervous. 'What I want to know's this,' he said. 'What're the Council going to do now? Have we got to wait for them to fill in the mine before we go home?'

Rex barely paused. 'Maybe Councillor Massen would like to answer.'

Maybe Councillor Massen wouldn't; but this was no moment to argue. I got to my feet.

'I'm sorry the City Engineer isn't here, but as Councillor Canning said, he's been unavoidably detained. I can't pretend to be an expert myself, but I'll tell you what I can. The next thing is for the engineers to finish plotting the course of the mine. When that's done we'll know which houses are affected and which aren't, and we should be able to let a lot more people go home. Obviously people whose houses are affected will have to wait, but I can't say how long, because we don't yet know what recommendations the engineers will come up with.'

'Come on,' someone shouted. 'They'll recommend filling in the mine.'

Did Rex expect me to pretend that this was so? I knew it wasn't, and I wasn't prepared to fib – although if I'd been less irritated with him, I might have found my way to an evasive answer. As it was I said bluntly, 'I don't think they necessarily will. Not all old mines get filled in, only unstable ones.'

'This one is bloody unstable. It fell in, didn't it?'

'Only in one place.'

'One place is one too many. We're not going to sit on top of a bloody great hole and wait for our houses to fall down round our ears.'

The noise level was rising again, and I had to shout. 'Nobody's asking you to. The engineer won't clear your houses unless he's satisfied they're safe.'

'Only one way to make them safe, and that's to fill up the mine.'

I seemed to be sinking ever deeper into the hole Rex had dug for me. 'Maybe that's so,' I said. 'If it is, the mine will have to be filled in.'

'The Council going to do it?' Utting demanded.

'I've told you all I can, Mr Utting. We won't decide anything until we've had the engineers' report.'

'They bloody won't, will they?' another man yelled.

'We want a promise. You've got to agree to fill in the mine.'

Damn Rex. It was all his fault that I was in this mess. I said loudly, 'The four councillors here can't make decisions for the whole Council. I've told you, that hasn't been discussed yet, and it won't be discussed till we have the engineers' recommendations.'

'You go back now and tell them they've got to fill in the whole mine. We won't take anything else.'

Shouts of 'Bloody Council' and 'Fill it up' came from all sides. I gave up and sat down.

Rex threw me a dirty look and shouted, 'Quiet please! You won't hear the answers if you all shout at once. Let's have some silence. Mr Keylock, you had a question. Please be quiet so you can hear Mr Keylock ask his question.'

Quiet the audience weren't, but Fred Keylock got to his feet anyway, and turned his back to us, facing them. 'I'll tell you what I know,' he bawled. He had a Rotary-club-auctioneer's voice, which carried effectively across the hubbub. 'And I'm a pro, you all know me, Fred Keylock of Keylocks Estate Agency. I know all about buildings and subsidences and chalk mines, and I know it's all happened before, and I'll tell you this. The Council never fill in the holes, except under their own houses and under the roads. Private houses they don't touch, never have and never will.'

'They bloody will this time,' someone shouted.

'They will, too right,' Keylock agreed, 'because we'll make them. We'll get public opinion on our side, we'll get these councillors here to support us, and we'll make damn sure they get their mates to agree. We'll force the Council to make that mine secure; and I don't mean a couple of props, I mean proper filling-in. Tell you what, for a start we don't want any survey. That's just a waste of money, it'll only tell us what we already know, there's a mine under Flint Hill and it isn't safe. We're saying right now, we're not having any fancy maps, what we want is foamed concrete pumped into that mine, starting tomorrow. They can do it if they've got the will. They can call an emergency meeting and agree the funding, and it won't take any hundred-thousand-pound surveys, it just takes a good civil engineer with the right equipment.'

Rex was back on his feet. 'Now I'm no engineer, Mr Keylock, but I can tell you it's not a job you can plan on the back of an envelope.

Whether it comes to filling in the mine or not, first we've got to —'

'Sod the survey,' a woman shouted.

'Now be reasonable, madam. There are things the engineers have to find out before we can even think about filling in the mine.'

'The man there's right.' This was James Dunbury, shouting from the side of the hall. 'All we need's for the engineers to be sure they've found both ends of the tunnel. They should have, they've been down there. Find out how long it is, which way it goes, and fill it in. Easy as that.'

'That's right. We don't want no bleedin' surveys, we want the mine filled in.'

What I wanted was to get out of the church hall in one piece, preferably without police intervention, and certainly without committing the Council to anything. Fortunately Rex did appear to be determined to resist the audience's blackmail. He said loudly, 'I think there are things we all need to know before we do that.'

'Like bloody what?'

'If you sit down and calm down, ladies and gentlemen, I'll give you some more information.'

Did he mean the doors, I wondered? With the audience in this mood, surely he wouldn't tell them about the doors? They'd likely as not go rushing down the hill to turn over numbers two to twelve.

But if the police could prevent that... Maybe Rex had a point. If he could bring this meeting to a tidy close without making any promises, it would break the momentum of protest. We might face some irate residents afterwards, but we wouldn't be confronted with a near-mob again.

Even now people were sitting down and quietening enough for Rex to continue.

'You say it's a waste of time to investigate, but let's look at what the engineers have discovered. They've confirmed the tunnel doesn't go under the north part of Flint Hill, and enabled around half of you to go back home safely. Isn't that worth something?'

A hundred low grumbles answered him, not a lot.

'And I think you'll decide this is worth something too. The hole behind Mr and Mrs Bunting's house isn't the only way into the mine.'

A man shouted, 'You mean you already knew about it?'

'Me personally? No, and nor did the City Engineer – but maybe some other people knew. I'd like to know if they did. Because there are two passages leading into the mine, and before it's blocked off I want to know where they come out, and whether anyone knew about them before the collapse.'

'How d'you mean, passages?' James Dunbury shouted.

'I mean brick-vaulted flights of steps fitted with doors. We want to find out whose land they're on, and if the owners knew about them, and if they did, why they didn't tell the authorities. Don't you think that's worth investigating? I do. I'll ask some hard questions and get some straight answers before I let anyone close off the mine for good.'

'Eh.' Graham Bunting struggled to his feet, clutching little Ben to his stomach. 'You're sayin' someone knew about the bloody mine all along?'

'I'm saying I want to know if anyone did, and I'm saying the City Engineer plans to find out. I bet you want to find out too, don't you, Mr Bunting?'

Superintendant Ransome slipped back into the hall, and a couple of constables followed him. Bunting meanwhile yelled, 'If anyone did and they didn't let on, I'll f...in' kill 'em!'

'Calm down please, and listen. This is important. That mine's dangerous, and only the experts should go near it. We can't allow anyone to carry out their own search. The Council engineers will do that, and I'll personally make sure you're told what they discover. If any of you have information that will help, you should let them know. Talk to me after the meeting, or phone City Hall and ask for the City Engineer's Department. And please stay well clear of the area until it's been fully investigated and made safe. Remember there's a danger of roof falls, and there's also a risk of gas in the mine, so it's no place for amateurs.'

'Let's find out now,' Mr Utting shouted. His face had turned salmon pink. 'I don't see why we have to wait. I'm asking you, folks – does anyone know where those passages come out?'

His only reply came from Superintendant Ransome.

'I'd advise you not to answer that, ladies and gentlemen. Tempers are high tonight, and that's understandable, but it's best if you give them time to cool down. I'm going to ask you to break up the meeting now. Leave in an orderly fashion, please, and don't hang about outside the hall. Please go straight home, and even if your house has been declared safe, don't move back in until the morning. We have a police presence in the area twenty-four hours, so everything's quite safe. Thank you for coming, and let's have you going now.'

Half a dozen policemen were now spread around the walls of the hall. Rex looked left and right, blank-eyed, then sat down.

Relieved, doubtless, as I was. Mind, I wouldn't have felt nearly so relieved if I'd been the owner of a mystery door.

Who was?

From the front I'd been able to look into most people's faces, but I hadn't noticed any strikingly guilty expressions. The Keylocks were still sitting, whispering to each other on the front row. The Dunburys were standing, both now with their backs to me, not touching each other. Daniel Duchêne had an arm round his wife as they watched people file out of the hall. Allie and Phil, Raze and Steve were talking – animatedly, but not in a way that triggered alarm-bells.

Who else? I couldn't see John Utting any more. The hall was emptying, and Jack Wells was standing by a sitting Rex, hand on his shoulder, telling him something in a low voice.

'Well,' I said to Dilys, 'what do you suggest our Caring Council does? Do we pay to have the mine filled in and get clobbered by the government for spending too much, or do we say too bad to all these nice people?'

'If you didn't spend so much on loony left projects, you wouldn't have that choice to make,' Dilys said coldly.

'Which loony left project would you like us to cancel? Cheap bus passes for senior citizens? The new swimming pool? Our small business advice service?'

Dilys wasn't listening. I resisted the temptation to inform Rex what I thought of his tell-the-people exercise, and went to see if Allie and Phil were ready to head for home.

9

ALLIE and Phil told me they'd watched Raze and Steve while Rex had been leading up to his announcement, and felt sure neither had known about a door. They hadn't recognized the Duchênes, and hadn't been able to see the Keylocks' faces, but they had also kept a close eye on the Dunburys. Norice had looked worried, they said, and Allie reckoned James had been angry. Phil was less sure.

Phil added that he'd asked Steve about the Uttings. Steve didn't know them well, but he did know John Utting ran a bicycle shop on Farmer Street, and they had two teenage daughters. Utting's wife Lucy was a rather complacent woman. She had barely reacted when Rex had mentioned the doors, but John had seemed furious.

'Someone'll go down the mine overnight,' Allie predicted, but Phil wasn't having any of that. Only an idiot would go blundering around a mine, he insisted, and by and large the inhabitants of Flint Hill were not idiots. He conceded that Raze and Steve could sometimes be crazy, but both had been in a sober mood at the meeting. Just before I'd joined them at the end, they had told Phil they would go back to their house in the morning and check whether they had a mystery door. Apparently their house had a cellar but they had never been down to it.

Phil couldn't see why they should have lied to him; and that night the place would be crawling with police, so he didn't think they would look sooner.

I DIDN'T have to ask myself whether I should go back over to Flint Hill next morning: I'd already agreed to do so. Allie and Phil were moving into their new flat, and I'd promised to help them retrieve their possessions from Phil's house.

Phil had phoned the engineers a few days earlier, and had been told he shouldn't go into the house himself: the fire service would bring everything out. Bill might have overlooked a clandestine nip inside to fill a suitcase, but a wholesale clear-out had to be done properly.

We got to Flint Hill at eight-thirty, and the fire service arrived a few minutes later. Farther up the hill police officers were relocating the barriers, and a couple of returning families appeared with suitcases. Down towards the ring road there was no sign of life.

The flat in Hunter Court was let furnished, so Phil was planning to have most of his furniture put into store. That would be done later, and the house boarded up; for now it was mainly a question of collecting cardboard boxes from the fire officers at the door and carrying them down the path to the van he had hired.

When we'd finished, around ten, Allie suggested we see if Raze and Steve were at home, but we hadn't seen either of them arrive, and Phil doubted that they would have come. Steve would probably be working, he said, and Raze never woke much before midday.

I guessed Phil was keen to get away. Allie might not have liked the place, but it had been his home for three years, and it was painful for him to see the house and his beloved garden left desolate. I offered to knock up Raze and Steve on my own. Phil and Allie had all day to unpack, and wouldn't want or need my help.

It was a pleasant morning, and I liked the idea of walking home. Hands in jacket pockets, I ambled down the hill, taking the pavement on the eastern side. At number ten the Duchênes offered narrow-slatted white blinds pulled halfway down and an elegantly curved blue vase on the windowsill. Number eight was hidden behind neatly cut privet; number six – Raze and Steve's house – scrawled over with uncut privet.

Behind the privet, the front garden was dull but surprisingly tidy: grass which had known a mower the summer before, and bulbs coming up in the flowerbed. The front door had a stained glass panel, and ridged mouldings which were heavy with dust. The bell was painted over, and there was no knocker. I tried ringing, and heard a tinny squeal somewhere deep in the house.

No reply. I tapped on the stained glass as well, but I couldn't see any movement behind it.

As I emerged from the gate, a police constable was coming up the hill. 'Hey, you!' he shouted.

Annoying, and not only because he'd broken into a sprint as if I was about to cut and run. I hadn't tried to avoid being seen, but in retrospect I could see I might have been wiser to, because now I'd have to explain what I'd been doing in Raze and Steve's front garden.

It would hardly have been a major crime if they had been home, but strictly speaking they shouldn't have been, and I didn't want to get them into trouble. And if I hadn't been expecting to find them in, why should I have been knocking on their door?

'This area's closed to the public,' the constable panted.

I gave him a professional smile. 'I know, officer. Erica Massen, from the City Council.' I held out my hand, and looking bemused, he took it. 'Our public meeting last night got a little out of hand, and since I was in the area, I thought I'd check that no damage was done afterwards.'

'That meeting was up the road.'

'True, but the people at it were interested mainly in ways into the chalk mine, and there's an entrance somewhere close to this row of houses.' I gave him what I hoped was a winsome shrug. 'I know the people who live here, and I didn't want them to come home and find a mess.'

'We've had a watch on the area all night.'

'I felt sure you would,' I gushed. 'You probably think it's stupid of me to be so over-concerned.'

He probably did, but he couldn't tell me off for that. 'Not at all, miss – or should I say councillor? We like to have people keeping an eye open. Only this area's supposed to be evacuated, so it'd be as well if you left it to us this time.'

I assured him I would in future, and he let me go.

WITH Phil and Allie gone, my house seemed as quiet as the evacuated zone. Not even Mao-mao was around. There was a buff-enveloped circular on the mat, and my answering-machine tape held three messages: from my mother, the Labour Group Whip updating me on decisions made at the pre-Council meeting I'd missed, and Louise Hoggett.

'I didn't have a chance to tell you yesterday,' Louise's voice said, 'but I did find Bill's number, and his wife said he hadn't come home from work. It worries me a bit. Will you ring me back?'

I did so, and learned that Bill's wife had been very apologetic when Louise had told her he'd missed the meeting, and had kept saying he didn't usually let people down – which, as Louise and I both knew, was true. But she hadn't seemed particularly worried where he might have got to, and when Louise had asked if she had any ideas, she had been vague and offputting.

'Isn't that strange?' Louise demanded.

'Well... yes and no.' I thought it understandable. Quite a few women find themselves not knowing where their men are – or worse, knowing but wishing they weren't there – and it's no fun to be interrogated by someone who doesn't realise the situation. I'd hit the problem myself once or twice. 'Louise,' I went on, 'I get the feeling you want me to phone Mrs Baxter, and I don't want to.'

'What if something's wrong?'

'Obviously something's wrong, but it's not our problem. It was Rex who asked him to the meeting, and David North's his boss, and his wife's his wife, and as far as I'm concerned he can tell them his excuses. If they don't like them, they can yell. I'm not yelling. I'm sorry he wasn't there, but I'm not about to make a formal complaint; and if there's something up in his private life, frankly, Louise, I'd rather not know.'

'I hope you don't think I'm prying.'

'I don't,' I assured her.

'Only I think someone ought to make sure he's all right, and someone ought to let him know that Councillor Canning told people about the doors to the mine.'

'That's true.' Councillor Canning being the someone. But Louise had dug in, and if I didn't make some concession I'd be stuck on the phone to her till midday. 'All right, Louise, I surrender. Give me the number and I'll ring him.'

She did so, rang off, and I sighed out loud and phoned it. It answered on the second ring. 'Bill...' an eager woman's voice said.

'Oh. I was hoping he was there, but obviously he's not.'

'No he's not. Who's speaking?'

I told her. There was a short silence before she spoke again, this time in a voice as flat as a car computer. 'I'm sorry, councillor. He's not available at the moment, but if you give me your number I'll ask him to call you as soon as he gets back.'

'Thanks,' I said, and gave her it. I had the impression her desperate eagerness had survived a long stream of callers, none of whom had been Bill. If she had known where he was, she would have got onto him by now; if she didn't, there was no point pressing her. I cracked a feeble joke about minding the mines, rang off, went upstairs and began to strip my spare bed. I was humping the sheets down to the washing machine when the phone rang again.

This time it was a lazy-sounding man. 'Hey, that the councillor?'

'Raze?' I guessed.

'Too right. Hey, we made discoveries here.'

'You're at Flint Hill?'

'Num-ber six. Down in the cellar. A door. Just like the man said, a door. We goin' explorin'. You wanna come?'

I'd felt relieved for a second; one door discovered, quickly, and Raze sounded as if they genuinely hadn't known about it before. Alarm rapidly took over.

'Don't do that, Raze. You were told last night that it's not safe.'

'We'll be safe. You ain't comin'?'

'Seriously, Raze, it's too much of a risk. There could be —'

'Down the chute, man,' Raze interrupted, and hung up.

Sweet heavens. I couldn't leave him to it. I'd have phoned Bill, but I knew he wasn't around. Should I phone another engineer? Or the police? The fire brigade?

I rang the City Hall emergency number, and had an abrasive and none too helpful conversation with the woman who answered. Apparently I was the third person that morning who had asked for Bill Baxter. Forget it, I told her, and leafed through the phonebook. There was only one Brennan, S, listed, and the number didn't answer. No Temperley, G was down in the book, and David North, the Chief City Engineer, didn't reply.

Would Raze and Steve really be such idiots as to go down the mine, or had Raze been winding me up? I didn't know him well enough to judge.

I rang the police, and told them I thought someone was about to go into the Flint Hill mine. I was put through to the control room, where a woman listened and took details with audible scepticism. So I was in Morton Street, nowhere near Flint Hill? So I hadn't actually seen anything? So I wasn't absolutely certain what was happening? I pointed out that there was a constable stationed in the area, and asked her to have him check, but I wasn't sure I'd infected her with my own sense of urgency.

There was only one way to find out what was happening. I grabbed my car keys and headed back to Flint Hill.

10

HIGH pressure falling was the danger combination, according to Phil. I didn't possess a barometer, and all I knew was that it wasn't raining. I'd have liked to have a better idea of the risk of carbon dioxide build-up. I was worried about roof falls, too. I had no idea how common they were. Mind, just being in the dark underground would have felt dangerous enough to me.

Saturday morning traffic jammed the roads solid. I should have taken my bike: I'd been in too much of a panic to think of it. I slotted Mahler's Fourth into my car cassette player to calm myself.

When I got to Flint Hill there was nowhere to park. I had to cruise round the neighbouring streets before I found a short space into which it took me three attempts to reverse.

I wondered if I should have stopped to changed into jeans: I'd got flattish shoes on, but a chalk-blue jersey skirt I was fond of, and a new angora sweater I didn't want to have to wash. I hadn't thought of going right down into the mine, but I thought now, what if there was no sign of them on the surface? I flipped open the glove compartment and slipped my torch into my jacket pocket. Then I ran.

Shoppers were trudging to their cars, shoulders drooping under the weight of their bags. Late-rising families were moving back into their houses and calling out greetings to each other. A flop-eared spaniel nosed around the barrier across the road. I slid between two parked cars, vaulted the barrier, and headed into the evacuated zone.

Beyond the barrier, the place was even more deserted than it had been earlier. There was no sign of Raze or Steve, the police or anyone else. I dashed down to number six, rounded the gate and, panting, pressed the doorbell. And again, and again.

No one came. My chest stopped hurting, my breath came smoothly. I tried the handle. It didn't give.

It must have been twenty minutes or more since Raze had phoned me, but I couldn't believe he and Steve would have checked out the mine and left in that time. Might they have decided not to check it out, and left? Maybe; but equally they might have gone down, and not come back up.

Extreme actions don't come easy when you're English, let alone North Anglian, steeped in North-Sea reserve. I thought of bashing in the door, but I couldn't bring myself to do it. Instead I went back to the street and found a passageway between numbers two and four. It took me to the rear of number six, but the back door was shut and locked, and all the windows were closed.

I went round to the front again and tried the windows there: no luck. These guys had gone through the front door and straight down to the cellar – they hadn't aired the house en route.

Where were the police? Was a constable still in the area? The woman I'd spoken to had been so noncommittal that I couldn't be sure. North Anglia Constabulary weren't exactly overstaffed on Saturday mornings, and they might have had to send all their officers elsewhere. Nor would they necessarily give top priority to answering my call.

If a police officer appeared, maybe he would break in. Then again, maybe he wouldn't.

Standing on Raze and Steve's path wasn't achieving anything. I went back out to the street, and looked down it: nobody. Looked up it – and surprise gave me a kick in the ribs. Rex Canning was barely ten feet away, and heading closer. He was a study in brown like an Edwardian sepia photo: milk-chocolate trousers and v-neck, beige shirt, bitter-chocolate overcoat flapping loose, hands in pockets, his fair hair and blue eyes adding touches of vividness.

He stopped two feet from me, and gave me an Edwardian dandy's knowing smile. 'Well, councillors' corner. Visiting the Dunburys' disreputable neighbours?'

'There's a crisis,' I told him succinctly. Small relief, the smile died. In a more reasonable voice he enquired, 'Need help?'

I did, sufficiently that even his was better than nothing. I explained who and what, and Rex said, 'Damn. You're sure they've gone down?'

'No, but Raze said they would, and I can't see that we can cross our fingers and hope he was fibbing.'

'That's true.' He frowned. 'I tried to get Baxter over this morning, but I couldn't get hold of him. And Ransome promised me there'd be a watch on all these houses, but I'm damned if I've seen a policeman.'

'There was,' I said, 'but there isn't now.'

'What were you planning to do if you got into the house? Go down after them?'

'Call out, at least. See if they're really down there, see if they shout back, yell to them to come out. Tell them they're crazy. Jesus, I don't know. I've phoned the police. Any other suggestions?'

'Is the door locked?'

'Doors and windows, front and back. I've double-checked.'

'We can hardly break in.'

'I know, but what if they are down there, Rex? What if they walk into a pocket of gas?'

'If they did, they're probably dead already. Don't explode, I'm only thinking out loud. We'll do what we can, and hope the police turn up soon – and bloody Baxter as well. Let's go to the shaft.'

'Let's what?'

'If you were thinking of shouting, we can shout down there.' He didn't wait for a reply, but turned and set off at a stiff pace up the hill, his overcoat flapping about his legs.

Sound travelled well in the tunnels, as I knew from Bill's exploration, and the shaft wasn't so far away: if they were down the mine, they might hear a shout from there. I couldn't think of a better idea, so I followed Rex up the passage between the Buntings' house and Phil's.

At the end of the passage was a barrier of scaffolding firmly buttressed with planks, about four feet high, with *Danger – No Entry* written in red across it.

I came close enough to look over. Nothing much had changed on the other side: the crane was still there, and so were the nettles, the old tyres and the chalk rubble. The roadmen's shelter had gone, but the hole was as large and black as ever.

'What the hell...?' said Rex. He shrugged off his coat, tossed it to me, and to my surprise, proceeded to climb the barrier.

'Can't you shout from this side?' At times I wouldn't have minded seeing Rex fall down a black hole, but this wasn't one of them. There were only a couple of feet between the barrier and the edge of the hole, and I lacked his faith in the stability of the rim.

'Shouting isn't all I... Intriguing.'

I leaned farther over. Whatever he'd discovered, he was between me and it, bending down at the foot of the scaffolding that buttressed the devastated back corner of the house. I had to wait impatiently until he raised his head and said, 'Look at this.'

He stood, bringing it into view. It was a rope, yellow plastic, good and thick. One end was knotted round the scaffolding, and the other disappeared into the hole. Rex had hauled out enough to loop between his hands, but the loose end hung straight as if there was plenty more out of sight.

'Was this here before?' he demanded.

'Before what?'

'When you last came, when Baxter went down the mine. Did he use this for anything?'

'No,' I said, bewildered. 'What would he use a rope for? And if he'd wanted to, I wouldn't have thought he'd have fixed it round the scaffolding. It isn't safe, is it? Yank on that and you might pull the whole place down.'

Rex took this suggestion seriously enough to give the scaffolding a brief appraisal. 'I won't test that hypothesis,' he said, 'but I wouldn't think it was so very risky. He might have fixed it like this if he wanted to drop something down the hole. Did he?'

'Drop anything? No. The rope wasn't there, anyway. I spent hours hanging around on the day he went down, so I'd have noticed if it was.'

'Weird.' Rex began to haul the rope out of the hole, hand over hand, letting an uneven coil build up on the broken patio. It was tug-of-war rope, I thought. Climber's rope. There was a knot every three feet or so. I wouldn't have fancied doing so myself, but anyone good at climbing could have gone down the hole using that rope.

'Rex,' I said, 'fascinating as this is, we did come here to shout to Raze and Steve.'

'Shout then.'

He had a louder voice than I. Oh well. I arranged his coat across the barrier and climbed over. It was as well he wasn't looking, since this didn't improve the coat. I took a small step towards the rim, clutching the barrier tightly, and peered down into the black nothingness.

'Raze! Steve!'

There's a built-in English inhibitor which makes us squeal when we mean to yell. I took a deep breath and tried again. My voice seemed to lose itself very fast in the immensity of the blackness. The third shout wasn't bad: Rex jumped and dropped the rope.

I waited till the echo had faded, then asked him, 'Would they hear that, d'you think?'

'Half Costhorpe must have heard that. Shut up or you won't hear if they call back.'

He had a point. We stood in silence in the mud at the rim. Nothing. Not a rumble, not a twitter.

'Shall I call again?'

'Feel free,' said Rex, and put his hands over his ears.

Yelling's a good feeling when you get used to it. Standing up here, deafening Rex, it was difficult to remember that two men might be unconscious or even dead down the mine. I had to remember. I couldn't stand here all morning. We'd had enough of a go to discover this didn't work, so we'd have to think again. 'What now?' I said out loud.

'First we'd better get the rope out of the way,' Rex said briskly. 'If we leave it here it'll be a temptation to every child in the neighbourhood. Then we'll phone the fire brigade – better choice than the police, I should think, because they'll have breathing equipment. If the police haven't turned up by the time we've done that, we'll take a cautious look at the mine ourselves. I'd rather not have to, but I take your point: if they are down there, every minute could be vital.'

'If we're going to go down, it'd be stupid to take the rope away,' I pointed out. 'Or were you suggesting we break into number six?'

Rex gave a short-breathed sigh. 'Neither. There is another way in, so we'll use that. I'll handle Mrs Dunbury: just don't say anything to annoy her.'

'Oh. So the other door —'

'Or me,' Rex added.

For once I took his advice, and watched in silence as he hauled out the rest of the rope – there was nothing at the end except a big knot – and untied it from the scaffolding. He humped the coils over the barrier and said, 'Do you need a hand?'

'No.' If I'd been thinking straight, I'd have climbed over when he wasn't looking. I couldn't put my muddy feet on his coat while he was watching me, so I moved along a couple of feet, and gave a silent sob for my skirt.

We hurried, but didn't run: it seemed pointless when so much time had been lost already. Rex dumped the rope on the Dunburys' crazy-paved front garden, and banged on their door. After what seemed like an age, Mrs Dunbury opened it a crack. 'There's an emergency,' Rex said. 'Phone the fire brigade, please, and tell them to bring a tender and breathing equipment. A couple of men may have passed out in the mine. Where's your torch? We'll have to go down.'

'I've got one,' I offered, and wasn't flattered when he raised his brows: heavens, competence from Erica! But his manner had done wonders with Mrs D, I had to admit: she had fallen back against the wall, her face hazed with adoration.

'Oh, and keep an eye open for the police,' Rex added. 'Erica's sent for them: if they come, show them the way down. Come on, Erica.'

There wasn't a murmur from Mrs Dunbury as he shouldered past her and along her hallway, which was dadoed, picture-railed, anaglyptaed and hung with Victorian watercolours. I followed while she was still in a daze, hoping she'd revive in time to do as he'd asked.

It wasn't hard to deduce that Rex had been there that morning. He led us unhesitatingly to a door set in a small lobby between the hall and kitchen, and only had to fumble briefly for the light switch on the other side. Stone steps led us down to a large stone-flagged cellar with white-painted brick walls.

It was filled with mahogany dining-chairs upended on each other; battered chaises-longue oozing stuffing; tables top-to-top, legs in the air; bureaux, chests, desks and blanket boxes. The place looked like an antique dealer's store.

On the far side of a stack of chairs a big battered dresser was set at an angle from the wall, with the most accessible end poking outwards. In contrast to the polished oak and walnut, it had been painted white a long time ago. One drawer was open, and full to overflowing with hammers, screwdrivers, pliers, unravelling rolls of upholstery webbing and heaps of old tobacco tins.

Rex disappeared behind this. I followed, and wasn't too surprised to find that in the wall behind the dresser was a heavy white-painted door. It was shut, and an iron key projected from an efficient-looking lock.

'Don't say it,' Rex said. 'Where's your torch?' As he spoke he turned the key. The door opened with well-oiled ease, revealing an oblong of solid-looking darkness.

'It's in my hand.'

'Pass it over.'

I took a breath. 'Don't laugh, Rex, but I need to hold it myself. I'll go first.' I threw the switch and stepped past him. A feeble cone of light revealed a flight of steps leading steeply downwards, with a white-painted brick barrel vault over them.

'Okay, if you must.' Rex's hand clamped round my upper arm. It made me jump; made sense, though. 'We're not going to do anything dangerous. We'll call out again first, and if we don't hear an answer we'll go and check whether the other door's open. If it is, we'll go fifty yards in each direction, but no farther. Then if we haven't found them we'll come back and wait for the police and the fire brigade.'

I thought of suggesting that one of us stay by the cellar door – what if gas overcame us both? Imagine being found dead with Rex. But I wasn't volunteering to be the one who went in alone, and fifty yards sounded like a fair compromise. 'Shall I shout?' I asked.

'Why not? You do it well.'

I shouted. 'Raze. Steve. Are you down there? Call out if you hear us. Raze. Steve.' We stood in the doorway and listened: nothing.

'Let's go down,' Rex said in a low voice. 'Take it slowly, I'm holding onto you.'

'I know you are, but I can't walk down steps with you grabbing my arm.'

His hand slid down and into my free one. It felt warm and reassuring, and I didn't protest.

Two steps, and I felt the temperature fall. It wasn't damp, just chill and dark. So dark, thick darkness everywhere the light didn't shine. Before we were at the foot of the steps the light from the cellar deserted us. I couldn't even see Rex by my side. I tried to play the torch methodically: over the brick vaulting, the worn brick steps, a few sooty graffiti, names and nineteenth-century dates.

We came to the end of the steps, and the torch showed a vaulted tunnel running left and right. It sloped a little, down to our left, and in the other direction I could see where the vaulting ended, giving way to rough chalk walls and roof.

'That way?' I was trying to remember what Bill had told us. It was hard to make my mind work. The darkness seemed to press in on my brain, and it took all the effort I could muster to keep it from overwhelming me.

'I'm just orienting myself,' Rex murmured. 'The cellar's behind us, and the wall with the door's parallel to the hall, so... Yes, go left.'

We crept along the tunnel. I was trying not to hold Rex's hand too tightly. I'd never normally have let him take charge in the way I had in the last quarter-hour.

I could see the arch of the vault over the other steps. Not far. Just a few yards more.

The other steps were dustier than the Dunburys'. Nodules of chalk crunched underfoot as we climbed them. Half-way up we saw that the door at the top was open. The cellar behind was unlit.

We went right up, and shone the torch in. Unlike the Dunburys' cellar, this one was thick with dust and festooned in cobwebs. As far as I could see, the reason the light wasn't on was that there was no light. The only contents were a stack of old newspapers and another of orange crates hacked up into kindling, both so dust-encrusted they could have been left behind by the previous occupants.

The door was an indeterminate dark colour in the torchlight. Agglomerations of spiderwebs cascaded from the top and frame. A black-iron lock hung half-off, and the wood all round it was broken and splintered, pale against the old paint.

'No key,' Rex said. 'They got the bolts undone, then they used a crowbar. Is that it over there?'

My torch tracked the bolts on the door, shiny with oil applied over rust, then followed his pointing arm and searched the pamment floor. The worn silver end of the crowbar jumped out at us. It too was black iron, heavy, well-used.

'They've broken the lock, but they could have closed the door and bolted it,' Rex went on. 'I can't believe they'd have gone off and left it open.'

'Then they're down there somewhere.'

'It seems all too likely. Let's go back to the main tunnel, and I'll shout this time.'

As soon as we reached the foot of the steps he did so, boomingly. The echo crashed and rumbled. How long was the tunnel, I wondered? Not very long. Sheila at the foot of the shaft had heard Bill shout from each end. Surely they would hear, if they were down here and alive.

It was hard to believe they werc, though. It was all so crazy; and it was ages now since Raze had phoned me. If they had come down, surely they wouldn't have stayed this long?

Rex's fingers tightened convulsively, crushing my hand.

'Did you hear that?' he said in a hissing whisper.

'What?'

'Listen again.'

We did, but to silence. Rex yelled again, and we listened again.

Fighting the echo, I heard a sound. A voice? Yes, yes. What else? It had to be a voice.

Rex loosed his hand, although he didn't, thank goodness, let go completely. I was shaking. I wasn't relieved, it was too extraordinary for relief. Rex shouted again. 'This way. South of you. By the steps. Shall we come and find you?'

We waited so long that I began to think we'd imagined the first sound, then there was an answer, louder than before. A man was shouting, although I couldn't make out the words. Most likely he hadn't made out Rex's. Echoes and darkness. At least they were there, they were alive, it was all right.

'It was the same voice, wasn't it?' Rex whispered.

What did he...? Oh. My hand tightened round his again as I realised what he was getting at.

'It'll be all right,' he murmured. 'Let's go a little way farther.'

I didn't want to, but nor could I manage to speak, even to say no. Rex tugged my hand, and not wanting to lose him I followed him down the tunnel.

The brick vaulting ended just beyond the Dunburys' steps, and the torch beam revealed rough-cut chalk walls and roof studded with sticky-looking black lumps of flint. The chalk was eerily, lightlessly white, like snow seen at midnight. There was a ledge just over half-way up the wall, with vertical streaks of black above it. Think, think, I told myself. Keep calm, keep thinking. All this was in Bill's report. That's a candle ledge, a well-known feature. Those are soot stains. Men mined down here, centuries ago. This tunnel has been here for ages, it's stable, it's safe.

Now I could hear footsteps, rapid but uneven, as if a man was stumbling as he ran. Rex tugged me again: I'd stopped to listen. My torch beam was drooping. He took a step back, and his free hand came across me and closed around my torch hand, forcing the beam upwards. We stood in a clumsy half-embrace in the dark behind the beam of light.

We saw his torch first – the vee of its beam, bright in the distance where mine faded, moving jerkily up and down. Then we made out the silhouette of the man who held it, and Rex released me and ran forward. I felt the chill of his withdrawn touch, and ran after him.

It wasn't Raze, it was the other man, Steve. Rex got to him first, and caught him by the arms as if he was about to collapse. Steve was more than a head shorter than Rex, and was still breathing raggedly when I got to them. His face was covered with chalk dust, and he was shaking.

'All right. All right,' Rex said. 'Get your breath first.'

Steve's head fell forwards. I could feel the pain in his throat and his chest. He took a half-dozen more heaving breaths, and began to choke out the words.

'Call – the – police. An – accident. Dead. A man – dead – down there.'

'Dead? You're sure?'

'Dead.' His breath was back now, and he repeated it firmly. He added, 'Oh Christ,' and crumpled like a puppet, so suddenly that Rex, who still had him by the arms, almost unbalanced and fell on top of him.

11

'LET'S get him out,' Rex said.

'Rex, shouldn't we...'

'If the other guy's dead, there's no hurry to see to him. If I take his shoulders can you take his feet? It's not far.'

'I can't hold my torch as well.'

'Put it in your pocket, beam up. Don't rush, give yourself time.'

I took a deep breath, then wondered if it was full of carbon dioxide. My heart was racing, and I felt light-headed. Raze dead? Down the chute, man.

I put the torch in my pocket, an action which made more difference to the light level than I'd hoped. 'Give it time,' Rex repeated. I gave it a minute, by which time I could just about make out Rex's tall figure, his hands under Steve's shoulders, and the indistinct shape of Steve's unconscious body.

We lugged him, somehow. Rex did most of the work. Halfway there Steve began to revive, and Rex said sharply, 'Keep still.'

It was a huge relief when we reached the steps, and the first light from the Dunburys' cellar. Rex backed up and I followed, trying not to bump Steve too hard. We got through the doorway and past the dresser. I loosed Steve's legs once we were right in the cellar, and grabbed a dining chair with a red velvet seat. Rex dropped Steve onto on it and shoved his head between his knees.

The two of us were panting, Steve silent. Where was Mrs Dunbury?

Steve gave a mutter. I knelt by him and said, 'Repeat that slowly.'

'Raze. He's down there, in the dark.'

Darkness wouldn't matter to him now, I thought numbly. Rex said, 'Erica, are you okay? Go and make sure the police and the fire brigade are coming, and tell Mrs Whatsit to make some tea.'

An urge to tell him he could do it himself reassured me I was returning to normal. I held it back, and made for the stairs, only to run slap bang into Mrs Dunbury, who had been lurking at the top. When we had both recovered our balance I said with an authoritativeness Rex himself would have envied, 'Make a strong cup of tea. There's been a death, and a man's in shock. Any sign of the emergency services?'

'Honestly, you come barging in here and – A death? You can't...'

'I do mean it. A cup of tea. Right away. Please.' Not having the time to amplify or reassure her, I headed down the hall and out of the front door.

Thank God, they were just arriving. The fire engine narrowly beat the blue-striped white car to the barrier. It couldn't get past, since the way was blocked by a row of parked cars festooned with tickets. I broke into a run and met the officers half-way.

'What's up, love? Where do we go?'

I was out of breath again. I had to wait till I could speak clearly, and in the process it struck me that there was no rush any more: Steve was safely out of the mine, and Raze wasn't going to notice how long we took.

I told them the gist of what had happened. The police constable went back to his car to call whoever the police send to the scene of fatal accidents, and a fire officer went back to the engine to phone and update the fire station. The other police officer, who introduced himself as Sergeant Starling, slid into step with me as we went back down the hill.

'This your house, love?'

'No, it belongs to the Dunburys. But I don't think Mrs Dunbury knows much about it – they came from the house next door.' I paused on the front step, recalling Mrs D's touchiness. Should I ring? No, the social introductions could wait. With luck she was in the kitchen making tea. I opened the door myself, onto what sounded like all hell breaking loose in the cellar.

'Gawd,' muttered Sergeant Starling, and pushed past me, followed by a couple of fire officers. I brought up the rear, and when I got to the cellar the sergeant, Rex and Steve Black were such a muddle of limbs that it took me a moment to work out who was restraining whom. Mrs D appeared to have wisely kept out of it.

Steve's yells of 'Let me go!' provided an answer. Clearly Rex wasn't about to do so, and nor was Sergeant Starling. In another minute he and Rex had one arm each, their legs were safely out of kicking range, and an acutely uncomfortable Steve was strung out between them.

'Now what was all that about?' Sergeant Starling demanded.

Steve and Rex began to talk at the same time. The sergeant told Rex to shut up, and Steve to carry on – which, resentfully, he did.

'Hell, you can't just leave him down there. He hasn't even got a torch – we'd only got the one, and I took it. It's all right you saying hold on, but how'd you like to be stuck in the dark with a dead body?'

Rex and I twigged at the same moment.

'You mean —'

'Isn't it —'

'Now now,' Sergeant Starling said. 'Your turn, sir.'

Rex said, 'Are we to understand it's not your friend who's dead?'

'What?' Steve said. 'No. Christ, no. Jeez, you didn't think...'

'Actually we did,' I said, since it seemed Rex wasn't about to. Sergeant Starling added, 'Do you know who it is then, sir?'

'How the hell should I know?' Rex and the sergeant had freed Steve's arms, and he rubbed the sore patches aggrievedly. 'It's bloody dark down there, and there's a ton of chalk on top of him. It wasn't a skeleton or anything, just a man, not all that old. All I saw was trousers and a tweed jacket. Raze said he'd stay there, and I came for help.'

His last words were almost drowned by a clatter on the steps: Mrs Dunbury, with our cups of tea. She hadn't spilled a drop, and she'd made it strong, which betokened an admirably swift recovery from the shock. A body under your house isn't something I'd have liked to find, even when it wasn't...

Where was Mr Dunbury? I couldn't bring myself to ask.

'Can I go and get him now?' Steve said.

'I don't want you going back down there, laddie,' Sergeant Starling told him. 'It's the scene of a suspicious death. There's procedures. We'll get your friend out, mind, if you tell us which way to...'

'Officer,' Rex said, 'could I have a word with you?'

WHEN they felt the need, North Anglia Constabulary could turn up plenty of officers. A dozen must have come to the house in the next ten minutes. A constable with spiky brown hair and a thin moustache took Rex, Steve, Mrs Dunbury and me up to the Dunburys' living room, which had a thick beige carpet, small-print wallpaper and a collection of prickly antique armchairs. Rex and I sat on a chaise longue, the others on the chairs, and we drank the tea Mrs D had made.

Steve looked no more than eighteen, although he must have been a little older if, as Phil had claimed, he'd graduated from the university. He was wearing brown Doc Martens, denims and a nice, if dusty, Viyella shirt with pale and dark blue stripes. He hunched in his corner chair, and didn't look at the rest of us. I assumed he was still shaken, and (remembering the record I'd heard about) maybe wary of the police as well.

Mrs Dunbury didn't speak to me either, although she issued a general moan about the amount of dust on the carpet, and when the constable asked where her husband was, told him he was at work.

So it wasn't...

I glanced at Rex, who had not spoken at all. He was looking down at his empty cup and frowning.

He seemed to sense my look: he turned to me and held my eyes. He had dropped his normal ironic manner, and for once looked serious, even sympathetic.

I remembered then, and guessed what he had told Sergeant Starling.

I should have made the connection sooner. Obvious enough, if fear hadn't kept me from thinking straight – a child's fear of the dark, never outgrown, dwarfed by my feelings now. They weren't knowledge, weren't emotion, but were something born of both and neither. There was a man dead in the tunnel beneath our feet, and all too likely it was a man I knew.

I couldn't have brought myself to question Steve. Perhaps Rex couldn't either; or perhaps he was holding off so as not to make it worse for the rest of us. It wouldn't help to think about it. I looked away from Rex, and at the constable, who looked blankly back at me. The room prickled with silence. I heard a couple of men pass by in the corridor, one asking the other what lighting he'd need. Taking photographs down in the tunnel?

Mrs Dunbury was sitting rigidly upright, clutching her teacup handle. Her dark grey flannel skirt was cut unflatteringly straight – she had heavy hips – and her sweater was a particularly yucky shade of pink, but again she was wearing good jewellery: this time a necklace and earrings of what looked to me like uncultured pearls.

Taken feature by feature she was quite attractive, I thought, surprised. She might have been beautiful when she was younger. Maybe that explained why the unlikely Mr D had married her.

Disapproval and disappointment had soured her since, though. Did he have other women? It seemed a silly thing to wonder at such a time, but I'd have liked to know. Maybe, even, he was gay.

WHEN Raze came up we were all shepherded out of the Dunburys' house and in twos into police cars, each with a couple of officers. I went with Raze, and had the impression the officers had deliberately separated me and Rex. My unasked questions now filled my mind. Did you see a bright sweater? Brown hair? A ton of chalk, Steve had told us.

We were reunited in the front office of Costhorpe Central Police Station, but several officers stayed with us, and these too seemed to have orders to discourage us from talking. Then we were led off one by one, presumably all to interview rooms like the one to which I was taken, which had faded cut-velvet wallpaper and discreet steel bars across the window.

What I said, I can't remember, except it was an account of what I'd done that day, as full and accurate as I could make it. I felt almost unnaturally clear-headed, and little details kept coming into my mind. I was rather disappointed afterwards to read the plain statement the constable had written down.

I asked if the victim had been identified, and was told he hadn't, as far as the constable knew. Then I signed the statement, and was told I could go. A policewoman asked if I wanted a cup of tea, and I said no thank you. I was escorted to the door of the police station, and released onto a street on which nobody I knew was visible.

I wanted Rex. I wanted my mother. I wanted nobody. Best to settle for nobody. I needed my car, and I'd left it over near Flint Hill. I'd walked from there once that day, but it would do me good to walk again.

12

MARGARINE'S spreading power has nothing on news of a disaster. There were twenty or thirty people by the barrier at the bottom of Flint Hill by the time I got back there. On the other side were police cars, a couple of utilitarian blue vans, a fire engine and what looked like a television news crew. Two constables had been stationed to keep the crowd on the right side of the barrier.

I'd walked so often through the exclusion zone that it came as a shock to realise it wasn't allowed. It occurred to me then that I was literally in shock – a surprise, because I'd had an idea I was particularly together.

I walked on past the Flint Hill roundabout, along the ring road. In a haze, I missed the Flint Avenue turning which would have taken me up to my car. I shook my head, and took the next turning. Then I decided, halfway up the hill, that I wasn't in a state to drive at all.

It'd be best to walk home – and I'd been stupid to go a mile in the wrong direction. Best to sit down and have Mao-mao pound my stomach and drink a cup of strong coffee and go up to bed and fall between cool sheets.

I got as far as the ring road again, and stopped once more. Sudden death. How vulnerable it makes us all. And in the dark, the roof falling in... It was too close to my nightmares.

'Hey. Hey, councillor lady.'

Raze was standing in front of me, six foot of dreadlocks and spaced-out grin. It was unexpected, and yet as inevitable as an incident in a dream.

'You okay?'

'Yes and no. I'm sorry... it just hit me. What are you doing here?'

'I thought, go back to the house. Shit, the police. You know what they'd find if they searched that house? Hey, d'you think they'll search the house?'

I had to think before replying.

'I doubt it,' I said. My brain seemed to be working again. 'There are rules about what they can search and when, unless they think you... No, I shouldn't think so. What were you planning, to go back there and get some stuff out?'

'Shit, the police...' Raze giggled. I wondered, vaguely disgusted, if he was high. I hadn't noticed earlier. Maybe he was simply as far off balance as I was. In the dark, with a corpse, the roof fallen in...

Why had he stayed there? In the tunnel, with the body? Why hadn't they both seen the body and ran?

'Hey,' Raze went on, 'can't go back, not now. There's a mate not far off, you comin' there?'

I didn't want to; or maybe I did. I'd intended to like Raze and Steve, out of a combination of liberal principles and solidarity with Allie and Phil, but liking isn't a matter of conscious intention and I was beginning to realise I didn't. Steve – where was Steve? – had struck me as weak and self-absorbed, and I wasn't sure I believed in the cute vulnerability he projected. As for Raze, I found him unfathomable. He had shown no sign of appropriate emotion at any time that morning.

'This way,' he said, and took a couple of steps, lingering as if he expected me to follow.

I don't know why, but I did. We went across the ring road and down a narrow street behind the cathedral, to a row of small houses which fronted straight onto the path. Raze stopped at one halfway along the row. He didn't knock, but tried the handle. It turned a fraction – it was a little loose, and clattered slightly – then stopped; locked.

He didn't persist. He turned to me and gave another high giggle. He said, 'He been dead hours, man. He was co-o-old.'

His words were chilling, but his manner made them oddly inoffensive. My head still felt clear. I could see why he'd said that. He'd thought I might think he was to blame for the death in the tunnel.

'It must have happened long before you found him,' I agreed.

'Them two next door, the an-tique man and his lady, they known about their door for years.'

I thought this remark through, and said, 'They maybe think the same of you.'

'You think so?'

Raze was standing very close to me: I could smell a distinctive mix of hair oil, sweet soap and a trace of hash – or was it incense?

'No,' I said. 'We looked in your cellar and saw the crowbar.'

'Ah, the crow-bar. Steve got that from Big Nick. First we came down and found the door, then he went to get the crow-bar. That door was ha-a-ard to open.'

'You shouldn't have opened it.'

'Our door. Hey, what that woman next door say?'

'To me? One sugar or two.'

'To that other guy from the Council.'

'I don't know yet.'

'He say she say she just found the door?'

'Raze, I told you, I haven't had a chance to ask.'

My tone was getting more tart, but Raze didn't seem annoyed. He began to walk back along the street towards the ring road. I didn't know where he was going, and I didn't know where I was going, but I kept in step with him.

'That man down there,' Raze said. 'That dead man. How d'you think he got in the tunnel?'

'I don't know,' I said. 'I'm not sure yet who it was.'

'Engineer man from the Council.'

I stopped. Raze went on a step or two, and stopped as well. 'I seen him round about,' he added helpfully.

It wasn't a shock. I'd guessed as much, so it shouldn't have been a shock. But Bill Baxter dead? In the tunnel? Why? How, and why?

'There must have been something,' I said slowly. 'Something he had to find out.'

'He weren't workin', man.'

'What do you mean?'

'What I saw. You want to know what I saw? Heap of rocks, and that man lyin' under them, and his head all cracked open. Marks on the ceilin', and I'd say, someone took a pick to it. No hard hat, no torch, no fancy equipment.'

No hard hat? No torch? But Bill couldn't have gone down the tunnel without equipment. He was a pro, and he knew the rules.

'Maybe his equipment was buried under the roof fall?'

'Nope.'

'Just him?'

'Just him. Hey, you okay?'

The honest answer was no. I tried to frame a reply that would be more ambivalent without quite being a lie, but the words didn't come.

'I'll give you some stuff,' Raze offered. 'Got some on me. Hey, the pigs, they never looked. You take some, mellow you out.'

'No,' I said.

'You seein' Allie soon? You take some stuff for her.'

In spite of my brusque refusal he'd made this second offer easily, as if it had never crossed his mind I might disapprove. But... Maybe it was irrational – I'd have taken up an offer of a stiff brandy, and wasn't that a stronger drug? – but I didn't want to be mixed up in illegal dealings.

'I think I'd better not.'

'Then you tell Allie I got some for her, good Colombian.'

'I ought to go home, Raze. I'll go this way.'

'Hey, the pigs like you. You do something for us? Tell them we called you. You tell them you saw me open the door.'

Saw you open...?

I was being so slow. I should have seen what he wanted from the first. The police to him meant trouble, and he was lining up his allies to bail him out.

Only I wasn't sure I wanted to be an ally of Raze and Steve's. I didn't know what was going on. Why had Bill been down the tunnel? What did Raze think the police would think? If I'd taken up his offer of dope, I belatedly realised, I'd have given him a hold on me. I suspected he wasn't too spaced-out to have calculated that.

'What I do with the police, Raze,' I said, 'is tell them the truth, okay?'

Raze giggled again. 'Don't you tell them about the Colombian.'

'I won't do that,' I agreed.

He stood on the path, an incongruous figure in a quiet English cathedral city, watching me walk away.

THE barometer hadn't fallen. The sun had come out from behind the clouds, and the parked cars sparkled. Spring had arrived, and Bill Baxter would miss it.

What really mattered was that Friday morning Bill had been alive, and now he was gone. Death had crept up on him underground.

Dear God, I thought, when I die let it be in sunlight. Except there is no god, or none which makes any sense to me.

I hadn't shopped yet, hadn't eaten all day. I went into Tesco and in a fog of indifference bought bread, cheese and paté. *'Chalk tunnel mystery'* read the Argus-seller's stand outside Marks and Spencer.

My copy wouldn't hit the mat till five-thirty, so I dug in my pocket, found him twenty-seven pence, and took a look at the front page as I walked on.

My mind wasn't working right: even my five-year-old niece could have told me Bill's death wouldn't hit the headlines quite that fast. The mystery was the doors, the story was Rex's meeting. Colour photographs of Dilys Drake and the back of the Buntings' house filled most of the front page, with the text spilling over to the inside. I turned over and saw a subhead, '*Open Sesame!*'

On page three was a photo of Bill.

A shopper blundered into my back: I'd stopped in the middle of the pavement. I apologised, listened to her grumbles about how her arthritic knee couldn't stand any more knocks, and hugged the shop windows as I headed past Boots to St Matthew's Church. The church isn't open Saturdays, but there was an unclaimed bench in the churchyard. I sat on it, my Tesco bag on my lap, and read the story.

'Mines are dangerous,' Patty had written: *'don't go into them.'* To make sure the message came over, the subeditor had reprinted it across the bottom of the page in heavy type like a Government Health Warning.

All too true. But Bill had known that. Why would he...?

I folded the paper and lobbed it into a litter bin as I went on. It was a pity Allie and Phil had gone: I could have used their company.

Back home, I discovered I'd forgotten to switch on my answering machine before I went back to Flint Hill. I made coffee, and learned from my kitchen calender that I had a squash date with Jenny at four-thirty. I could get through the next two-and-a-half hours in eating and putting the place straight, and the combination of Jenny and squash would bring me down as well as anything – or was it up?

I put the sheets and towels I'd abandoned earlier in the washing machine, and assembled a cheese and paté sandwich. I did it carefully. It occurred to me that I should be grateful for being alive.

The phone went as I was eating. I swallowed a mouthful of bread and cheese, and picked it up on the seventh ring.

'Erica?' a bright female voice enquired. 'Patty Fowler here.'

'Oh.'

'I gather you were there when the body was discovered.'

I felt an ache in my arm, right up to the receiver.

'How do you know that?'

'From the police, of course. There's nothing odd about it, Erica –

all journalists get information from the police. This is a matter of public concern, and we have to cover it.'

I supposed she was right. It was something I'd expect to read in the paper; only I didn't want to help put it there.

'Erica? Are you still there? I just want a few comments, you know the sort of thing, some atmosphere. And I'm not clear yet what you were doing there?'

I gave it some thought.

'Acting as ward councillor.'

'Oh, come on, Erica.' Patty sounded rattled. 'I'm not being ghoulish, but I need a story.'

'A man's dead. That is the story.' I hung up on her. I was beginning to shake. A man was dead.

I didn't yet know his story.

13

I FOUND it hard to know what to say to Jenny, because I knew her reactions would be coloured by Nick. If she saw I was off balance she'd hear me say it was because of Bill's death, but all the same she'd think I was more upset than I let on about splitting up with Nick.

Maybe it was true. Going down the mine, Steve rushing out at us... I'd been nervous as a white mouse, and yet I hadn't really been in danger. Bill was a man I'd barely known, and his death didn't demand more than a moment's sadness from me. Everything had hit me too hard recently, and maybe that had more to do with splitting up than I liked to admit. I wasn't missing Nick, but I was missing my cosy niche. These days it felt like I was out in a cold draught, and shivering.

So I said nothing to her. It was enough to have her company for an hour; I could do without her concern as well. She'd mind, of course (and so would Nick) if she subsequently learned from someone else that I'd been at Flint Hill, but I didn't think she would. I hadn't given Patty any quotes she could use, and I couldn't see why I should figure in any other reports: I hadn't personally discovered the body.

I played hard, and beat Jenny for the first time in weeks. After my shower (my third that day, I realised) I really began to feel the chalk dust was off me. We had a drink of orange juice in the sports centre bar, and I stalled when Jenny asked what I was doing that evening. The answer was nothing – my fault, I hadn't phoned most of my friends for weeks – but I didn't want her to hear it.

Maybe I should go out, I thought. Give Sally a ring, or Judith; go on my own to the film at the Regal. Jenny and Nick were going for a pizza with friends. Even without Nick, I could have – should have – fixed something similar. Council meetings and decorating my front room weren't about to turn my social life around.

Back home, I watched the national news – a multinational on the brink of collapse, whispers of fraud; a minor war in Africa; the Prime

Minister arguing about the CAP in Brussels – and kept the television on for the local headlines. Was I becoming obsessed with the media? I felt I needed to know if the story would be covered. It was, as the second item.

The reporter said the police hadn't ruled out foul play. David North, Bill's boss, was interviewed saying what a fine man Bill had been, and there was film of Raze and Steve leaving a big shabby-looking terraced house, turning their faces away from the camera. The commentary was studiedly neutral, but the pictures made them look... guilty.

An outsider watching might have thought Bill had been murdered, and they were the prime suspects. Had Bill been murdered? I'd known from what Raze had told me that it looked suspicious, but even so I'd been thinking more of an inexplicable accident than of a man with an axe. And if he had been murdered, why should anyone suspect Raze or Steve? I couldn't imagine what their motive could have been.

The item left an unpleasant taste in my mouth. Where there had been a good man, there was now only the squalour and indignity of public death. As soon as the news ended John Utting phoned, demanding to know if Bill's demise would slow his return to his house, and I wasn't exactly cheered by this either. Recently it seemed everyone had showed me their meanest face.

I wasn't wasting my breath on rats like him, so I told him I'd speak to the engineers on Monday, and rang off fast. I thought of switching on the answering machine, but before I'd done it the phone rang again. This time it was Rex Canning.

'Erica,' he said briskly, 'I need to talk to you.'

'I was about to go to the cinema,' I hedged.

'This is more important. Can you cry off?'

'Can't you talk to me over the phone?'

'Not about this. I'll be over at eight.'

No 'may I?' No 'okay?' He put the phone down before I could argue.

I'd built up to annoyance even before he rang off, and it soared to temper once I'd taken it in that he actually meant to turn up on my doorstep. I hated myself for not having said a flat no.

I couldn't imagine talking to Rex Canning about anything important. His interests and mine were too different. I supposed it was something to do with Bill or Flint Hill, but I didn't want to discuss those subjects that evening, especially with Rex.

The phone rang again. So much for solitary evenings, it seemed all Costhorpe was after me. I switched on the machine this time, and didn't stop to listen to the message. Instead I went into the kitchen and opened a bottle of Koonunga Hill. Phil and Allie had left me half a dozen as a thank-you, and I needed something to 'mellow me out', as Raze had put it. I wasn't inclined to get drunk, though: I poured one glass and corked the rest. Then I carried the glass through to my living room, flopped on the sofa and drank it while glancing through the morning and evening papers.

The phone rang continually. I turned the machine to 'broadcast' and listened to assorted Hillside residents, fellow councillors and other acquaintances leaving messages. What do we do now about Flint Hill? (Mike Soley.) When can we go home? (Daniel Duchêne, almost as aggressive as Utting.) Do you know anything about Baxter? (Three of these: Nick and Judith Armitage, neither of whom knew I'd been there, and Harry Dent, Group Whip, who did, somehow. I was supposed to talk to him before saying anything in public – not that I intended to.) How awful; are you okay on your own, or shall I come over? (Allie, from a phone box: I hadn't expected her to be so thoughtful, and was touched.) No engineers, no council staff – they'd ring each other, not the politicians.

I even had an offer of work: a woman who had got my name from Yellow Pages wondered if I could help her arrange a trip to Bulgaria. It wouldn't pay much, but I needed any work I could get. Surely I knew someone who spoke Bulgarian, or someone who knew someone who spoke it. I wound back the tape and noted down her name and number.

By now it was five to eight. I switched the machine back to silent recording, drained the wine and took my empty glass out to the kitchen. I supposed I'd have to let Rex in, but I wasn't going to encourage him to linger.

Rex arrived at one minute past eight, and entered my living room with all the aplomb he'd shown with Mrs Dunbury. Before I'd had time to speak he had thrown his overcoat across the arm of my sofa, claimed the precise spot I'd just been sitting in, and pushed a lock of fair hair back from his forehead with theatrical weariness. 'I won't stay long,' he informed me. 'It's been a hell of a day. I spent three hours at the police station, and I didn't get rid of Jack Wells till past one last night.'

If he was expecting sympathy, he was misjudging me. 'You can be as brief as you like,' I said. 'What exactly did you want to say?'

'I want to talk about the Dunburys.'

'I warn you, I'm not inclined —' I put on the brakes. My anger was shallow, rooted in weariness, vulnerable to my usual curiosity. If Rex meant to talk, not question, I decided I might actually be interested in hearing him. I fell into the chair opposite his sofa, and said, 'Well. You know what I saw. If you want to tell me they're fine folk because they vote Tory, I won't listen. But if you've something else to say...'

'I think it would be useful if you knew what happened before we met up this morning.'

Useful? Why?

Rex was doing much what Raze had tried to do, I supposed. 'Poor cops,' I said. 'They take all that trouble to keep us apart, and as soon as they turn their backs we run around swapping accounts.'

'For heaven's sake, Erica, we're not accomplices in some dreadful deed. We're material witnesses, but that's all; only I expect the police will interview you again, and you might find it helpful to know more of what happened.'

Yes, but helpful in what sense, and to whom?

I'd reserve judgement on that, I decided. Hearing him out might not gain me anything, but I couldn't see I would lose more than a few minutes of a dead evening. Since I was so unsympathetic to Rex and his attitudes, he wasn't likely to persuade me I'd seen anything I hadn't.

'Okay,' I said, 'tell me all.'

'Right. James Dunbury called me about ten this morning, and told me he and his wife had come back to their house about half an hour earlier. They'd been worried by what they'd learned at the meeting, and of course they wanted to check if they had a hidden door. So they went down to their cellar, moved the dresser you saw, and discovered the door behind it. They said they hadn't tried to open it because they were worried about the safety aspects, and could I come over?'

'Why you?'

'I did chair the meeting. Of course I phoned City Hall, and I tried Bill Baxter at home, but I couldn't get him on either number. So I went over to Flint Hill, we all went down to the cellar, and Mr Dunbury unlocked the door.'

'Where was the key?'

'They found it in the lock,' Rex said levelly. 'We didn't go right into the mine, we just opened the door and shone a torch down the steps. Then Mr Dunbury had to go to work and I had a cup of tea with Mrs Dunbury, and when I left her I ran into you.'

The key in the lock made sense. It would have been fishy if they had claimed to find it in a kitchen drawer.

'Did they oil the lock and hinges in front of you?'

'They did, actually.'

Even so, I didn't believe they'd only discovered the door that morning. More interestingly, Rex hadn't told the story as if he believed it.

'How terribly convenient it would be,' I said, 'if the Dunburys could persuade everyone they didn't know about the door until then.'

'Terribly,' Rex solemnly agreed.

'But they can't, can they?'

'I think not.'

'So are they going to admit they staged this little scene?'

'No.'

'Oh.' That surprised me. 'But if they don't, and you or I or both of us say we don't believe them, it won't look too good, will it? Considering what happened on the other side of the door.'

'That's why I've come,' Rex said. 'Obviously they planned the charade when it was a question of the neighbours getting angry if it turned out they'd known all along. They wanted to put a little pressure on me to confirm they hadn't, and if that had been the only issue, maybe I'd have obliged. But the game's changed. Now it's a question of when and how Bill Baxter went down the mine.'

It sure was. 'If I were the Dunburys,' I said, 'I'd tell all that to the police. Mind you, if I were them I'd have gone to Bill and told him about the door as soon as the mine was discovered. They must have known then that he'd find out about it.'

'He might not have. The Buntings' hole needn't have led to the same tunnel, or there could have been a blockage between that and the doors, or...'

'But there wasn't, and if they'd looked they'd have known that.'

'I doubt if they did look,' Rex said. 'Not everyone cares to roam around underground – you know there are serious risks. Anyway, I suspect they had an additional reason for not letting on.'

'Which was? Is?'

'This isn't something I'd wish to suggest in public, Erica. So if I tell you, I hope you won't attribute it to me.'

'Is it something you've told the police?'

'I've tried to nudge them towards it.' He paused. I snuggled down in my chair, and examined his body language. Sprawled, still unreasonably at home; but shoulders squared. Eyes alert, fixed on me.

He said, 'You know James Dunbury is an antique dealer.'

I sort-of did, so I nodded.

'It's not always the cleanest of businesses. Antiques don't come from factories, and...'

'And sometimes dealers don't want it known where they did come from.'

'Or where they're going,' Rex agreed. 'In short, they have reasons for not putting their goods on public display. So if you had a house with what was effectively a second, hidden cellar...'

'You might use it,' I finished for him.

'It sounds a little strange, I know, but life is. Certainly they chose to hide the door, even though their cellar can't have had too many visitors, and it's worth asking why. That's the answer I've come up with.'

His theory deserved consideration. I gave it some.

'What you're suggesting,' I said slowly, 'is that when the tunnel was discovered, James was caught with his inlaid marquetry cabinets down. He couldn't let on about the door until he'd got rid of them, and if he couldn't say anything straight away, there wasn't any point in saying anything unless and until he had to.'

'Precisely. That explains why he acted as he did. I'd like to make sure the police understand that, so they don't waste too much time investigating his cover-up.'

'You mean you think the Dunburys might be guilty of handling hot antiques, but they couldn't be guilty of murder.'

Rex gave me a disapproving look. 'I can't say I'd put it like that, but I won't disagree.'

'If Bill was murdered, somebody did it.'

'If he was, obviously someone did. But it would hardly have been the Dunburys.'

'Why?'

Rex gave a shrug, as if to say, it's obvious.

It wasn't obvious to me. Did he have some other suspect in mind? But who would...

I thought back to the television news.

'Steve and Raze next door?'

Rex didn't answer.

A renewed spurt of anger sent me to my feet. 'Oh, that's great,' I said. 'What a fine theory. Tories might fence antiques but they'd never stoop to murder, so to find a suspect for that you look next door where you find gays with dreadlocks. Even, dare I say, socialists.'

Rex was only taken aback for a second. He stood up too, cancelling my height advantage. He was taller than most of the men I've argued with, and I can't say I liked glaring upwards.

'Such wonderful characters they seem to be,' he said. 'You could smell the marijuana on that black guy.'

'The incense, actually.'

'Don't be so naive! The other man's got a record. They deal in the stuff.'

'It was still incense you smelled,' I retorted. But I was uneasily conscious that he was right about the record, and that a smell either way wouldn't convince him of their innocence. I switched lanes. 'Anyway, what if Raze and Steve do take marijuana? It's not called the peace drug for nothing: people don't generally kill because they're high on hash.'

'People go to jail for dealing in that stuff.'

'So what's that got to do with Bill's murder?'

'Maybe Bill was on to them.'

'It's a lot more likely he was onto James Dunbury's stolen antiques,' I snapped back. 'I'm sick of your cheap little stereotypes!'

'You think your socialist stereotypes are any better than my Tory ones?'

Yes! I mean – I didn't have any. Well, all right, I did. And stereotypes are dangerous, because they lead to prejudices. But my prejudices were only cancelling out Rex's.

This spat wasn't taking us anywhere, though, and I was getting a crick in the neck. I took a deep breath and a step backwards.

'Obviously I do,' I said. 'Being a socialist. And obviously you think the reverse, being a Tory. Those are our conceptual frameworks. Everyone needs a conceptual framework, even if they do distort things. You tell me your perception and I'll tell you where it's biassed. Actually I suppose I could even tell you my perception and let you tell me where that's biassed.'

'Are you offering me a truce?'

I held his eyes for a moment. Rex has striking eyes. They look at you in a fixed way which can almost make you believe he's honest.

Misguided, of course, but in his way honest.

A second later, it occurred to me that he was also a chronic Lothario. Women can't be frank and friendly with a man like him, because he takes everything short of downright hostility as a come-on. Most of his mind was on Flint Hill, but I could sense a detached part making sexual calculations.

I broke off the contact and retreated right back to my chair. 'Truce, maybe,' I said. 'Peace treaty, no.'

'I wasn't asking for one, but since I've told you about the Dunburys, you could tell me about Garron and Black. I'll listen.'

Listen maybe, but would he hear?

He might, I thought. Rex wasn't a black-and-white type, and what I told him might lighten his grey image of them. Anyway, he'd already taken advantage of my hesitation to settle down again and look expectant.

I heard myself say, 'I've a bottle of wine open.' And a detached part of my own mind jumped.

Rex gave me a ruminative smile. 'I should have brought one with me. I'll owe you it.'

'This is just because we're off balance. Because of what happened today. I don't want you to take it —'

'Erica, you're safe with me,' Rex interrupted. 'I'd love a glass, and I'm not reading anything into the offer.'

I wasn't sure I believed him, but I knew I wanted another drink myself. I went to get the remains of the Koonunga Hill and two glasses, and returned to find Rex inspecting my cd collection. 'May I?' he asked, and at my nod, put on Schubert's Great.

Cosy: maybe too cosy. No: superficially, deceptively cosy. Neither of us had forgotten we were political rivals.

I certainly didn't forget it in telling Rex about Raze and Steve. I wouldn't have told him I didn't like them, any more than he'd have spelled out what I knew perfectly well, that he disliked the Dunburys. I did tell him how I'd come to meet them through respectable Allie and Phil, and how Raze had phoned me as soon as he and Steve had discovered the door.

Rex knew already that their discovery was a genuine one, because he too had seen the cobwebs and the newly-scraped rust on the bolts. Wherever Steve kept his stashes, it couldn't have been in the cellar or the tunnel. Anyway, James Dunbury would hardly have kept antiques in the tunnel if there had been another entrance in use.

'That's true,' Rex agreed. He'd been listening silently, drinking his wine. 'But what it comes down to is, you didn't see them prise the door open, so you can't prove they didn't discover it the evening before.'

'I think that's in their favour,' I told him. 'They didn't bother to fix up an alibi because unlike James Dunbury, they had nothing to hide. Anyway, what difference would it really make if they did go looking for the door straight after the public meeting? Bill had gone missing hours before. You can't be suggesting they somehow tracked him down after the meeting, knocked him on the head, dragged him through their house, dumped him in the tunnel and engineered a roof-fall to hide the evidence.'

Rex said. 'I agree it would be incredible, but I'd point out to you that the whole business is incredible. Did Baxter go down the tunnel with his killer? Was he ambushed there? Or was he killed on the surface, and if so, why was the body dumped there? None of it makes any sense.'

I could agree with that. Fortunately, though, it wasn't my job or Rex's to make sense of it. The police would do that.

Fine, said Rex. We leave it to them. Then there was silence – or rather, Schubert.

He broke it, halfway through the third movement.

'Were you drinking alone? Before I came?'

I'd been lulled into a Germanic contentment, but that deceptively lazy enquiry sure jerked me out of it. 'That's an impertinent question,' I said.

'Don't growl, Erica. I'm not looking for ammunition, I'm just concerned. Friendly concern, okay? You need people to be concerned about you, because you're on your own, you've had a bad experience, and you're not as hard as you pretend to be.'

First Allie, now Rex: I don't like being called hard. Nor do I like being accused of pretence; and I wasn't such a weak-spined heroine that I needed Rex Canning to play protector. Half an hour in my house, and the man was acting proprietorial.

I was too tired to play games with him; that, or the wine was hitting me. 'I don't need you to be concerned, Rex,' I said curtly. 'And I don't know about hard; what I know I am is whacked. You said you wouldn't stay long, and I'm going to hold you to it. As soon as you've finished your wine, I'll throw you out and go to bed.'

'How direct you are.'

'It's a socialist virtue. I suppose by the standards of Tory ladies, I rate as uncouth.'

'I didn't say so. And not all my ladies are Tories.' He drained his glass with commendable speed, stood up and held out both hands. Short of being rude, I could only take them and let him pull me to my feet. 'However,' he continued, looking down on me at very short range, 'all of them are quite different from you. Not that it matters. You're very tense.'

'Let go of my hands.'

'Why? Does it make you uneasy when I touch you?'

'Imagine what the Labour whip would make of this. Or the Tory whip, come to that.'

'I'm not going to tell them. Are you?'

'There won't be anything to t—'

Except there was. He kissed me. He knew how far to push his luck: it was short, more friendly than passionate, barely enough to give me the feel of him, warm, firm, overlaid with Australian Cabernet. He let me go with a wry smile, and I stared at him like a savage transfixed by a television set.

His hands were still holding mine. Self-hatred gathered in my gut and crouched, ready to spring.

'We both know it's there,' Rex said with disgusting self-assurance. 'Why deny it? Now I'll leave you to your solitary bed.' He swept his coat from the arm of the sofa, and let himself out of the door before I could say another word.

14

I'VE NOTHING against the police. Except for parking on the odd yellow line, I obey the law. I'm on friendly terms with the Chief Constable, and when my car was broken into an officer took the details promptly (although I didn't get my radio back). But when I returned to Costhorpe Central Police Station on Monday afternoon I couldn't help thinking: how would I feel now if I were a gay Rastafarian whose partner had a record for possession?

In Costhorpe at least, the police still means short-haired white men in blue. Fifteen percent women, dotted across the lower ranks. No black faces. They talk about equal opportunities, but Costhorpe's immigrant communities are tiny, and no one from them has ever applied to join.

A sandy-haired detective constable in a green flak jacket showed me into an interview room, told me to sit down, and sat himself. A blonde policewoman sat next to him. He did the questioning, she did the writing. I asked their names, and was told: Detective Constables Sunley and Allen.

On Saturday the police had concentrated on that day's events, but now they wanted absolutely everything I knew about Bill Baxter and Flint Hill. After my fencing match with Rex, it all seemed pedestrian. Sunley wouldn't tell me what he already knew, so I had to go over a lot of tedious territory. Ask a question myself, however innocent, and I felt the chill like an open freezer door.

I described my phone conversation with Bill on Friday morning, and how I'd gone over to the engineers' office. I had no idea what Bill had been meaning to tell me. Sunley asked if I thought it was relevant to his death, but I could only say I didn't know.

Friday afternoon I'd done my monthly accounts, weeded a drawer of my filing cabinet, spent a while despairing that I hadn't any proper work, and a while longer making a list of old clients to chase up. I hadn't seen anyone till Allie had come back around four-thirty, and hadn't made or received any phonecalls. If they were looking for an alibi, I'd failed miserably to produce one.

I'd had company afterwards, though: first Allie, Phil as well after six, and a roomful of people all evening. When exactly had Bill died? I still didn't know, and Sunley's flat manner gave nothing away. He had me list all those people I knew who'd been at the public meeting, then took me just as patiently through Saturday morning.

I'd been at Flint Hill from eight-thirty onwards, but only for the last few minutes had I been out of sight of Allie, Phil and the firemen. I'd seen residents returning home at the top of the hill, but I didn't know most of their names. I was asked if I'd seen the Dunburys, and said no – then it struck me.

'What is it?' DC Allen asked.

She hadn't spoken up before, and wouldn't have then, I guessed, if Sunley hadn't failed to notice my slight hesitation. I'd paused because I'd realised that if I said more, I'd have to mention my conversation with Rex. I didn't like that prospect, but I had to go on.

'According to Rex Canning, the Dunburys came over to their house about nine-thirty to see if there was a door in their cellar. But that can't be right, because we were there at nine-thirty, and we didn't see them. Whether they came up or down the road, we couldn't have missed them.'

'Could you have been in your friends' house when they passed?'

'We didn't go in. The fire service brought everything to the door, and we never spent more than a half-minute at a time in the van.'

The police exchanged glances. Sunley said, 'You say you came at eight-thirty, and left at ten?'

'That's right. I know I left Phil and Allie at five to ten, because I looked at my watch. I walked down the hill and looked at the Dunburys' house – well, their privet hedge, which is high. I didn't see anyone, although I mightn't have noticed if they'd been indoors. I knocked on Raze and Steve's door, and went round to the back, so I was briefly out of sight of the road, but I'd surely have noticed if somebody had arrived next door. Then I talked to a police officer, so I must have reached the bottom of the hill around ten-fifteen.'

'What time did you return?'

'I walked home... spent a while on the phone... drove back again. I shouldn't think I was home for much more than twenty minutes, so I'd have been away altogether for... I'd guess, about an hour.'

'Were they there when you came back?'

'I saw Rex Canning less than five minutes after I arrived, and he'd just come out of their house. I see what you're getting at – but add it up. The Dunburys had to go down to the cellar and move a heavy dresser. They phoned Rex, and Rex tried to phone Bill Baxter, so he can't have left home straight away. Allow a while for him to get to Flint Hill: I think he lives on that side of the city, but the traffic was heavy. The Dunburys took him down and showed him the door, and they messed around oiling the hinges and unlocking it and fetching a torch and looking at the steps on the other side... Rex should have told you about that. Half an hour? Surely not less than a quarter. Afterwards Mr Dunbury went to work and Rex had a cup of tea with Mrs Dunbury, so you have to give her time to boil the kettle, make the tea and drink it. Can you fit all that into an hour?'

I didn't expect a direct answer, and didn't get one. Sunley asked, 'Do you think it's possible the Dunburys were there at eight-thirty?'

'It's conceivable. I wouldn't recognize their car. If they already knew about the door, they knew the tunnel didn't go right under their house, and it's brick-lined in that section anyway. They would have realised there was no real subsidence risk, so maybe they stayed in the house overnight – although the police should have noticed if they had.'

DC Allen said, 'Why do you say, if they already knew about the door?'

'Take a look at their cellar, and see if you think they could have not known about it.'

This produced no reaction; however if they had spent three hours interrogating Rex, it would have come as no surprise. Sunley moved on to my encounter with Rex on Saturday morning, through our search for Raze and Steve, and to how we'd found Steve in the tunnel.

He asked me a lot of questions about Raze and Steve – more than he'd asked about the Dunburys. His expression was as deadpan as before, but I reckoned his ears had pricked up. I meant to tell all, so I threw in the fact that both Phil and Mrs Dunbury (inaccurately) had told me of Steve's conviction.

Sunley said, 'Do you disapprove of drug pushers?'

What had he expected, haughty distaste? I said rather shortly, 'I don't use the stuff, and I don't approve of people letting it take over their lives. I know some people turn to crime to pay for drugs, and that's an evil; but when it comes to making criminals of people who smoke the odd joint, I get uneasy.'

'You've never heard of the ladder effect?'

A fence had gone up, and we weren't on the same side of it. However, I wasn't prepared to fib about my opinions just to cosy up to the police. 'I've heard of it, yes,' I said. 'I dare say people who take crack often started out on pot, but that doesn't mean everyone who enjoys a joint ends up in the gutter. I honestly think marijuana's less harmful than tobacco: the main difference is, one's legal and one isn't. All right, you have to enforce the law – and personally I try to keep it, even when I think it's stupid – but that's my opinion of it.'

'So you're friendly with Garron and Black?'

'Is that supposed to be a logical conclusion? I hardly know them. They're voters in my ward, and we've a couple of mutual friends. I've met them twice; I'm not even sure I like them. Maybe you come to a judgement on people the first time you meet them, but I try not to.'

It wasn't maybe: they had, and I knew it. The atmosphere couldn't have been more hostile if I'd admitted to killing Bill. Only they didn't suspect me of that: they suspected Raze and Steve, and me of covering up for them.

This was my thesis, at least, and so far everything fitted it. Sunley grilled me about Raze and Steve like Brian Walden launching into a particularly slimy politician.

I didn't admit I knew Allie and Phil smoked dope, and I didn't mention Raze's offer to me, but I told them everything else. I was sceptical, though; more than that, I was getting annoyed. I couldn't believe Raze or Steve had killed Bill, or that his death had anything to do with drug dealing, and I didn't want to help the police chase at full speed down that particular cul-de-sac.

When I told them about the crowbar Rex and I had seen on the floor of Raze and Steve's cellar, they could hardly keep their expressions blank. For heaven's sake, I almost said out loud. You know what they used it for: to get the door open.

'Did Garron say where it came from?' Sunley asked.

'Yes. From Big Nick's garage on North Road, where Steve works.'

'When?'

'That morning, I think. I can't remember his words exactly, but I think he said, when they discovered the door was locked, Steve went to get the crowbar to break it open.'

'So they came to their house, went down to the cellar, found the door, Black went to North Road, took a crowbar, came back, they levered the door open, and phoned you?'

'I see what you're implying.' He'd turned my point about the

Dunburys neatly back onto me. 'North Road isn't far from Flint Hill, though. They could have done all that in an hour.'

'An hour?'

'That's how long I —' I stopped in mid-sentence. Stupid, Erica. It hadn't been an hour after I'd left Flint Hill when Raze had phoned me – it couldn't have been much more than forty minutes.

'All right,' I amended, 'it's tight. Most likely I'm wrong about when or where they got it. Perhaps Steve had it in his car all the while. I told you, I don't know them well.'

'He had the crowbar in his car?'

'It's just a suggestion. You'll have to ask them.'

'We will,' said Sunley, and I silently cursed. I'd have to watch my words more carefully if he was determined to take everything I said as evidence against Raze and Steve.

'Miss Massen?' DC Allen said.

'Oh; sorry. I wasn't concentrating.'

'Are you tired? Do you need a break?'

'Are you going to take much longer?'

'We're not finished yet. Would you like a cup of tea?'

'Yes please.'

I'd expected they would send out for one, but in fact DC Allen led me up to an utilitarian canteen. A couple of uniformed constables were smoking over a corner table, and a sergeant was reading the Sun and eating an iced bun. I suggested coffee, and Allen bought me a cup. She didn't get one for herself, and when she'd seen me to a plastic-covered table by the window she excused herself and went off.

What was this, amateur psychology? Leaving me to mull over my misdeeds in the hope that I'd decide to co-operate? Hell, I had been co-operating! I wanted Bill's murderer caught as badly as anyone did, but I simply couldn't see that an obsessive interest in Raze, Steve and their predilection for illegal soft drugs would do anything to help catch him – or her.

Whatever the motive for Bill's killing, I didn't believe drugs had anything to do with it. Nor did I believe I could provide the police with any more useful information. I had no idea what had happened on Flint Hill. I'd barely known Bill, and I knew Raze and Steve even less. If the police had taken three hours questioning Rex, and planned to take at least as long with me, I supposed it just demonstrated their lack of solid leads.

I wished I could guide them to a more fruitful line of enquiry, but how? All I knew about Bill was that he had been the Council expert on chalk tunnels, and there was no obvious motive connected to that. And that he'd wanted to tell me something – I'd had the impression, something not directly connected with the Flint Hill collapse – but I didn't know what, so that wasn't much help.

Why had he picked me to tell? I didn't even know that. I wished he hadn't picked me. In a strange way it made a connection between us, and I'd have preferred to think of him as a distant acquaintance.

No, I was exaggerating. He had been a distant acquaintance. Connection, huh! When engineers say they've something interesting to tell you, it invariably turns out to be as boring as a lump of chalk. As much of a let-down as the prizes in a five-p lucky dip. The mystery was interesting, the timing was – more than interesting, indeed shiver-inducing, but the information itself could hardly have been the kind to justify murder.

I returned to my cooling cup of coffee, and wondered when Sunley or Allen would come to retrieve me. The constables stubbed out their cigarettes and left. I swivelled round and looked out of the window, which provided a view over City Hall carpark. My bike was still locked to the railings. I watched Harry Dent drive in, park and go through the back entrance. Then I sensed movement behind me, and swivelled back.

A tall dark-haired man with a bandit moustache had come into the canteen. He was a man I'd have noticed even in a crowded room, which it wasn't. He ignored the woman at the counter, the Sun-reading sergeant, and fixed on me. I wasn't going to fake coyness, so I watched him as he headed over. He was wearing jeans and a denim jacket, but he looked at home as only coppers can in police stations.

'Councillor Massen?' he asked, stopping by my table.

'Ten minutes ago I was Miss Massen.'

'Ten minutes ago you were talking to a DC.'

'You're his boss?'

'Two rungs up. Detective Inspector Zahler.' He held out his hand, and I stood up and took it. He had a warm, firm grip. I'm generally wary of the police – who isn't? – and the altercation with Sunley had made me even warier, but I liked this guy instinctively. I assumed Sunley had sent him, though, and was asking myself why.

He asked – asked! – if he could join me, and I agreed. So he sat down across the table, and we looked at each other with the uneasiness of two strangers who aren't sure who ought to speak first.

'Maybe I should explain,' he said. 'It's normally constables who take interviews, however important they are, because they're the ones who're in practice. They do it every day, and I don't.'

I find it amusing, mostly, when people think local councillors are important.

'So is this an interview?'

'If it is, it's an off-the-record one.'

'What did Sunley tell you?'

'That he'd rubbed you up the wrong way.'

That was honest. I liked him for it. 'It was mutual,' I said. 'And I admire him for having stopped the interview when he did – although actually Ms Allen did that. Sunley didn't argue, at least.'

'He wouldn't. Not in front of you.'

Well trained, huh. Zahler had spoken with parental pride. I said, 'But I didn't admire his line of questioning.'

'You think he asked leading questions?'

'Not in the legal sense. I think his prejudices showed.'

'Against blacks?'

'Black, gay, drug-takers: Garron and Steve Black have it all.'

Zahler nodded. 'Believe it or not, we noticed.'

'Prejudice against women,' I said. 'That was patronizing.'

He dropped eye-contact. I'd spoken without thinking, it was the kind of bitter repartee Nick and I had grown expert in. Allie's remark skidded through my brain, the one about being too aggressive to attract a nice man. Hell, who was I kidding? Police officers are not nice in the sugary Mills & Boon sense, and sane Labour councillors do not try to attract them.

Thinking this, I'd dropped my gaze too. When I looked up he was ready for me. It was one of those connections so direct it carries a kick like an electric shock. It cost me an effort to hold his eyes.

'You're right, of course,' he said. 'You can work to minimise prejudice, you can work so bloody hard you reverse it even, but not many of us manage to tread a dead straight line. What I'm trying to say is, we're conscious of the political dimension, and we wouldn't be so dumb as to arrest Costhorpe's only gay Rasta without a hell of a solid case.'

'Which you don't have.'

'I guess I can confirm that. I've nothing definite on either Garron or Black.'

'So the case is wide open.'

'Sure is. That's why we value your help.'

'I'm giving it,' I said. 'I'm not going to censor my opinions on soft drugs just to please you – you plural – but they don't make me your enemy.'

'I don't believe you are.' There was no softness or flattery in Zahler's tone. He went on, 'You're a Labour councillor, aren't you?'

This was a dubious follow-on, I thought. 'How did you guess?'

'Not all policemen are Tories; although most are, I'll admit. What I mean is, you have a political attitude to Garron and Black? They're – I'll get this wrong – clients, in a sense? You feel you need to protect them?'

'I wouldn't swear they're Labour voters,' I said drily, 'and I certainly wouldn't ask them. Point taken, though – I'm biased in favour of anyone who's asked for my help, particularly if they're from a minority and the system's biased against them. It's a necessary corrective. The Tories – Rex Canning – hold a brief for the establishment types, the Dunburys etcetera. It's not as strong as a lawyer-client relationship. If I have evidence against them, I'll give you it.'

'And Canning the same?'

'He's tricksier than me.' I wondered if I should have said that, but it was the truth as I saw it. I added, 'I can't imagine he's spelled out his doubts about the Dunburys, but I think he's made sure you've noticed them. He made sure I noticed them too.'

'Big of him.'

'Game playing.'

Zahler gave me a quizzical look, but made no comment. He let a silence grow, then asked, 'Have you told us everything?'

'Sunley hasn't finished with me. I've cooled down, I guess he's cooled down, I'll go back in the ring after the break. There's not much left. I've been trying to remember what Bill said to me Friday morning, but it isn't coming.'

'Do you think it's important?'

'I hope it's not.' I gave him a rueful smile. 'In the sense that it was me he meant to tell it to. I don't want to feel involved, if you follow. Hope it's not, but don't know. I remember the word obsession. I won't feel happy till I've pinned down the rest. If it doesn't come I'll sleep on it.'

'Do that.' He stood. 'I'm glad we talked.'

'So am I,' I said; and I meant it.

I SPENT nearly two hours more with Sunley and Allen. Friendly they weren't, but I had no further hint of disapproval from them. We went over every moment of Friday and Saturday and discussed every issue I could think of. They soft-pedalled over Raze and Steve. Even so, by the time they let me go I felt like a dirty dishcloth.

I flopped against the outside wall of the police station, and glanced at my watch: nudging four o'clock. An Economic Development Committee meeting I should have attended had started at two. I was asking myself whether I should go to see if it had finished when the swing-door banged and Fred Keylock came out of the station.

'Afternoon, Fred,' I said without thinking.

Keylock whipped round to me with alarming speed for a sizeable man. Alarm was on his face as well.

'Sorry,' I said. 'I shook you. Erica Massen. City Council – you'll remember me from the meeting at Flint Hill. I guess you too have just been questioned about Bill Baxter?'

'Oh – uh – yes. Well...'

'It's a sad business. Did you know Bill?'

Keylock's eyes flickered to the road. I knew he didn't want to talk, and I don't know why I pressed him. Presumably he was also feeling wrung-out.

'Not intimately. Yes... well... Police doing a good job, eh?'

'I guess so. And the Council, I'd like to think. Fred, I heard what you said about infilling the mine without surveying it, but I'm sure you really understand it's not practicable.'

Fred stared at me.

'I mean, it's...' I paused, trying to find the energy to choose my words. I suspected I'd made a mistake with the 'Fred's: 'Mr Keylock' would have gone down better. 'It's not a political issue, basically,' I said. 'I know Mrs Drake wanted to make some capital out of it, but I think the Tories on the Council accept that we can't just infill. So it's... unhelpful to everyone to suggest it in public.'

'You trying to censor me?'

'No,' I said insincerely. 'I just thought – you surely knew we couldn't agree, so I wondered why you'd called for that.'

'You'll have to agree to do something for the residents.' Fred's face was reddening. 'That's what I'm pushing for, the Council to pay.'

'I suppose you are.' I shouldn't have talked to him, I thought: it'd probably only increase his determination to embarrass the Council.

'I'm sure you meant well.'

He stared again, then turned and walked off. I shrugged and went round the corner to City Hall. I didn't mean to try the committee room, just to grab some of the black sludge they call coffee, and wind down before cycling home.

Interrogations. Imagine hours of it. Trying to peer at blurred pictures in your mind, when willpower alone won't bring them into focus; to recall sequences of events which jiggle and slip. Imagine days of it. No wonder people confess to things they didn't do.

There were no councillors' cars in the carpark – Harry had evidently stayed only a couple of minutes – and nobody else was in the Members' Room. The coffee was end-of-day thick and vile. The one sip I took was more than enough: I went to the kitchen up the corridor and threw the rest down the sink. I drank two cups of cold water and took another back with me, then slumped onto the sofa with that morning's North Anglia Herald.

The Herald's a sister-paper to the Costhorpe Argus, covering a larger area. It doesn't always give the same space to Costhorpe news, but Bill's death was a big story by any standards. It took up most of page four: story by James Donohue, with additional reporting by Patty Fowler and A N Other.

There was a photo of Bill, and an account of how his body had been found down the mine. It held me. In all those hours at the police station, I hadn't had the sense of a tragedy, just of a boring but necessary work routine. But there was tragedy here, a man who had been alive and was no longer.

It was a while before I moved on to the small photos of me and Rex, and a little box of text headed: *'Local councillors led police to the scene'*. Depressing. The Labour Group wouldn't be so stunned by Bill's death that they'd overlook the chance to gossip about us running round Flint Hill together.

Maybe I was exaggerating; my guilty conscience speaking. It wasn't a sin to talk to a Tory, and nobody else could know we'd more than talked. Not much more than talked, really, and it wouldn't happen again. I didn't even fancy him. Okay, he wasn't exactly ugly, but his squeaky-clean Trevor-Howardish looks weren't to my taste: I preferred Nick's kind of amiable scruffiness. Rex had such vanity, too: Jenny and I had a running joke that one day we'd discover where he worked out, and sneak a candid shot of him on a rowing machine or humping weights. Admittedly his manner was slick, but only those impervious to oil would call it charm. Mrs Dunbury might think he was wonderful, but that didn't mean I had to agree.

He wasn't worth thinking about. I turned back to the paper. There were two other text-boxes. One, heavy-black-lined, gave details of Bill's family and career. He'd had two children, a boy of seven and a girl of five. He'd lived just outside the city on a modern estate, and his widow was called Freda. I remembered the eager voice on the phone saying 'Bill', and hoped the police and press had been gentle with her.

The third box summarised the mine story to date. It was illustrated with an artist's impression of a brick-vaulted tunnel and a flight of steps, and a rough sketch-map showing Flint Hill and the tunnels underneath it.

I stared at this with growing amazement. Surely the engineers wouldn't have released this information? Now we'd have a dozen families poring over it, deciding their house was safe, and going home without official clearance.

I rang David North, the Chief City Engineer, made the usual sympathetic noises and asked him if he'd given the map to the press. He assured me that it hadn't been drawn up by his staff, and that he was just as angry as I was. A team of his officers was already contacting all the evacuees, and he had also alerted the police, who would continue to patrol the exclusion zone and make sure no one went there without authorization.

Maybe the map hadn't been drawn by an engineer, but someone had told whoever had drafted it where the tunnels went. In fairness, though, I could see it needn't necessarily have been one of North's staff. I could have sketched a map like that myself; so could any of the City Works men who had been around when Bill and Sheila had come out of the mine; so could Phil, Rex, and who knew who else?

I thanked North and rang off, then asked myself whether I needed to make any more calls. I reckoned not. Since North's staff were contacting all the evacuees I wasn't obliged to go back to John Utting and Daniel Duchêne, and anyone else who needed me would know where to find me – only I hoped they wouldn't, because my head felt like I'd been listening to hip-hop through headphones for the last ten years.

15

When I got home I discovered the second post had brought a report I'd agreed to translate weeks before. It was dusty stuff about agricultural machinery, but I'd have welcomed even a chunk of the Belgian telephone directory. I gave myself an early night, and in the morning, early – eight's impressive for me – out came the dictionary, my files of technical terms and my list of expert contacts. I switched on the answering machine, and there ensued ten hours with no interruptions – just the word processor, a steaming coffee pot and Mao-mao on my lap.

That was the longest time I'd spent without thinking about Flint Hill since Graham Bunting had first phoned me. Murder and danger seemed distant and unreal. I stopped work at six, did half an hour's exercises, had a quick shower, ate a takeaway pizza, and as I fished my sage-green council-meeting suit out of the wardrobe, told myself I was even feeling up to fending off awkward questions from Nick.

Maybe, at that, he wouldn't ask any. I'd become a little paranoid perhaps: not everyone in Costhorpe was mean, miserable or downright villainous. Under his wisecracks Nick was a decent, caring man. Unlike Rex; well, not so unlike Rex, to be fair. Rex might be politically misguided, but he too was involved in local politics because he cared about the city and its inhabitants.

Monthly council meetings are nearly all ritual: the real business is done in committees. Our chairs make speeches saying how wonderful the Council is, and the opposition make speeches claiming we've made a mess of everything. Flint Hill wouldn't come up unless the Tories or Liberal Democrats asked a question about it; and even then they'd get a bland answer.

I arrived barely on time, and wasn't sorry: the only person I wanted to talk to was David North, and I'd have a chance to grab him in the tea interval. As I slipped into the Council Chamber the mace bearer was ordering everyone to stand for the Lord Mayor's arrival.

Costhorpe City Hall is New Brutality out of Arts and Crafts. The

Council Chamber boasts semicircular leather benches, quantities of polished oak, over-varnished portraits of nineteenth-century mayors, and dim Thirties-style flambeaux. We sit in named seats, well separated, so there's little room for intrigue during the meeting.

My seat's in the middle row, with Nick right in front of me. Rex was watching me from the Tory benches. I avoided his look, and fixed my eyes on Nick's broad shoulders, the stub of his ponytail and the grubby neck of his rugby shirt.

At the tea interval I filed out of our benches in the opposite direction to the Tories, which took me towards Jenny. I couldn't avoid talking to her, so for safety's sake I grabbed a topic before she could. 'You made a good speech on the Housing report.'

'You're not often that transparent, Erica,' Jenny said. 'You know what I want to hear, and it's not your flattery.'

I let myself sigh. 'One,' I said, 'I did not discover Bill Baxter's body. Two, if you read the Argus, you already know why I came to be on Flint Hill. Three, it was an accident that I ran into Rex Canning. Alas, it happens: we do cover the same patch.'

Jenny gave me a thoughtful look, and I resigned myself to a lot more questions about the mine and the murder; but I didn't get them. Instead she said, 'I wish you'd told me and Nick. We wouldn't have put you through the wringer, but I'd like to have had a chance to be a friend when you needed one. Or did Rex do that for you?'

'Hardly.'

'Do you get on with him?'

'Who would?'

'Lots of women, I should think,' Jenny said reasonably. 'I just thought, you're on your own, and —'

'So are a lot of men I don't want to know any better than I already do. Give me a break, Jenny – I've better taste than that. I need to talk to David North, so I'll see you later, okay?'

'All right. But Erica, don't forget, if there's anything you want to talk over, I'm always —'

'I'll ring you,' I said, grabbed my cup of tea, and set off in search of North.

It seemed I wasn't the only person who wanted a word with the City Engineer. After a search I found him halfway down a side-corridor, talking to Jack Wells, the Tory leader. North is tall and saturnine, with a vertically-creased face; Wells, who was back-on to me, is bald and tubby. Too glum to form a comic duo, they had heads close together and were making no gestures.

Were they talking about Flint Hill? About Bill? I couldn't get near enough to listen in without making it obvious. Worse, as I retreated through a pair of swing doors I almost crashed into Rex.

'Hi,' he said. 'Feeling okay?'

'Why shouldn't I?'

Rex looked a little taken-aback, but he went on, smoothly enough, 'I was looking for David North.'

'He's down there with your leader. And when Jack's finished, I want him.'

'I didn't realise there was a queue. Can you let him know I want a word?' He turned and stalked off.

He'd taken offence at my playing porcupine, obviously; and for a second I was sorry. I hadn't meant to be rude to him, merely to avoid encouraging anyone else to think on the same lines as Jenny. He should have comprehended that – surely the Tories gossiped too?

It was too bad if he hadn't, since I couldn't afford to explain. I stationed myself by the doors and waited. North and Wells had swivelled round, so North now had his back to me. Their bodies and faces still gave nothing away.

Maybe they weren't discussing Bill's death; maybe – most likely – their conversation was as tedious to hear as it was to watch. North could be short-tempered, but Wells was a dozy bore, whom it was all but impossible to stir into argument. I should know, the Labour Group tried all the time.

Still, they had enough to discuss to occupy them for a full tea interval, and as well as wanting to grab North, I'd have liked to know the subject. I hadn't a hope. Eventually the bell rang to summon us back, and Wells touched North on the arm and headed towards the door and me. I backed against the wall, let him pass, and grabbed North as he followed.

'David, briefly.'

'Councillor, I really have to —'

'I really have to ask you this,' I said, cutting off his protest. 'I know you're piled under, but it could be important, and I forgot it when I rang you yesterday. Last Friday Bill Baxter said he had something he wanted to pass by me.'

North's mouth closed. The familiar 'be polite to councillors whatever the provocation' expression came across his face. It was followed by a more introspective look, then a positively intent one.

'About Flint Hill?'

'I suppose so, but I'm not sure. He said it was something he wanted an outsider's opinion on.'

'An outsider?' North repeated, rather blankly.

'Non-engineer.'

'I can't imagine... If Baxter had something he wanted to discuss, he should have come to me.'

'And you'd have gone to Nick Halton, I know. All right, Bill wasn't following the proper channel of communication. I maybe should have thought of that at the time, but I didn't. I took it that he'd just had an impulse to talk to me, and I had the impression that whatever he wanted to tell me was something... off-centre. Not a policy issue.'

'I've no idea what you're talking about.'

The City Engineer, a dour Mancunian, was renowned for being unhelpful, so I wasn't too put off by his response. 'Nor have I,' I said. 'But I'd like to know, and so would the police, for obvious reasons. So I'm asking you to find out. It shouldn't be difficult, Bill must have left some clue. Can you run your eyes over his desk? Or I will, if you'd rather. Not that I know much about engineering, but probably I wouldn't need to. He might even have written my name on a piece of paper.'

North frowned, and for an instant I felt uneasy. After all, Bill had been murdered before he could pass on his information, whatever it was, and if I went around asking about it...

It was too late now to draw back. North said brusquely, 'Sheila Brennan's taking over Bill's urgent work. I'll have a word with her.'

That wasn't the reply I'd wanted, since I'd deliberately chosen to ask North and not Sheila, and not because of personal liking or its lack. I didn't believe Bill had discussed his 'obsession' with Sheila, or he wouldn't have spoken about it as he had to me; and I thought it might be significant that he hadn't chosen her, since she was the obvious choice.

However there wasn't much to be said for telling Sheila's boss that I didn't trust her; and I didn't trust North to not pass it on to her if I did. So I thanked him; then added, 'There's one other thing.'

'The meeting's started again.'

'This won't take a second. Did you find out who leaked the mine plan?'

'No. Excuse me, councillor.'

I let him go; and asked myself during the second half of the council meeting if I could do any more. I'd have to wait to see what North came up with, but I reckoned I could try Patty over the plan. She wasn't my favourite person at that moment, but I assumed she'd have realised that, and thought she might be willing to give me the snippet in order to restore our friendly relations.

So after the meeting broke up I drifted in a casual way over to the reporter's desk, where Patty was briefcasing her notes, and squeezed out an apology for being so short when she'd last phoned me.

Patty gave me a cool look, and told me she quite understood. Then I said, 'I wasn't too thrilled to see that plan of the mine in the Argus.'

'Weren't you?'

She doesn't give; or at least, only space for others to cavort in. It's a disconcerting technique. I was conscious of my own unease as I went on, 'What I thought was, it might encourage people to move back into Flint Hill when they oughtn't.'

There was a short silence. Patty snapped her briefcase shut then returned her attention to me. She set her head to one side, chin jutting, her cap of chestnut hair falling vertically. 'Oughtn't they?'

'Not till it's safe.'

'Some people think the Council could trim the danger zone.'

'Some people, meaning you?' She wouldn't say, I knew. She's more elaborately neutral even than the council officers. Instead she shrugged, turned away and picked up her case.

I said, 'So someone thought that if the plan was published, it would put a little pressure...'

'That's one way of looking at it.'

'I'd like to know who.'

'Erica,' Patty said with crisp near-disgust, 'you can't be asking me to reveal my sources.'

'It won't hurt. I'm just curious.'

'That's hardly a reason for me to tell you. You'll have to excuse me, I've still got to write up my copy. No offence, I hope.'

None; even though it was a fib. Of course she'd written up everything during some of the more interminable speeches. I knew when to give up, but I still had a lingering feeling I needed to know who had handed over the plan.

16

NEXT morning work hit me a bunch of ram-raiders. I still had the agricultural report to finish and phonecalls to make about the Bulgarian trip, and the postman brought a couple of long business letters which needed translating urgently. I'd no sooner started on that lot when I had a call to say an EEC document, Dutch to English, was in the post: together they gave me enough to tie up the rest of my week, and longer.

I stayed in my dressing gown, so I wouldn't be tempted to go out of doors, and left the answerphone on all morning. I hardly ever do that: I'm cat-curious, and it takes real willpower for me to listen to the phone ring and cut out, and not play back messages right away.

There were a half-dozen calls, and at lunchtime I went through the tape – an indulgence like the splat of Christmas mail on the mat, except this was mostly manila-envelope stuff. Least welcome of all was Graham Bunting. He didn't leave a message, only his name, spoken loudly, and a number. The threat of him would wreck my afternoon: I phoned him back to get it over with, and was rewarded with a tirade. What was going on about these doors? It sounded bloody fishy to him, but if someone had known about the tunnels all along, no doubt about it, he'd sue them. And how long were he and Mandy supposed to sweat it out in the dump they'd been sent to? The Council ought to give them a house with a garden. They knew their rights, and wouldn't let us pull a fast one on them.

I bit my tongue, and promised to get onto the Housing Department. That wasn't good enough for Graham, I'd got to see the dump for myself. He didn't want words, he wanted f...ing results.

Didn't we all? The result I wanted was the Buntings out of my hair. Strictly speaking they'd moved out of Hillside and into Cavell ward, Tony March's patch, but I didn't think it would be fair to shove them onto him, so I agreed to check the dump that afternoon at four.

I'd phone Louise Hoggett after lunch, I decided, and hope to learn something to tell Graham. Meanwhile I made myself a salad sandwich, and was just biting into it when the phone rang again.

'Erica, it's Allie.'

Guiltily, I remembered I hadn't returned her thoughtful call on Saturday evening. I apologised and assured her I was fine – but she hadn't called only to hear that.

'It's Raze and Steve, Erica. The police questioned them on Saturday, and had them in again on Sunday, and Eddy just phoned me to say they've gone back to the station today. What on earth do the cops imagine?'

I'd learned by now that Allie, so aloof to the outside world, was a clucking chicken with her inner circle. When she wanted something done for them she could be as insistent as Bunting, so I agreed it sounded too much like police harassment, and promised to investigate for her. I took the name and number of the friends Raze and Steve were staying with – the Eddy who had phoned, and Clara, neither of whom I knew – and told her I'd call round to update her that evening.

It looked like becoming a busy day. I do enjoy being everyone's agony aunt, but it doesn't always fit with earning an honest living. I went across to my bedroom and pulled a black cord skirt and black sweatshirt out of the wardrobe. I washed (again), dressed, went down to make a strong cup of coffee, and opened my office window six inches. I worked at the agribusiness till ten past two, then tried Louise's extension at City Hall, and got her straight away.

One mention of the Buntings, and she sighed so loud it sounded like Mao-mao's best purr. Apparently they had phoned the Housing Department every day. First of all, I should forget any idea that their new flat was cramped: it had two bedrooms, which was right for a family their size. Second, I ought to know they owed the Council two months' rent.

'Come on Louise,' I said. 'Special circumstances: find them a house somewhere round Hillside.'

'Come on Erica,' she retorted. 'Find me their back rent and I will.'

I pointed out that the Buntings deserved compensation for the upheaval, the carpets that wouldn't fit a different house and the fittings they'd never retrieve. Louise pointed out that they had already demanded twice the maximum the council ever paid, and hadn't exactly turned thirty-three Flint Hill into a palace before it fell apart. We haggled. Louise agreed that if I persuaded them to settle for a reasonable figure, she would try to get them allocated the first house that came available in Hillside. A deal, I said, hoping I could talk the

Buntings into it.

That was half a problem solved, but I still had to see about Raze and Steve. I dialled the police station and asked for DI Zahler – who was unavailable. I didn't want to tangle with Sunley, so I tried Superintendent Ransome next. He was in a meeting, but I was told I could leave a message.

I didn't. I wasn't sure I should even have asked for Ransome. I'd have spoken to Zahler if I could, because I'd only have had to hint my concern to him, but I didn't want to make things worse for Raze and Steve by coming over heavy in the wrong quarters. What power did I have, anyway? The police did make reasonable efforts to stay on good terms with city councillors, but we weren't the Police Authority, and hadn't any direct influence over them. I hadn't been asked to intervene by either Raze or Steve, and as far as I knew the police weren't holding them against their will.

Allie was right, though: heavy pressure had to be resisted. What was the legal position? Hell, I was no expert. I gave it five minutes' thought, and tried Justin Howell at Green and Green. A longstanding acquaintance, a Labour Party member, and by repute a good criminal lawyer, I thought with luck he'd give me some quick free advice.

Justin was out to lunch. No panic, Erica. The only urgency was my work deadline. I pushed the window sash up higher, and with the cold air on my face managed another page of French jargonese. Then I rang Justin again, and again every half-hour between one-thirty and three. I'd thought epic business lunches went out with the eighties.

At three-thirty I finally got onto him. We had a five-minute conversation full of 'if you were told' and 'these friends of mine' before Justin said straight out, 'This is the Bill Baxter case, isn't it?'

'Since you ask, yes.'

'Then I can guess who your friends are: Steve Black and his partner.'

'I knew you were the right person, Justin.'

'I'm their lawyer.'

'You must have picked a bad slot on the duty solicitor rota.'

'Not a bit of it, I've acted for Steve for years. And off the record, I wouldn't advise you to treat him and Raze like welfare cases. Steve's family have money and influence which they're not scared to use, and if there was any whiff of discrimination Raze would play it all the way to the High Court, with me to back him.'

'So can I tell their friend Allie you'll haul them out?'

'You can tell her to leave it to me; and no offence, Erica, but I'd like you to do the same. I know the rules, and so do Ted Zahler and his crew. You're right, it's time the police wrapped up their statement and let them go, but I want the whole thing played gently. Okay?'

'Fine by me,' I assured him. I wasn't looking for anyone to nanny, and if Justin was getting paid for doing the job, who was I to protest?

FOUR pm, early March. A bright afternoon fading to grey. The address Graham Bunting had given me was on a modern council estate a mile from the university. Square blocks of flats two and three storeys high were linked with arches and 'brightened' with stripes of yellow, giving an effect like a superior Lego set. There were beds of low-maintenance shrubs outside the windows. The grass looked dingy, and each square was quartered by tracks of bare earth. The balconies were festooned with limp washing, and a brown-haired mongrel skulked about the entrance to numbers ten to eighteen.

The only people in sight were a plump old lady carrying a shopping bag, and a thin young one two storeys up, yelling at her. 'You tell Pete he can park his own bloody car next time.' 'If you'd been looking where you were f...ing going...'

I'd livened the black outfit with a bright blue jacket, and tied my hair back with a chiffon scarf to match. Neither woman gave me a glance. I found flat number twelve on the ground floor, a location much coveted by elderly couples and young families, so Louise hadn't done badly for the Buntings.

Mandy, fag in mouth, gave me a bored look on the doorstep and stood aside to let me come in. I followed her down a featureless corridor to a living room painted sunshine yellow – not by her, I assumed. The baby was asleep in a cheap pine cot, and the toddler was watching television amid a scrawl of toys. Mandy made no move to switch it off.

She offered me coffee, which I accepted, and made strong instant. In the kitchen she told me Graham wasn't around. He'd gone to the Citizens' Advice Bureau to see if he had a legal case against the owners of the doors onto the mine.

These two didn't need nannying either. They'd called on me because they reckoned I could help them screw the system. When I went down the list of items they could claim compensation for, Mandy knew what to say about every one. The furniture they hadn't been allowed to take from the upstairs back bedroom, the carpets that wouldn't fit another house, the cupboards in the kitchen. Uh-oh, those cupboards came with the house, I said (Louise had told me) but Mandy shot back: it was Graham who painted them.

We argued for half an hour, during which I let her talk up the claim until she hit double the figure I'd agreed with Louise. I told her she wouldn't get more than half as much, and she narrowed her eyes and apparently decided I meant it. She ground out her cigarette in the sink. 'Could be worse. I vote Labour,' she said off-handedly. 'So would Gray if 'e bothered.'

'That's good. Mind you, I'd do the same for a Tory.'

I doubted she believed me, and wondered what strange sense of protocol had made not tell me until we'd finished bargaining. She lit a new cigarette, offered me the pack – no thanks – took a deep drag and stared at the window. The old woman was still outside. I could see her mouth opening and closing, but I couldn't hear her over the noise of Record Breakers coming through from the television.

Mandy in profile looked weary. I could see dark circles under her eyes, and a quarter-inch of dark roots under the blonde of her hair.

'That guy wot died down the mine. D'you know him?'

She asked as if it was a natural subject for gossip.

'Yes, but not well.'

'Someone kill 'im?'

'So the police seem to think.'

'D'you know why?'

'I haven't a clue. Do you?'

'Never met 'im, 'ave I?'

'You might have an idea anyway. You lived on Flint Hill.'

She turned to face me. 'You think it was about the 'ole?'

'I can't see how it could have been. A lot of people were upset about the mine, but why would any of them want to kill Bill? It wasn't his fault.'

'I never thought it was.'

Mandy had stressed the 'I' very slightly. 'Did other people?' I asked.

'Wot people say, Joan an' everyone... Hell, 'e made a mistake, we all make mistakes. It's Mrs f...in' Dunbury I'm livid at, 'er and that bleedin' pair of faggots next door to 'er.'

'I don't blame you,' I said. I thought of telling her Bill hadn't made a mistake, but I didn't think she'd believe me, any more than she would if I told her Raze and Steve hadn't known about the door.

'What Gray reckoned was,' Mandy said, 'they killed 'im so 'e wouldn't find out about this door arrangement.'

'That doesn't make any sense. Bill was only one engineer in a sizeable department, and anyone surely would have realised that if he didn't investigate the tunnel, someone else would. Anyway, Raze and Steve told me about the doors on Saturday morning – and the Dunburys told another councillor.'

'Cover their tracks, maybe.' Mandy lifted her shoulders and extinguished her fag-end under the tap.

It still made no sense. Nothing made any sense. What the Dunburys had done on Saturday morning, what Raze and Steve had done, what Bill had wanted to talk to me about... none of it fitted.

Maybe the police had made sense of it. Maybe they had some information – on Steve and Raze? – that I didn't have. If they knew Bill had gone into the tunnel through...

Something else didn't fit.

'Mandy,' I said, 'did you have a rope at Flint Hill? A thick yellow rope?'

Her speedy reaction made her gold chains tinkle. 'How'd you know 'bout that?'

'I saw it, that's how, tied to the scaffolding at your old house. I wondered if it belonged to you.'

'The police asked us that. No, it ain't ours. A climber's rope, they said. You see Gray as a mountaineer?'

'Not exactly.' I smiled, to echo her close-lipped effort. 'That's why I was surprised when I saw it. It didn't look as if it was yours, but if it wasn't, whose was it?'

'Dunno. I don't know any mountaineers round there. You think they went down the tunnel that way?'

'I've no idea.'

'Tell you one thing, I'm bleedin' glad I'm not goin' back to our old house. Could be a psychopath, couldn't it, some nutter who ran across 'im and done 'im in. Someone hidin' in our house. Gray said they knocked down the back, so you could get in easy.'

'It's a horrible thought.'

Even so, it seemed to me more incredible than scary. A wild-eyed maniac holding Bill at gunpoint and forcing him to climb down into the mine using a yellow rope... then what? Why leave the rope, in that case? Why not untie the end and drop it down after him?

'Mummee,' a yell came from the living room. 'Jade's woken up!'

This was promptly confirmed by a wail. 'I'd better go,' I said, and Mandy made no move to stop me.

17

It was barely a fortnight since the hole had opened up, and now the Buntings' children were watching television in a different living room, and I was en route to Allie and Phil's new flat. Life fell apart, and yet it didn't: the survivors still ate breakfast, lunch and supper, got up in the morning and wondered what to wear.

I'd seen the phlegmatic faces in the church hall after the evacuation, and I'd seen the same faces distorted with fury at Rex's public meeting. I didn't underestimate the anger people felt when their homes were endangered – or how it simmered on under the politest façade of resignation. But could it ever have risen to murderous rage? If so, in whom?

If someone had killed Bill, I wanted the police to catch them; but I couldn't believe anyone I knew could have killed him. Graham Bunting, James Dunbury, Fred Keylock, Raze and Steve... they weren't my favourite people, but I wouldn't have set down any of them as a potential murderer. Learning that one of them had done it – let alone someone I liked, such as Phil – would almost be worse than knowing an unknown murderer was still on the loose.

No, it couldn't be Phil. At least I was sure of that. A nice guy like Phil, who dealt with stress by making a list and opening a bottle... life wouldn't be worth living if you took that kind of possibility seriously.

Allie and Phil's new address was a block of privately-built Thirties flats. The paint outside was peeling but inside everything was dinky: carpeted stairways and lacy curtains and rows of pot plants at the landing windows.

I'd thought I knew what Allie was like at home, but it turned out I'd underestimated. In my house she had been no more than a faint smell of wine and casserole, a swish of long skirts and the warmth of a cup of tea offered every time I turned round. The essence she had bottled there had spilled across this place like a perfume spray dropped on concrete.

The furniture was landlord-standard-issue, ten-year-old Dralon sofas and autumn-leaf carpets, but it was effectively drowned by paisley shawls, Victorian silk fringes, Turkish rugs and a Moroccan bedspread. Watercolours of maharajas and elephants, detailed delicate scenes half-coloured in red and yellow and a clear light blue, hung in composed groups on the cream woodchip. Piaf moaned from the stereo.

I'd simply said I'd call in, but she had assumed I'd stay for supper, and I wasn't complaining. She opened wine without waiting for Phil (it was five-thirty when I arrived), and poured herself a glass even when I said I'd rather have water: I'd have to do some more work after I got home.

I followed her through to the kitchen, where she chopped peppers and onions and set rice to boil while I told her about Justin, and – where I could – answered her questions.

I'd been satisfied by Justin's assurances, but I soon discovered Allie wasn't. She was convinced Raze and Steve shouldn't be suspects. Neither of them had known Bill. Why had Justin let them give more than one brief statement? Why hadn't he told me straight out that he was sure they were innocent?

Because I hadn't asked, I protested. Anyway, how could he be sure before the investigation was over? You didn't have to know someone in order to murder them. They'd been on the scene, found the body, and if that made the police take a serious interest in them, I thought it was understandable. Presumably the police knew from long experience that proximity counted in murder cases.

'But are they home now?' Allie demanded. 'Did this Justin actually get them out? It's the trouble with not being on the phone here, nobody tells us anything.'

'I'll watch the rice if you want to go and phone Eddy and Clara.'

'We'll see if there's anything on the news first.'

Phil came home, and we ate vegetable and lentil curry and watched the television. Sure enough, the regional news reported that two men who had been helping with enquiries in the Bill Baxter case had now been let go, and the police had refused to comment when asked if arrests were imminent.

Phil said he wanted to know more, and I was curious too. I'd have liked to know if the police had harped on about the crowbar, and what Raze and Steve's explanation was, so when Phil suggested I come over with him to Eddy and Clara's, I agreed. Allie said she had some marking to do, and would stay behind. I had work to do as well, but I didn't mean to stay long at Eddy and Clara's, so it could wait until afterwards.

I'd biked over to the flat, so we drove to Eddy and Clara's in Phil's car. I'd seen their house before: it was the big shabby terrace that had featured on the television the previous Saturday, with a furtive-looking Raze and Steve leaving it. There were a dozen bells by the black-painted door, but Phil knew which to push. As we waited I could hear the muffled beat of rap played loud, coming through the wall from above our heads.

The ringing had no effect, so Phil tried the door, which proved to be unlocked.

'Most likely the music's theirs,' he said. 'They won't hear, or won't bother to come down if they do. We'll go straight up.'

When we reached the second landing a door above us opened. The rap hit me like Athens-August heat.

'Hey, Phil. Hey.' A short-haired black man peered over the banisters. 'Who's she? Not the plods?'

'No, she's okay. Raze and Steve here?'

'Around, but flat out. Come up and join the party.'

I'd have been wary on my own, but Phil went on up as if it was his second home, so I followed in his wake.

Even at the door of the flat the sweet smell of hash was strong enough to lure every cop between there and the seaside. Phil found and introduced me to Eddy, who was a Rasta like Raze, but shorter and thinner. Clara was tall and black and beautiful. The other people who filled the flat, spread across three or four rooms and a corridor, coming and going in a dim light made dimmer by smoke, seemed to be mostly male and mostly white.

Raze and Steve weren't so much flat out as rubber-doll bendy, hazed out of sight. After three bouts of interrogation... hell, I couldn't blame them for needing to mellow.

'Okay to stay?' Phil yelled in my ear.

I nodded out of politeness, knowing he wanted to; knowing too that I wouldn't get what I'd come for. The questions I wanted to ask weren't ones I could yell over NWA, and even if I'd tried, Raze and Steve were both far past answering. Phil disappeared into the crowd, and Eddy handed me a beer.

I thought of skipping off without telling Phil, then I thought about not skipping off. I wasn't on home territory, but parties are better sometimes when you're not. Although Raze and Steve weren't my friends, I didn't figure anyone around for a murderer, and Phil was there to keep me safe. The music was good, it made me feel like dancing. I hadn't danced in months. It occurred to me that I too needed to mellow a bit.

I pulled the tab on the beer-can, took a long draught, and threw my jacket on a pile in the corner.

I thought dimly of work, but I told myself I could afford to forget it for a few hours. I danced to the Bhundu Boys with a tall bony man I didn't know, and danced again with a sleepwalking Raze. Then I fell onto a sofa, a fresh can in my hand and Raze to my left. Someone passed him a joint, and he took a drag and passed it to me. I passed it right on. Habit, convention. Protesting I hadn't wouldn't cut much ice if the police walked in.

'Hey,' a voice said in my ear.

I took my time turning, and focussed slowly on an unfamiliar face, dominated by a pair of round red-framed glasses. The eyes behind them were watery blue, and the face neat-featured, with a vee of beard on the chin. He was in his late twenties, I guessed, and wearing clothes as preppy as Steve's.

'You're into this Flint Hill business,' I lipread over the music.

'In a fashion,' I mouthed back. He waved the hand that didn't hold a glass towards an open doorway.

I'd have sat and drank, I'd have danced to the music which vibrated through the floorboards and into my feet. He wanted to talk. I had come to talk, and I'd said nothing yet but hi and thanks. But I'd lost my inclination – and I didn't know if this guy was planning to ask, or to tell.

Habit and convention won out: I heaved myself up and followed him – standing, I realised he was short, only five-two or so – along a red-lit corridor and into a kitchen.

The ceiling was sloping, eaves-low. The light was bright in here, from a neon strip. Open shelves were loaded with scratched pans, packs of cereal and rice, unlabelled glass jars with spices in them, a half-used jar of coffee and a bottle of milk. Mugs swung from hooks, and a plump pink-faced boy and a shorter dark-haired one were arguing in a corner.

The man ignored them. He stopped by the stove and turned to me. The neon skeetered off his glasses, and I couldn't see his eyes. 'This subsidence business,' he said in a south-London whine. 'F...in' racket, innit.'

Wariness crawled across my skin. 'In what sense?'

'You're on the Council, you should know.'

Cosy party chat this wasn't. What did he want with me? 'Are you an estate agent?' I guessed out loud.

'Nah, buyer. Flats. Bedsits. All over.' He waved his hand as if he was dismissively claiming half Costhorpe.

'You own this place?'

'Yeah. Eddy's my friend. I'm okay, good landlord. Don't you jump to no stereotypes.'

How not? My mind had jumped, I was still cold-footing on behind it. Landlords and saints are mutually-exclusive classes – socialist dogma, but true, man, true. I was sobering fast. Who had told him what; and what was he telling me?

'Right,' I said. 'So far I've got subsidence, racket, landlord and council. Now give me a link, because I don't see it.'

If he heard me, he gave no sign. I had the impression he'd switched on a well-worn tape. He'd shifted a little, and now I could see the pale eyes behind his glasses, but they didn't look into mine as he went on. 'You know the villains in this game, and it ain't the landlords. We provide a public service. People like these, they gotta live somewhere, and we don't all go for the Marxist state. You go here, you go there, kick our asses, incompetence, bureaucracy. Free enterprise is the only way. Maybe it ain't perfect, but it's the only way.'

The only way to what? Not to win round a socialist politician. Was he sober? Was he gone on dope? There was a slight slur to his voice, but without knowing him I couldn't be sure it wasn't permanent.

I thought of walking out, but I'd drunk enough to keep on in there, if not quite enough to argue back.

'So what's the racket?'

'You know what this mine business does to prices?'

This sounded a comparatively sensible question. 'I've an idea.'

'All over Yorkshire, the Midlands, South Wales, you think we've the only mines in the world? A few pathetic chalk pits. You know how many yards of tunnel there are? You know how often they collapse? Once every twenty years, that's what. You with your f...in' surveys, the press with their scare stories, they got half Costhorpe thinkin' they're gonna fall down a black hole in the middle of the night.'

I knew he had his figures wrong. I'd asked Bill a couple of months before, and he'd told me that including the little collapses owners managed to keep out of the press, there were one or two mine-related subsidences in Costhorpe each year. I wasn't about to argue that point.

'Do you think we should pretend the mines don't exist?'

'Know when the last person died when a mine caved in? Fifty-seven years ago. There's people all over Costhorpe, got good solid houses with holes a hundred feet beneath them, and you blight the f...in' lot.'

I had it, I thought. He'd been stung. He owned property on Flint Hill – maybe Raze and Steve's house, that would make sense – and he knew he'd lost out. So like all the rest, he wanted someone to blame.

'I hate blight too,' I said, 'but by and large, I'd say there's only blight where there's a real risk. You can't get round that.'

'A risk? Hell, half the time in this place they make up the f...in' risks. Wanna know where the scam is? That's the big scam in this town, and much you f...in' care.'

'I can't see there's much for anyone in making up risks,' I said sarkily. 'Anyway, I think the chalk mine survey's a worthwhile —'

'And you're on the f...in' Planning Committee. Right load of angels you are. Some of you are in on it, I can tell you. Not you, you're clean, I've heard about you.'

'Thanks a lot.' I didn't believe him. Big scams indeed. Every now and then someone buttonholes me to tell me how corrupt all politicians are, but the only offer I ever get from developers is of a cup of lukewarm coffee, plus two digestives if I'm lucky.

'Now they'll stitch up Raze and Steve,' Red-glasses went on, 'and they ain't done nothin''.

Was this paranoia, or was he onto something? I couldn't work out what. I went back to what I hoped was safer territory.

'Are you the landlord at Flint Hill? You own number six?'

'Nah, that's Steve's house, used to be his grandmother's. Good house that. Now that'd make flats, you seen the space inside there?'

I shrugged. Two-storied terrace on a secondary road: we'd never give permission. It was against the Local Plan. More interesting was his argument. I was trying to make sense of it, but I hadn't made much of a beginning. 'Let's start at the start,' I said. 'Bill was doing a survey on mines, and if you had a house with a mine running under it, you might not like the idea of his finding out; although not many people know, I'd have thought. But if you did know, and you thought Bill was likely to find out too, then fair enough, you'd have a reason for stopping him. One person who could have known was Steve, because he had a house with a door that led onto a tunnel. Maybe he didn't know that, but maybe he did. Most people would in such a situation. So how's it clearing him to argue like that?'

'You think that's how the coppers argue it?'

I thought that in three interrogation sessions, the coppers would have tried every possible angle. This was an angle, and after a pint of beer I could see it; so surely DI Zahler would, surely DC Allen would. Sunley I wouldn't have sworn to.

How long had the police taken interviewing the Dunburys?

'I'll tell you now, they're in on the scam. Wanna know why they don't look too hard? I'll f...in' tell you.'

'Erica?'

It was a relief to turn from this tirade to find it was Phil who had called me. He was standing in the doorway, looking straight and sturdy and sober.

'I reckon I'll be going,' he said. 'You ready to come?'

I reckoned I was. The conversation had sobered the enjoyment out of me, and I doubted I was going to keep my temper long enough to find out if Red-glasses had a thesis that hung together. 'Yes, sure,' I said. 'Excuse me.'

Red-glasses nudged past me, and held out his hand to Phil. 'We met at Tony's,' he said. 'Alex Yelland. You need some advice on your house, you come to me.'

'I might,' Phil said cagily.

'Here.' Yelland put down his glass, reached in his trouser pocket, brought out a leather wallet and removed a card. He held it out to Phil. 'You need some advice?' he asked me. 'You want one too?'

'Maybe.' No way would I touch a guy who went on about corruption in the Council and the police; not unless he had proof, and I didn't believe he had. But I wanted to remember the name, so I could avoid it in future. I took his card and slipped it into my pocket.

18

PHIL seemed abstracted, heading back to his car. I asked if everything was okay, but all I got was, 'Oh yeah; just tired.'

So was I, but my mind wouldn't cut out of gear. Why had Yelland approached me? I couldn't fathom his motives. If he did know about a scam in the property market, why should he tell me about it?

Was there a scam? It occurred to me that I knew diddly-squat about the property business in Costhorpe. It occurred to me too that if there had been a scam, there was a fair chance Bill Baxter had uncovered it.

I thought the police ought to be given that lead; but it wasn't really a lead, I had nothing solid to tell them. I thought of asking around, getting some information together. Mentally I ran through the property professionals I was acquainted with. I couldn't ask Jack Wells for background, because he and I weren't exactly best buddies. Miles Keylock? I didn't rate his professional judgement: he'd warned Nick and me that our house was subsiding when it wasn't, then bought himself a place next to a chalk mine. If that was the general calibre of their staff, it was amazing that Keylocks were as successful as they were reputed to be.

Nick and I had switched to Black Horse, and they had done us a reasonable job. Maybe I could talk to someone there – but what could I say? Hi, good morning, know any good crooks?

'Bloody idiots,' Phil said out loud. 'Can't just collapse and have a beer, they have to haul half Costhorpe in for a bloody party. And the dope. Jesus, there are times. If the plods had knocked on the door...'

I hauled my mind around. 'Was that why you wanted to leave?'

'Uh? No, just tired. I'd have got Allie to come if I'd known we might stay. Don't like going places without Allie. I suppose it must be love.'

'Course it is,' I said; then on impulse I added, 'Phil, do you know any climbers around Flint Hill?'

'Wisteria, you mean? Clematis?'

'Phil! As in mountaineer.'

Phil flicked me a sideways look, and for a second I felt sharp-tongued and unlovable. He didn't criticise me, though. He swung into Morton Street, pulled up his car outside my house, then said evenly, 'There's more clematis than there are mountaineers in north Costhorpe. Can't think of any of the latter. Sinkers I know, though – Steve's one. He belonged to the pot-holing club when he was at the uni.'

'Steve? You're sure?'

'Course I'm sure. I remembered when we heard about him and Raze having a look down the mine – they would, it's Steve's scene. Not Raze's, as far as I know. I actually went pot-holing with Steve once, but it wasn't my scene either.'

'Would Steve have a climbing rope?'

'Haven't a clue. You okay to pick your bike up in the morning?'

I'd have liked to ask more, but the message coming over was that he was too tired to answer. 'Sure,' I said. 'Thanks for the lift. Love to Allie.' Phil didn't even wait till I'd unlocked my front door before driving off.

I fumbled for my key to the sound of his retreating car engine, followed by silence and darkness. Ah, empty houses. Beer hangovers. Mountains of urgent work I should have been doing that evening. Cold rooms.

I got through the door, and noticed there was a light on in the kitchen. Strange, that. I don't habitually leave lights on to foil burglars, nor do I generally forget to turn them off when I go out. I couldn't even remember entering the kitchen before going...

Out at three-forty, to bike over to the Buntings' flat. It had been light at three-forty.

'Mao-mao,' I called out. My voice sounded thin and high. Bluffing's not my forte, but I did belatedly realise no burglar would be struck rigid by my calling to my cat. I called on my recent practice and gave a full-blooded yell. 'Nick! I'm home, darli—'

A bang took my words away. It came from the kitchen, or at least, from the rear of the house. I backed against the wall. Even through my jacket, it felt cold against my shoulderblades. The front door was ajar behind me, and I hadn't yet switched on the light.

A draught whistled through the house and slammed the door shut. I jumped. My skin was loose, and shuddering around me. When I saw a shadow move, I almost fainted with fear.

It was only Mao-mao. She wove around my ankles, buzzing like an electric razor.

The light...?

Someone had been there, I knew. And left with the bang? There were other possibilities, and I wasn't feeling reckless. I felt for the front doorhandle. My fingers were like sausages, and I had to concentrate hard to tighten them round it. I turned it slowly, felt the click, eased the door open, slid through it and ran.

My friend Carol lives at the top of Morton Street. It was only just past eleven, and Carol's a night person. She opened up to my hammering, and made me strong tea as I was phoning the police. 'I'm being silly,' I kept repeating, but Carol said, 'Don't worry, love. They won't think so.'

I think the constable did for a moment, when he escorted me back into a tidy, empty house; but his scepticism died when we went into my kitchen, and saw the glass on the floor and the jagged hole in the pane in the back door. I'd left the key in the lock on the inside, and was given a lecture about my stupidity.

They had taken my stereo, nothing else. 'Video?' the constable prompted, but I didn't own one. Apart from the broken glass, they had made no mess. 'You're lucky,' said the constable, and I agreed I was. They hadn't touched my paintings, books, jewellery, anything that really mattered to me.

He and Carol both stayed with me till I'd finished the tea. Carol offered to let me sleep on her sofa, but I told her I'd be fine, and left the constable to take her and her empty mugs back home. I reckoned I was tired enough that it'd take more than a minor burglary to keep me awake; and I was right.

I'd set my alarm for five am. The early-morning radio news went through my head without connecting any neurons. The overnight DJ (no classical stations operate between twelve and seven) was just switching from supersoft rock to wake-up jive. Groan. Shower. Hairwash. I tied it back scrunch-dried, and made peppermint tea since I couldn't face more coffee.

I'd been indulging myself too much with running around: work didn't so much call, as scream to be done. I did it till a quarter to nine, and managed to fax my most urgent translation from City Hall before a Planning subcommittee meeting started. I couldn't skip the meeting, since I was the chair. Rex wasn't a member of the subcommittee, but

Nick was, and Patty was covering the meeting for the Argus. I hustled the debate along, and we turned out a verdict on a couple of dozen planning applications and a traffic calming scheme before twelve-thirty. There was nothing particularly contentious on the agenda, and Patty folded away her computer and left half an hour before the end.

Come the finish, Nick said, 'You're looking done in, Erica.'

'Partying too hard. And overworked, for once. I've got to go now, Nick, or I'll miss a deadline.'

'Women do panic,' Nick said. 'You can spare me ten seconds to pass on Jen's invitation to supper. Can you make tomorrow night?'

I'd no grudge against either Nick or Jenny, but I knew I wouldn't find them relaxing company, and I wasn't inclined to let myself in for an evening of monitoring every word I said. Nick wouldn't have let a curt refusal go untaunted, though, so I took the time to phrase it kindly.

'Thanks for the offer, but no to tomorrow. I want to keep on at the translations till I'm over the hump. Can I take a raincheck?'

I didn't expect the refusal to come as any surprise, but Nick gave me a real close look as if he hadn't anticipated it. It unnerved me that Nick should actually notice I was tired. He'd never been the teamaking sort of partner when we'd been together.

He said, 'So long as you're humping, darling – no, that's not the phrase. So long as you're on the jo—'

'Nick!'

My protest had Wilf turning to look at us, and a couple of the planning officers. Nick took me by the shoulder and twisted me away from them. I felt him take a deep breath. I was half-enveloped in bearlike male.

'All right, all right,' he said. 'I'm an insensitive ass and I don't know how to relate to you at the moment. Jen's already told me that at boring length, so we'll take it as read, okay? I wasn't trying to wind you up. I'm an idiot maybe, but I honestly thought you might laugh.'

'Wrong woman,' I said grimly. 'This is the one who's allergic to sexist jokes. Remember?'

'Dimly.'

At that I couldn't resist a smile. Nick smiled back, and for an instant I felt the old warmth, the kind we'd shared before it all went off the rails.

'Friends?' he asked.

'Yes, but... distant friends for now, please, Nick.'

I felt him hold his first response back, and choose the words for his second one. He loosed my shoulder, too.

'If that's what you really want. Thing is, Jen doesn't see it like that. You and I know, in a way... my stupid jokes... when you snap... it's all necessary realignment. But it can't help but be shitty when you lose your lover and your best friend at once, and when we read about you stumbling over bodies...'

'Jen's feeling guilty.'

'Chronically. So'm I, a bit.'

'I'm sorry,' I said, and meant it sincerely. 'But you'll have to work that off in some other direction, Nick.'

'We'll try. Erica... I know you've got lots of other friends, but you've never been great at leaning on them, darling. If you need me for anything...'

'I know the number. Nick, there is one thing you can do for me.'

'Yeah?'

'Stop calling me darling.'

That earned me an embarrassed smile. 'I didn't realise I did. Go back to your word processor. Oh – one last thing, Bill Baxter's funeral is tomorrow at ten. Apparently the coroner wouldn't agree to a cremation but he's released the body for burial, so they can exhume if they have to, gruesome thought. The service is at the new church on Newmarket Avenue, I forget the name but you know the one I mean.'

'I think I do,' I agreed.

'I'll aim to go but it'll be tight, because I'm lecturing at eleven. I think Judith's going, and she's sending a note round in case anyone else has the inclination.'

'Fine. One last thing from me, too. Do you know any Bulgarian speakers at the university?'

I SHOULD have turned down the request to sort out the Bulgarian travel group: it was taking hours, and I'd only earn a tiny commission. But Nick came through, and when I got home I persuaded his contact to make the phonecalls and write the letters.

The hump was coming closer – and there was no point in polishing off everything at record speed then finding myself workless for a fortnight. I worked on till two, then went to buy a new stereo – it could go on my credit card until I got the insurance money – a pane of glass and a tub of putty. I spent a messy hour fitting the glass into the back door, another half-hour wiring up the stereo, put Chopin on the cd player and my feet up on the sofa.

I know I closed my eyes, and I suppose I slept. When a noise woke me the room was darkening, I was out of preludes and my watch said six-thirty.

My sleepy mind said it was the hand-delivery of councillors' post – it splats through the letterbox some time after six – but I raised my head and nothing was on the mat. Then the doorbell rang, and I knew it was that I'd heard before.

Was I expecting anyone? If so, I'd forgotten.

Mao-mao appeared from nowhere, and attacked my ankles as I stumbled to the door. I opened it to find Steve Black on the step, looking pale and cold in a thin black windcheater.

'Oh,' I said.

'I heard you came over to Eddy's yesterday.'

Yeah, you were past seeing when I got there, I thought. I stood aside and in he stepped.

'Hey, nice place. That looks like a...'

Uninvited, he went across to my mantlepiece and picked up the sculpture. 'It's a Johnny Ahlberg,' I said in a discouraging voice.

'That's right, I forgot the name. Someone told me you were married to Jonathan Sayer.'

That was a line I hadn't expected. Ever since I'd come back to Costhorpe I'd been careful to keep quiet about Jonathan. It doesn't do for a local councillor to harp on about her ex-husband in the Shadow Cabinet – at least, that's the excuse I give myself.

'A long time ago,' I said.

'Did you get this through him?'

'What makes you think so?'

Steve shrugged. 'I know he and Ahlberg were schoolfriends, because I was at Ranborough too. We got the famous f...ing old boys rammed down our throats.'

I was pushed to find a polite response. 'Like a coffee?'

'I never touch it. D'you drink a lot of coffee? You shouldn't, you know, it gives you heart attacks. Coffee's about the worst stuff you can drink, even the decaffeinated's got all sorts of suspected carcinogens.'

I would, I would keep my cool. 'Water? Peppermint tea?'

'That'd be better. Hey, you'd better feed that cat.'

'I was about to, thanks,' I said through gritted teeth. I left Steve to prowl while I saw to Mao-mao and made peppermint tea for us both. I'd have preferred a double scotch. I wanted to be sympathetic – after all, Steve had had it rougher than I over the previous week – but he was certainly making it difficult.

When I got back to the front room he had my little Cotman watercolour off the wall, and was looking at the back as if he was trying to work out whether it was original. I could see grease stains on the backs of his hands.

'Yes it is,' I said. 'Now put it back.'

His head flicked round fast. 'Sorry.' He rehung it carefully, standing back to check the alignment, then said, without turning to me, 'Allie said you got onto the police to get us out.'

'I got onto Justin Howell, that's all. Before you ask, the City Council aren't in charge of the police, and I have absolutely no say in who they question or for how long.'

This silenced him. I could hear a faint hum from the stereo, and the slurps of Mao-mao cleaning up in the kitchen. The crowbar. The rope. DI Zahler sounding calm and rational. My back door banging, and a cold wind whistling through. I was trying not to run on too far from what I knew, but what I did know was mounting up, and none of it made me feel comfortable to be alone with Steve Black. I didn't sense any violence in him, though.

'Justin said, co-operate,' Steve said in a fast whine, 'but shit, three interviews. They think they've got something, don't they?'

'Have they?' I poured the tea, breathing deliberately to keep my hand steady. At least he couldn't be my burglar. I'd left him zonked at Eddy and Clara's, and my burglar was someone who hadn't realised my pictures were worth far more than my stereo.

'You knew about the tunnel. Come on, admit it, you must have known. That's what they said, but f... that.' He picked up a mug without pausing to thank me. 'My gran had this story about underground passages, but she was senile. I never went down the f...ing cellar.'

'That's how it looked to me,' I agreed.

'You saw the cellar?'

'From the tunnel, yes.' Curiosity beat my unease, and I added, 'Maybe you didn't go down the cellar when your gran lived there, but why didn't you look at it when you moved in yourself?'

Steve made a face. He hadn't sat down. 'Shit, what'd we need a cellar for? Raze opened the door once and it was full of spiders, and we thought, f... that, life's too short to clean that place. We'd got more room than we needed upstairs. I told the police all this.'

It took me a few seconds to work out 'the door' and realise he wasn't referring to the one they'd forced. Steve meanwhile was talking on. 'And the dope, Jesus, the way they went on about the dope you'd think we were South American drug barons, not f...ing hippies from Costhorpe. What else d'you deal in? C'mon, everyone has a little E hidden away these days. Don't want anyone bringing crack into Costhorpe. D'you hide your stash in the tunnel? I mean, f... that for an idea. If that's what they call an investigation...'

I was reminded of Alex Yelland. Steve had the same reckless indignation, and the same apparent inability to pick up on my negative response. 'Did they ask you about the crowbar?' I asked when he paused for breath.

It stopped him. His hand jerked, slopping a little of the peppermint tea. His eyes narrowed onto me, and for an instant I wondered if I'd been too rash.

'How'd you know about that?'

'I saw it in the cellar. What did you tell them about it?'

'Look, you're a friend of Allie's, right? You do believe we're okay? Why would we kill this bloke? We never even met him.'

'I'm not saying you did, Steve. I just want to know what's going on. For instance, why are you here?'

'Allie said you helped us,' Steve said resentfully. 'I came to say thank you, right?'

If so, he hadn't made much of a job of it. But presumably public-school manners lurked under his belligerence: I could half-believe it was the truth. And maybe his resentfulness was justified; maybe I was being aggressive. A minor burglary wouldn't normally have knocked me far off balance, but coming on top of everything else, perhaps it had. I told myself to cool down.

'Consider it said.'

'Did you tell the cops about that crowbar?'

Whenever possible I tell the truth. 'Yes,' I agreed. 'I told them what I know about it, which isn't much. Raze said you went to Big Nick's to borrow it.'

'Hang on. I got it from work, yes, but not on Saturday morning. Was it you who told the police I fetched it then?'

'I told them I didn't know when you fetched it.'

'You listen. I borrowed it weeks ago, for a friend who had some slabs in his garden he wanted lifting. He did the job and gave it back and I put it in my car. So f... this going over to North Road, all I had to do was go out to my car and get it.'

'Where did you park?'

'Canon Road, I wasn't driving up to the f...ing barrier and having them nab us. I can prove this, the police have checked it all out, there's no blood, no hair or anything on that crowbar. They've got nothing, nothing at all on us.'

Steve said this with real vehemence. It sounded truthful to me; and surely if the police hadn't been satisfied they wouldn't have let him go. So I told myself.

'Then you should be okay now,' I said.

'Shit, I dunno. The media...' Steve's voice trailed away. 'The other thing is, this woman.'

My other thing was the rope. It wasn't the moment to ask about the rope. 'What woman?'

'Mrs Brennan. She phoned me this morning, when I went over to the house to get some clothes. It was all official, a copper came with me, a constable' – he said this contemptuously – 'and when we were there this bloody woman phoned. She had all these questions. She wanted to know whether Baxter had a torch with him. What colour hard hat was he wearing? Hell, he wasn't even wearing a hard hat, how'd anyone bash his head in if he was? This bloody constable was listening in and wouldn't say a word, and I had to get rid of this f...ing female, and I didn't know what I was supposed to say to her.'

'Did you answer her?'

'With a cop listening? I said excuse me, Mrs Brennan, but if you want to know these things you should call Costhorpe Central Police Station.' His voice had changed as he said this: he mimicked a public-school accent perfectly. Although it wasn't mimicry if he'd been to Ranborough, I reminded myself: he must have spoken like that once. He'd chosen to alter his voice, just as he'd chosen to follow up his philosophy degree by working as a car mechanic. He couldn't have had an apprenticeship: had he learned car maintenance at school?

I said, 'She worked with Bill. Did she tell you that?'

'No. I said, what d'you want to know for, but she wouldn't say. I thought maybe she was a journalist. Then she got angry and started yelling at me over the phone, and I thought f... this and hung up on her.'

'What did the police say?'

'Not a word. I told the constable, Mrs Brennan, write it down, B-r-e-double-n-a-n, and write down that I don't know who she is. Did he f... They think we did it, that's the trouble. They're not looking for anyone else, are they? Shit, I might as well look myself.'

I sat back on the sofa and took a long drink of hot peppermint. I couldn't object to his comment, since I'd been thinking much the same; and much as Steve annoyed me, I still couldn't imagine how or why he or Raze could have killed Bill Baxter.

'I'm curious, Steve,' I said. 'Someone gave the press a map of the tunnels under Flint Hill. I'd like to know who.'

'Why?'

'I'm not sure. There are lots of ideas half-connected in my mind. I won't tell anyone, but it's nagging at me. So if it was you...'

'That little sketch they had in the Argus?'

I nodded. 'It wasn't anyone from the City Engineer's Department.'

'Maybe it was Miles. He knows all that sort of thing.'

'Miles Keylock?'

'Yeah. And he butters up the press, it's Fred's policy.'

But would he have known the tunnel layout? Maybe he would. Miles would have professional contacts, and he certainly had a motive to find out the layout – and to make use of it, to get his house cleared quickly for re-occupation. 'You know him well?' I asked.

Steve shrugged. 'I see him around.'

'One other thing. Did the police ask you about the rope?'

'Uh?' It took him a moment to orient himself. Then, 'Yes,' he said. 'Sure they asked us about the rope, a yellow plastic climbing rope. They asked us every f...ing thing. I used to do some pot-holing but I don't have a rope. It wasn't my rope they found, I don't know whose it was. Are you looking into all this?'

'I'm not investigating,' I said, 'but I'm looking at what comes my way. As you said, you might as well do the same. If you can find out whose rope it was, that's a line for the police to follow which won't lead back to you.'

'I'm not going to the police with anything I find out.'

'You won't have to,' I told him. 'You can bring it to me, and I'll make sure it's passed on.'

19

RED dots were swirling in front of my eyes by the time I got Steve out of the door. I turned up the radiator – it was too late to light the fire – put a Mozart flute and harp concerto on the stereo, switched the lights off and lay back on the sofa in the dark.

Thoughts and questions chased Mozart's themes through my head. How could Bill have gone into the tunnel? Had he put the rope there? If not, who had, and why had they abandoned it? There was no reason I could see for Steve or Raze to kill Bill – but had his killer had a reason? Mandy had said, some psychopath. No one would plan, surely, to kill a man by engineering a roof fall in a tunnel...

I WOKE, freezing, at three am, and stumbled upstairs. I forgot to set my alarm and when I woke again, thick-headed, it was past eight o'clock. Peppermint tea shouldn't cause hangovers, but it felt as if I had one.

I didn't want to drink more peppermint, but I couldn't face coffee either. I went down to London Road and bought camomile and Orange Grove teas in a delicatessen. It started to rain as I was walking back home. I drank a cup of the camomile and read The Guardian while my toast was grilling. I had a nagging feeling there was something I'd —

It was twenty to ten when it hit me: Bill's funeral was that morning. Maybe no one else would care if I was there or not, but I felt I needed to go. I scrambled from my jeans into a skirt, tied back my hair, hauled an old black coat from the back of my wardrobe and made a brake-squealing drive to the city outskirts. The row of cars on the verge of Newmarket Avenue alerted me a hundred yards before I reached the new church.

There was a queue in the rain, stretching from the church door back to the road. Two-mourner funerals depress; two hundred mourners depress differently. So many lives had been affected. The limp queue brought it home more bloodily than the corpse itself could have done.

At first I couldn't make out a single familiar face under the umbrellas, but once I'd joined the back of the queue I noticed Gary Temperley perhaps twenty feet ahead, and Nick just in front of him, scrunched into a rarely-worn suit. I thought of joining Nick, but without much enthusiasm; anyway it was beginning to be obvious that we wouldn't all squeeze inside the church, and I had no right to queue-jump.

It occurred to me I hadn't sent flowers. I hoped the Labour Group Secretary had done so.

The queue had stopped when I'd reached it, but now it began to shuffle forwards. The man in front of me had half-inch stubble and a luridly-jacketed paperback poking out of his overcoat pocket. Ahead of him was an elderly woman in a headscarf, whispering to another in a wedding hat. The last funeral I'd been to was in France: they'd known how to do it there, but the English become gauche and embarrassed when called upon to dramatise grief.

We inched farther forward: it was past ten already. A black-suited man was walking down the queue, apologising to us and picking out a few people to send inside. I shook my head when he came to me, and settled for joining the cluster of latecomers under the porch. It was high-roofed and narrow, not much good for keeping out the rain, and I hadn't remembered my umbrella.

They'd left the church door open, but I could barely hear the service. I stuck my hands in my pockets and thought of Bill. Images flickered through my mind. Gaudy sweaters, orange overalls, mud and chalk dust. He'd been a decent man – at least, he'd looked it from the outside. An ordinary sort of man, whom I'd imagined to live an ordinary, even boring life.

Murder was such a melodramatic deed; or maybe it wasn't, in real life. This wasn't an opera, this was a world in which people read whodunnits in the queue to mourn a friend's death. Maybe when – if – I ever discovered what had happened I'd think, how stupid. Instead of finding a grand passion or a criminal conspiracy hidden under the debris of normality, the police would uncover a pathetic foul-up.

The hymn was Dear Lord and Father of Mankind, but no one outside was singing. We could barely hear it: I found myself straining like someone irritatingly aware of a radio playing next door. The organ sounded so dull I thought it maybe wasn't a real one, only a recording.

A prayer followed. Comprehension seeped through the crowd under the canopy till we'd all clasped our hands and bowed our heads. I wasn't feeling prayerful. I cheated, and looked up and around before it had finished.

DI Zahler, black-suited, was leaning against a drainpipe watching me. I was too slow-witted to take evasive action. Our mutual awareness flooded across the rain-dewed heads: gallons of it, drowning the drip-drip of the funeral service.

Lust was the word, and direly inappropriate it was. I was embarrassed more at myself than at him. Life fighting back against death, all the old clichés... but it seemed so unequal a contest, as if a gorilla was struggling to get out of a cage of soggy cardboard. I should have been moved by the funeral, firmly overcoated in – not grief perhaps, considering how little I'd known Bill, but at least solemnity. I'm not a Christian, but I can recognise a spiritual force and respond to it. There wasn't one to set against the man. I've reacted more powerfully to a heavy metal concert than I was doing to this shuffling group of strangers and the words I couldn't hear.

Afterwards maybe, but hell, not now...

My eyes floundered: suddenly there was nowhere to look except at him.

There had to be someone I knew, some detail on the flat brick wall, something to distract me. Sheila Brennan, along at the end of the porch: she'd do. His name was Ted, Justin had told me. No, look at Sheila.

Sheila was wearing the green suede jacket I'd coveted before, and a dark green skirt. Her head was bowed, her eyes were closed. My concentration might be a shattered eggshell, but hers was clearly intact. I battened onto it, hoping to leach some sense of the respectable from her.

I could feel her ache. There was no strong expression on her face, but the stance of her body, the tilt of her chin... I couldn't have analysed her body language, but watching intently, I could read it.

The ache was too strong, considering.

Once I'd had the intuition, everything confirmed it. Sheila must have been in front of Gary in the queue, or I'd have noticed her earlier – but while he'd gone into the church, even Nick had, she had stayed outside. She was a careful dresser, and she'd avoided black. That charcoal suit with the velvet collar – she'd looked it over, I could swear, and decided not to wear it.

The phonecall to Steve was the clincher. The evening before I'd barely asked myself why she had rung, but it was so obvious now. Inappropriate hunger. Not respectable at all. She'd wanted to know how, why, when, all the questions which tact should have kept her from asking. She'd wanted it even more strongly than I wanted to turn round and switch back on the invisible circuit that linked me and Ted Zahler.

I barely noticed the prayer ending in time to look away from her. My eyes flicked across Zahler, but he wasn't looking in my direction, which wasn't surprising, since I felt sure he wasn't the type to behave unacceptably in public. How much more of the service was there to get through? It was years since I'd been to an English funeral, and I couldn't remember the order.

Nor could I have recalled it afterwards: I'd been given to much else to think, to feel. Or not to think, not to feel. I was getting wet, I remember that; and the relief when a blast of Bach, decently loud, told us the service was finished. We shuffled aside into the rain proper to allow the pall-bearers space to emerge into.

Zahler and I ended up side by side. Feeling him there, I didn't need to look. We stood in silence watching the bearers bring out the coffin and stow it back in the hearse. The congregation followed them out. There wasn't a churchyard, so presumably Bill would be buried in Donne Road cemetery.

There were a few hundred people I didn't know, but there were also plenty I did. David North was there, and at a glance, all his staff. Harry Graham, Chief Planning Officer, had come with a half-dozen others from the Planning Department; so had the Council's Chief Exec, his secretary, and a couple of committee clerks. The Labour Party was represented not just by me and Nick, but also by Judith Armitage and three other Planning Committee members. The Lib-Dem and Tory leaders were there, and so was Rex Canning. I recognised the Council's union officials, the car-park attendant, and maybe a dozen others whom I knew from different contexts. An old neighbour, several teachers I knew from acting as a school governor, the County Archivist – had he met her while researching the chalk mines?

The family I didn't know, but they were easily made out, a large, self-insulated group. A tall old man, tears streaking his face. Old ladies on Zimmer frames. Bill's own generation: brothers, sisters, in-laws, cousins – I couldn't have guessed which were which. It was easier to identify his widow, who was all in black, and hollow-eyed with shock, tears and sleepless nights. A couple of other women held the children's hands. The children. What this death had meant, to so many...

Nick came over and touched my shoulder. I was conscious of Zahler watching and listening. 'I haven't time to come to the cemetery,' Nick said. 'Everything okay with you?'

'Nick, did the Group send flowers?'

'I haven't a clue, but Judith would know. See you around.'

When he'd walked off, I risked a glance at Zahler. He looked straight back. 'Do you have a car with you?' he asked in a low voice.

'Yes. Do you?'

He nodded, then went on, 'I'd like to talk to you, but now's not the time.'

'My number's in the phone book.'

'I'll call it.' He turned and strode away.

Had he been talking about his investigation, or about us? What had he made of Nick? Was he married, or otherwise attached? Hell, surely he was. Good-looking men over thirty are never single: women who want them have to filch them from somebody else. I knew that, but I'd always shrunk at the prospect of doing it. I wanted him, but I didn't want all that hassle. Come to that, I wasn't even sure I wanted him in any serious sense. Some of the remarks he'd made in the canteen... Men I meet through thc Labour Party I trust to think my way, but that one I didn't.

It was just as well we had separate cars, because I wouldn't have known what to say to him on the journey to the cemetery. When we arrived he stayed well away from me, as if similar thoughts had occurred to him. I joined Judith Armitage instead: hers was safer company in which to stand through the committal, make suitable remarks to the other mourners, and learn through the grapevine where the funeral breakfast was being held. Also, she had a large umbrella.

The funeral breakfast was to be at the Guildhall, so we weren't required to thin down to numbers that would fit into a living room. Judith had to get back to work, so I agreed to go along and say the right things on the Labour Group's behalf.

In spite of the rain, few mourners were yet moving off. Presumably we had to give Mrs Baxter and the rest of Bill's immediate family time to get to the Guildhall first. I went to say hello to my ex-neighbour. Zahler had left, and so had Rex, I noticed.

'Councillor Massen?'

The voice at my back made me jump: I hadn't thought anyone remaining was likely to look me out. It belonged to Gary Temperley. Hair wet-slicked to his head, acne flaring, he looked embarrassed, as if he'd been sent over with a message he didn't want to deliver.

It turned out all he wanted, though, was to beg a lift to the Guildhall. David North, with whom he had come, had left to return to work, and he couldn't find Sheila. The Guildhall was a mile and a half away, and I couldn't blame him for not relishing a hike in the rain.

I was happy to oblige him; in fact, glad to have a chance to talk to him. I still wanted some information from the City Engineer's Department, and it wasn't a time when I'd have chosen to approach Sheila. I doubted Gary was so grief-stricken that he'd find it difficult to turn his mind to chalk mines. But the moment, the rain and his awkward manner all made it difficult to find a lead-in, and we walked in silence back to where I'd parked near the cemetery gates.

We continued in silence till we were halfway back to the city centre, when Gary suddenly offered, 'He was a nice guy. It's so unbelievable.'

'Death is, especially for atheists.' It was the sort of thing I'd have said to Nick; to Zahler, even. As soon as I'd said it, I thought it was wrong for a stranger like Gary. I probably sounded like a hard politician, while in fact it reflected my irritation at his platitudes. To soften the phrase I added, 'It must be rough for you, and even worse for Sheila Brennan.'

'Sheila? Oh... maybe. I suppose she knew him fairly well.'

Even if he hadn't noticed what I thought I'd noticed, it seemed a thin thing to say about one's two closest workmates. 'Obviously she did,' I said sharply. 'They worked together for years, didn't they? Maybe they didn't always see eye to eye, but...'

There was a pause while I turned onto the ring road, then Gary said, 'They didn't quarrel or anything, don't get me wrong; what I meant is, Sheila's tough. She's not the kind of cookie to cry for anyone.'

Brittle perhaps; tough, no. I didn't think I was wrong, just that Gary had been uninterested in them both, so unobservant. He was the type who'd have a closer relationship with his computer than with any human being. But since he'd evidently read nothing into my comments, I could afford to ask on.

‘She’s divorced, is she?’

‘I think so. We don’t talk about that sort of thing.’

Not a man worth pumping for gossip. I turned to an alternative interest. ‘I gather Sheila’s dealing with the chalk mine study?’

‘She’s doing some of Bill’s old work, but I’m doing quite a bit.’

‘You’re working on the next stage of the report?’

‘Yeah, that’s a big part of my work now.’

‘Maybe you’re the person to tell me what I want to know. There was something Bill had been meaning to pass by me, and I never got to find out what it was. If you’ve taken his work over, I guess you’ll have come across it.’

The car was heating up, and we were drying out. A mingled back-of-wardrobe-fustiness and sweat smell was building up. Gary didn’t reply straight away.

‘I’m not sure I know what you mean.’

‘David North didn’t say anything to you?’

I got no answer, and assumed he’d shrugged: with eyes on the road, I wouldn’t have noticed. I went on, ‘It was something he’d found out... a new bit of data, or a pattern he’d seen in what he’d already got...’ I wished I could remember Bill’s words, but I’d been mulling over them for days and they wouldn’t firm up in my mind. ‘Possibly a way of forecasting collapses?’ I hazarded.

‘If anything like that came up, we’d look into it.’

‘Obviously you would.’ The sweat smell was winning. Either this guy had a social problem, or he didn’t appreciate my questioning. It occurred to me that he’d quite likely exaggerated his own importance, and was afraid I’d catch him out. It might have been kinder to drop the subject, but I still hadn’t got an answer. ‘However,’ I added, ‘that needn’t stop me looking into it too. It might seem odd to you, because you’re the expert and I’m an idiot when it comes to engineering, but there are non-technical aspects to the subject. Political aspects. Those are my business.’

‘I – I see.’

‘So if you come across anything – anything Bill had marked, that it looks like he’d meant to show me – or anything else that you think I’d be interested in – I can rely on you to give me a call?’

‘Oh. Yeah. Sure. Anything we ought to tell you...’

If this had been a date, I wouldn’t have been caught hovering by the telephone afterwards. The boasting apart, he had shown a less than minimal interest in what I was saying. When it came to dealing with councillors, even Sheila Brennan could give him some lessons.

I couldn't push any harder, not on the way to a funeral breakfast. I said instead, 'Can I ask you something else? I know you couldn't predict the collapse in Flint Hill, but can you give me some idea of the risk level in that neighbourhood? If someone had been planning to buy a house there before the mine collapse, would you have warned them off?'

'Depends if it was subsiding,' Gary said.

'If there were no signs? Say, would you have bought one there yourself? Before all this happened?'

'Depends on the price,' Gary told me; and I gave up.

20

A HALF-HOUR of funeral breakfast persuaded me I'd been exaggerating the connection between Bill Baxter and Flint Hill. The man? He might have died there, but he hadn't lived there. None of the Flint Hill residents who haunted my life were at the Guildhall.

I came away instead with the sense of a life I hadn't known. An aunt of Bill's had grabbed me in a corner by the buffet – damp sandwiches and sausage rolls – with the fixed idea that I was his daughter's Brown Owl. A man who'd lived next to him in his last house but one had told me about his passion for model trains. One of Freda's friends had recalled being a bridesmaid at her wedding.

Random information, sparking only feeble curiosity in me. Bill's life hadn't been my business – and the funeral over, perhaps his death shouldn't have been either. But there were plenty of unanswered questions in my head, and Bill's murderer was still undetected.

I went home and checked my tape to see if Zahler had yet called – he hadn't. I thought of exercising, but switched on the word processor instead because it would leave me closer to the phone. That's not me; that was discomfiting. I hadn't clutched at the receiver since I'd been a student staying home nights to make sure I didn't miss Jonathan's calls. I'm used to being in control of relationships, but I could feel my self-sufficiency slithering away like satin sheets.

It was as much loneliness as him; and he couldn't realise it. So I told myself. When the phone did ring I made myself count to ten before picking it up.

I rang off five minutes later still not knowing what he had in mind, beyond a drink at the Lord Nelson – his choice, although he'd offered me mine. I never normally went into the Lord Nelson. Why was his choice surprising? I knew that wherever he generally spent his time, it wasn't any of the places where I spent mine.

If I'd known he was single I'd have been flying, but I hadn't dared ask. Imagination wouldn't provide an answer, so I exercised instead, hard, for the first time in days. I showered and washed my hair, took the time to condition it, and spent twenty minutes trying to decide what to wear. That's not normally my style either.

If he's married you'll opt out, I told myself sternly. No heartbreak, Erica. Tell him everything you've discovered about Flint Hill since you last talked to the police, then plead work in the morning. No, it was Saturday in the morning. Plead shopping or something.

I'd chosen black, a jersey top and leggings. I made coffee, with a guilty sideways glance at my new packs of herb tea, and took it up to my office. I looked at the pages of French, although not much English text grew on the screen. Jenny rang, to confirm our Saturday squash date and try again to persuade me to come to supper. Nick clearly hadn't spoken to her, except to say I'd refused for that evening, and irritation at them both chafed me. She talked of my needs, but the subtext was her guilt. This time, though, I hadn't the inclination to argue it through, and I ended up with a commitment to eat a lasagne with them after the squash, sufficiently casual that I'd be able to leave early if I found it a chore.

Allie rang to ask me over for Sunday lunch, and I converted that to an invitation to Wednesday supper. Sunday I'd be with my parents. Suddenly my life seemed full, almost too full. How could I fit anyone else into it? Maybe I didn't want to fit anyone else in. Maybe the starving don't admit to feeling hungry.

I brushed my hair through again, tried the effect of a red chiffon scarf tied round my black top like a low belt, wondered if he'd think it eccentric, and decided it'd be too bad if he did. Then I tried to work some more, since I meant to be ten minutes late to the Lord Nelson.

I managed to be five minutes late. By then his pint of bitter was half-drunk, so I reckoned he'd been ten minutes early. He was looking at the door as I came in, and was standing by the time I reached his corner table. He was my height, allowing for the heels on my shoes. I'd known that before, it wasn't really a surprise. I'd known he had brown eyes, slightly hooded, giving him a lazy look, and his hair was straight and silky and not as short as it looked at first, and his smile was the kind to make my insides flip.

He wouldn't have smiled like that if he'd asked me there in order to pick my brains about Flint Hill. So my intuition told me, although he said nothing more revealing than 'What are you drinking?' I asked for bitter, sat, and watched him go to the bar and order it.

He moved economically, in a space of his own. He had a low-pitched voice, and he dressed plainly: he was in denims tonight, as when I'd first seen him. I'd thought him devastatingly attractive, but maybe I was uniquely susceptible – no, hang it, he definitely was a very good-looking man. But he didn't call attention to himself, as so many of my colleagues did: in a crowd (most of the pub tables were full) he blended. I supposed a plain-clothes detective would need to. The bandit moustache was an indulgence, though.

'The name's Ted,' he said, returning with my glass.

I wasn't letting on that I'd known. 'Erica,' I said.

He nodded. 'I wasn't thinking when I phoned you, but I hope you weren't taking it as an order to come along this evening. We normally try to avoid demanding interviews with people on Friday nights.'

I didn't know how to read that. 'So this is off the record again?'

'There's no agenda. I wanted to reassure you about Garron and Black – Justin Howell mentioned that you'd been asking. Then there's the information Baxter didn't give you, the thing he phoned you about – I'd like to be updated on that. Otherwise I'm... feeling around.'

'The case is still wide open.' I tried to say it levelly, but I could feel disappointment crawling up my throat.

'Exactly.' He sat back and took a gulp of his beer. 'I won't apologise for interviewing Garron and Black at length. They're important witnesses, and I believe it was warranted. Howell accepted that too, and we kept to all the guidelines. But I will say we're fairly certain now that Baxter didn't go into the mine through their house, and we're not planning to bring them in again.'

Fairly certain now? Hell, their cellar had been so deep in dust that the police could have mapped every footprint – I couldn't see how it could ever have been a possibility. But I didn't feel in control enough to risk a show of temper.

'You know Steve Black's a pot-holer?'

At a guess Zahler hadn't, although he was too practised to make it apparent. 'Did he tell you so?'

'More or less. He called round; and he also told me Sheila Brennan had phoned him. Your lot know that, because there was a constable with him when she rang.'

'You're thinking of the rope?'

'Obviously. Steve told me he'd told the police it wasn't his.'

'Was it?'

'His? He didn't tell me he'd lied to the police, if that's what you're asking. I barely know him, and we're not exactly friends.'

'But you talked about the case to him.'

'Is that a crime?'

I must have sounded irascible, because Zahler lowered his brows and gave me a careful look. 'No,' he said. 'In a way it's useful when people talk about big unsolved cases – it can bring up new information, and what you just told me's a good example. But there are times when it seems like the questioners are falling over each other. We'll go to interview people after a crime sometimes, and find the press have already been all down the street.'

'I'm not doing it for the press,' I protested. 'Nor am I investigating in any serious way, Ted. I have to do my translation work, and my Council work, and those leave me with neither the time nor the inclination to take over from the police. It's simply that I've had reason to see people from Flint Hill, and when I see them, we talk.'

'Who else have you seen?'

I told him, briefly: Phil and Allie, the Buntings, and I'd had phonecalls from a half-dozen others.

'The Keylocks?'

'No. I only see people who ask to see me – I haven't chased anyone. And I suspect the Keylocks are Tories.'

'Do you know Miles?'

'Minimally. We thought of using the Keylock agency when we sold our house, but Miles rubbed us up the wrong way so we moved elsewhere.'

'Who's we?'

He'd picked that up fast. I shot him a sideways look – I'd been focussing on my beer glass as we talked. I still didn't know what to make of his attitude. 'I shared my last house with Nick Halton, who's a fellow councillor.'

'But not this one?'

'That's why we moved.'

'So who do you live with now?'

'My cat. She's a three-year-old female tabby called Mao-mao. Nick chose the name: puns are his speciality.'

I looked straight at him as I said this, and he looked straight back. I hadn't imagined it, hit those brown eyes dead on and I felt myself fizz. I started to frame a similar question to him, but he got in with another one before me.

'What did Keylock do wrong?'

I had to swallow fast, to hide my disappointment. Signals as mixed as these weren't safely read as a come-on. 'Nothing dramatic,' I said. 'Topical, though – we got annoyed because he warned us about subsidence. Chalk mines, etcetera. Okay, all Costhorpe agents make a few gloomy mutters, but to listen to Mr Keylock you'd have thought we'd never sell the house at all. It's weird, when you think he bought a house on Flint Hill himself.'

'There's no mystery about that,' Zahler said promptly. 'The house was cheap. There was nothing dubious, he bought it through a different agency, and it was a genuine bargain. Apparently there was no sign of subsidence, still isn't, and from what I can gather, if you red-lined every house that might conceivably have a tunnel beneath it you'd rule out most of Costhorpe.'

I was a little sorry – I'd almost enjoyed fingering Miles for questionable dealings. But what did I have on him? Even if he was the person who'd given Patty Fowler a map of the chalk mine, that wasn't an indictable offence. 'I keep asking myself if Bill's death was somehow connected with his work,' I said, 'but I can't see how.'

'Nor can we. And if it was, that's no reason to tie in Keylock, because he didn't know Baxter at all, and he has an alibi for that Friday afternoon – he was miles away, in Cromer. Which reminds me, did you find out what Baxter had wanted to tell you?'

I shook my head. 'I've asked David North, and I've asked Gary Temperley – only today, admittedly – but nothing's come up. I don't suppose the police have turned up anything?'

'No,' Zahler said. 'We've interviewed Baxter's workmates, but they all say there wasn't anything worrying him. According to everyone he wasn't the fretful type.'

'Maybe not, but that department was jumpy.'

'How do you mean?'

'I mean jumpy,' I said. 'I won't exaggerate, I don't know any of the department well, but just about every time I've seen Gary or Sheila Brennan, I've come away with the sense that they were... antagonistic. Short-fused. North has the reputation of being a dour boss, and maybe it's nothing more than that it's not a happy department. I'd thought when I first met Sheila that she disliked me, but now I've reconsidered, because the attitude's common to all of them.'

'Temperley dislikes you too?'

'Not precisely. He's very young, and he seems very self-absorbed.' I summarised our discussion on the way back from the cemetery. 'I don't suppose he'd have begged the lift if he was agin me,' I went on, 'but I've found him... obstructive's maybe the best word. Generally council officers treat councillors deferentially. I don't encourage that, and when they do it to excess it makes me squirm, but after a while you get used to being called 'councillor' and treated like a mini-VIP. When we phone with a request, we're given the impression the officers will drop everything and do it. Of course half the time they don't – it's a game, they flannel and flatter and manipulate us so we'll make the decisions they want. But Gary doesn't play it. Nor does Sheila, and nor does North, very well.'

'So when you asked them what Baxter had meant to tell you...'

'They didn't give me the impression they'd try to find out. They ought to realise it could be important – after all, Bill's dead, and that's hardly trivial – but they acted as if I was being a nuisance. They behaved as if they don't want to know about Bill's obsession. Maybe they're miffed that he'd chosen me to tell, but even so...'

'What did Sheila say exactly?'

I hesitated. Just as I'd not wanted to talk to Patty Fowler about Bill's death, so I was reluctant to tell Zahler about Sheila's pain. It seemed prurient. Nor was it directly related to the murder – or was it?

I had to admit it was relevant.

'I didn't ask her. Partly because she'd already been antagonistic, but partly because of... female intuition, you'd maybe call it. I reckon there was something between her and Bill.'

'Something as in an affair?'

'Possibly. I've no firm evidence, and it's not a piece of information I'd want to go into your computer, especially not with my name next to it. But it fits. When I rang Freda Baxter on the Saturday morning before Bill was found, the way she handled it – Bill being away overnight – made me think, was he...? Then when I saw Sheila at his funeral I thought, of course. There's no more to it than that. But if it were true, it would make for an uncomfortable atmosphere in the office, and explain her attitude to me – she was insecure and nervous of other women who might be rivals.'

'And people let you into their houses...'

'I don't see any more than a million other women do,' I said, stung.

'Don't you believe it. Accurate intuition's rarer than you'd think.'

'Maybe it's just that policemen are no good at it,' I lobbed back.

'I think they are good, actually. In spite of the system, which isn't geared that way; and in spite of people's attitudes to us. We're trained to see, and we do see, maybe more than you realise; it's good to have confirmation, but we already knew about Baxter and Sheila. Mind you, I didn't go to the funeral to look for guilty expressions – only to pay my respects.'

'I wasn't intending to play the amateur detective either,' I retorted.

'I wasn't suggesting you had been; but since you noticed, I'm glad you told us. We may look hard and question hard, but we also need to use informants, messy though it can be, because some people clam up when they see us coming.'

That was me, I supposed – an informant. Useful female with access to assorted suspects, willing to help in order to redeem her lost credit with the cops. I winced.

'No wonder,' I said. 'I know it's all necessary, but spew your thoughts out to the police and you end up feeling dirty and used.'

'There's a man dead, Erica. We'll do whatever we have to in order to find his killer.'

Maybe I'd deserved the rebuke. Zahler didn't dwell on it, but went on to milk me of the other snippets I could provide.

He hadn't known Graham Bunting had worked for James Dunbury. I'd almost forgotten I knew it myself. I had to admit, he had a good technique for worming out information – arguably the better for being 'out of practice' at interviewing. He didn't plod like Sunley, he thought and probed.

'Mind you,' he explained, 'somebody else in the team might know. The difficulty with a big investigation's collating all the information.'

'You know what Rex Canning thought about James Dunbury?'

'I can guess,' he said. 'I know you noticed a few gaps in the Dunburys' story. So did we, and we've been working on filling them.'

'Do you think Bill was brought into the mine through their cellar?'

Zahler regarded me consideringly. I thought he'd refuse to answer, but after a longish pause he said, 'We haven't ruled it out, but neither are we certain of it. It's equally possible he was brought down the shaft behind number thirty-three. There's no firm evidence either way.'

'Was he dead before he was brought down?'

'It's likely; not certain. We're assuming he was knocked out, at least, before the roof fall was engineered. That was deliberate: whoever did it was probably trying to prise out a large lump of flint, but he brought down a lot of chalk as well. He was lucky to get out in one piece.'

‘So he – I suppose it was a he – knocked Bill over the head, dragged the body through the tunnel, chose a likely spot, and tried to bring the roof down.’

‘That’s roughly our hypothesis, except the body wasn’t dragged – at least there are no marks indicating it was. Possibly there were two or more men involved, and they carried him between them.’

‘So it wasn’t a crime of passion.’

‘Those that are don’t always look like it, but it’s unlikely to have been his wife or Sheila Brennan acting alone. And it didn’t require a great degree of engineering knowledge.’

‘None, I’d have thought. An engineer would have provided some props, a hard hat and so on.’

‘It depends whether the engineer double-guessed us,’ Zahler remarked. ‘Or whether he or she had props readily to hand. Appearances can be deceptive, but basically this has the marks of an unpremeditated crime, and a crude attempt at camouflage afterwards.’

‘Someone who hoped that if Bill was dead, nobody else would go down the tunnel?’ I guessed out loud. ‘Or someone who...’

‘What is it?’

‘At the meeting, Rex’s meeting, several people argued that we ought to fill in the mine by pumping in concrete without doing a proper survey first. We shouldn’t waste time and money by sending men down again – just shove in the nozzle, or whatever they do.’

‘That sounds a little improbable.’

‘So I thought at the time, but they argued it quite convincingly. It’d be a cheap permanent solution, they claimed. It was Fred Keylock’s line, and I think James Dunbury’s too. I’m not sure if there was anyone else...’

Zahler was silent, letting me think, finishing his long- neglected pint. I shook my head. ‘I can’t think of anyone else who said it.’

‘No matter. I’ll check the computer, and maybe ask Ransome. Have you eaten?’

His question caught me off balance. ‘No,’ I said, ‘but don’t feel you have to —’

‘I don’t,’ he said drily. ‘I’d like your company over supper, and I don’t much want to send you home at nine, thinking of murders in dark tunnels. Your cat won’t miss you for a few hours yet. Would a pizza suit you?’

‘I should think it would,’ I agreed.

21

TED picked a place where the lighting was low and the music soft and jazzy. We split a carafe of red, and he began to open up.

He was married, yes, but separated – I asked, and he answered unhesitatingly. He worked long hours, he said, and his wife had grown sick of it, so she had given him an ultimatum he had failed to meet.

I asked if he was sorry, and he said he was. It was honest – I liked him for that. They had two kids, a boy of ten and a girl of eight. He admitted the passion had died, but he hadn't been itching to get free, and he hated the whole business of living alone and access visits to the kids. Yes, he'd probably go back if she would take him, but he hadn't changed – he worked even harder now there was not much else to do – so he doubted whether she would.

This was honest too, but I liked it less. What man with an eye to seducing me would have told me that? I couldn't see any real barrier between us – I didn't even mind about the work, it's not as if I'd sit at home every evening waiting for any man to come home – but he was acting as if there was one. Maybe the barrier was in his head.

Maybe I could be patient. I wanted him enough to try, and if I stuck around I'd have a chance to learn what the barrier was, and possibly how to break it down. Separated wasn't what I'd hoped for, but it was better than married and together.

When he wasn't working he painted, he said. It was relaxing. He said his paintings were very bad, but without seeing them I couldn't judge whether that was modesty. They wouldn't be sentimental-bad, at least: I couldn't see a fluffy-kitten streak in this man. We searched for common ground in books we'd read and films we'd seen, and what we found was on the serious side – thrillers, yes, but he watched arthouse stuff too.

Not much comedy. I hadn't seen him laugh yet.

Two calzones came and went, and so did the wine. We passed on dessert, and over coffee Ted switched back to the Baxter case. We tried to think up a way a property dealer could make money out of chalk mines, but neither of us could see one. If you could tell where the mines were located you'd avoid expensive mistakes, but that wasn't the kind of get-rich scheme to justify murder. Maybe it was blackmail? Your house is in danger, and I'll file the details with the Council unless you pay me? Both of us found it unlikely. Then there was Alex Yelland's strange comment about people pretending there were mines where there weren't – but where was the scam in that?

We both reckoned there was more mileage in investigating whatever Bill had intended to tell me. I'd tried to tell myself it could only have been trivial, but that was a wish, not a conviction. Bill had, after all, judged that it justified a special meeting.

It seemed nobody else in the City Engineer's Department knew what it had been, or North would have come back to me. But why hadn't Sheila at least known? Add their personal relationship to their close working relationship, and there surely couldn't have been many things that were important to him which she hadn't known about.

I wondered if North had omitted to ask her, but Ted quickly killed that idea. After interviewing me his men had questioned not only North himself, but every member of his department, and had drawn a blank all round.

It didn't really need Ted to tell me that if Bill had been murdered because of what he knew, then the murderer must have known – or at the least, guessed – that he knew it. And that he was about to pass the information on?

'But he didn't get to pass it on,' I said.

'So there's nothing you know. But you're uneasy, aren't you?'

'Of course I am. I feel singled out. As if I ought to be able to work out what it was; but also as if the murderer's expecting me to work it out.'

'You haven't been threatened in any way? No strange phonecalls, no letters, nothing odd happening?'

'Noth—' I began; then I stopped.

'What is it?'

'It's probably a coincidence, but there is something. I was burgled a couple of nights ago. Someone broke in during the evening when I was out, and nicked my stereo.'

'Just your stereo?'

'Yes. Mind, I interrupted them. I didn't see them, they slipped out the back when I came in the front.'

'Much mess?'

'No. Nor any clues.'

'Mmm.' His hand went to his moustache and stroked it. 'It's probably not relevant, but I'm glad you told me. I don't want to worry you, but I'm going to send someone round to check over your security arrangements.'

I agreed I'd appreciate that.

'Don't ask the engineers any more questions,' Ted added. 'There's no need, anyway: that's our job. I want to get to the bottom of this business, if only to eliminate it. We haven't yet searched Baxter's office, but I'll see about getting that done now.'

By someone like DC Sunley, I wondered? I said, 'It's easy to order me not to ask questions, but I can't help feeling Bill chose me for a reason, Ted. Maybe whatever he had to tell me was something that I'd understand more readily than anyone else would.'

'Maybe, but that doesn't mean you're the right person to look for it. You're not as experienced at searching through papers as my officers are, and I'm not prepared to put you at risk.'

'If your team don't find it, though...'

'If they don't, I'll think again. But I doubt that'll happen.'

I didn't argue any further. After all I wasn't an engineer, and how much sense would Bill's papers make to me, without Bill himself to explain what was in them? I drained my coffee and said, 'I did ask myself whether Bill's secret might have been something he saw down the tunnel. He was the only person who explored the whole tunnel, because although Sheila went down with him, she stayed at the foot of the shaft. If there had been something down there that somebody didn't want anyone to know about...'

'Like stolen antiques?'

I nodded.

'You think that was his obsession?'

'It'd be a strange word to choose, if that was what he meant; and that's the word I recall. Find a load of furniture down a mine, and you might be intrigued; worried; but obsessed?'

Ted shrugged. 'We haven't lost sight of the Dunburys, I assure you. That's confidential, by the way – I don't want the press fingering any more suspects.'

'I don't give them that sort of information,' I told him.

'I'm glad to hear it. The difficulty with a case like this is, tell our informants how far we've got, and we risk telling the offenders too.

You maybe think everyone's trying to help us, but someone out there is doing the reverse. Don't forget it, Erica.'

'I won't.' A waitress came over with the bill, and once Ted had paid I got to my feet. He followed suit immediately.

'I'll see you home.'

It was polite of him; maybe no more. We'd both been drinking, so we took a taxi back to my place. Ted got out with me, but told the driver to wait. Up my ten-foot front path, we were barely out of the driver's earshot.

The streetlight's three doors off, and my house was dark. I couldn't make out Ted's expression, and I told myself it was as well.

He put one hand on the door, shoulder level; reached out the other, and touched my arm. The night was silent around us, and I sensed the emptiness of the house behind me. Ted wasn't the only one who didn't like to live alone.

'I'll talk to you when we've checked out Baxter's office.'

I nodded. 'You've got my number.'

'Yes.' This was followed by a silence just long enough to make me wonder whether I wanted to wait for his next line. I'd framed 'thanks for supper' in my throat when he spoke again.

'You have to understand, till this enquiry's over I'll be working nights, days... all the time it takes. Till it's over, you're a witness to me. I can't afford to compromise you as a witness.'

I could feel his hand through my jacket, feel the relief ooze through my bones as I understood what he was trying to say.

'So it would compromise me if you came in for another coffee?'

'It could – as well as distracting me, when I know I can't afford it. If you were needed to give evidence at a trial, the defence would use any relationship you had with me to undermine that evidence. They'd suggest I'd primed you, and that would affect the jury. I've seen cases lost that way before.'

It made sense. I didn't like it, but I could see it made sense. And if that was all that was holding him back... hell, I could almost have cheered.

'I sure hope you catch them soon.'

'We will. Till then – don't run away.' He squeezed my arm, turned and strode back to the cab.

22

A SMILE, a touch: it's odd how little it takes to change someone's outlook. It was enough to clothe me against the dread self-pity, and by Saturday morning I was almost looking forward to supper with Jenny and Nick.

Jenny, playing squash, was cheerful and determinedly non-introspective. I beat her, although she played well. We gossiped about fellow-councillors driving back to her and Nick's house, and Nick, in jovial mood, met us at the door with wine and a demand that I admire the premises.

I hadn't seen their house before, but even if I'd visited a month previously I'd have noticed changes this time, they told me proudly. In less than three months they had decorated three rooms. Maybe that was the secret of living with Nick's jokes – you had to get too tired to notice.

Nick and Jenny would never be wine and food buffs like Allie and Phil, but Nick's lasagne was well-practised and tasty. By silent agreement we drank sizeable quantities of Tesco Bulgarian Country Red and kept the talk to concrete subjects.

Rex Canning wasn't one of them, and nor was the murder, although Nick did update me on the Flint Hill mine investigation. I learned that Sheila Brennan had taken charge of plans for a full survey of the tunnel complex, and that consultants had been hired to advise the Council and the other owners of affected land about the work that would need doing. Nick had been liaising with Jack Wells and the Lib-Dem leader, and there was broad all-party agreement on what was being done, and on how to present it to the press.

We talked about politics, as we always had when the three of us had met up, and Jenny talked fake-casually about single men of our acquaintance. It wasn't like old times, we all knew the ice wasn't thick beneath our feet, but there were a few moments of genuine good humour. I'd warned that I was overdue for an early night, but it was eleven when I left.

Lasagne on top of calzone, followed by my mother's Sunday lunch – by the time I drove home from Fursham Sunday evening, I was feeling as if I could live on sandwiches for the next week and not suffer a pang.

I didn't get edgy about Ted till Monday; then I jumped every time the phone rang, and sulked a little every time it wasn't him. I took his point about being a witness, but surely he could have checked in.

The phone rang a lot that day. My most unexpected call was from Miles Keylock. 'You're the councillor for Flint Hill?' he demanded, after giving his name.

'One of them.'

'I need your help. I know this damn tunnel doesn't run under my house, but still the engineers won't let me go back home. Can you put some pressure on them?'

'The tunnel must run pretty close to your house,' I pointed out.

'Close doesn't mean there's any real danger of subsidence. I'm in the property business, so I know what I'm talking about. I want to go back, and I'm prepared to agree that it's at my own risk.'

I told him I'd talk to the engineers, and rang Sheila, who was predictably short with me. I'd been surprised that Miles should have chosen me to contact, but it turned out he'd rung all three of the Hillside councillors, and I was the last to get the same answer: she had cleared as many houses as she thought safe, but she wasn't clearing Miles'.

I didn't owe Miles much consideration if he'd only used me as a longstop to Hillside's male councillors, so it was curiosity, mostly, that took me drifting down to Keylocks' office when I went into the city that afternoon.

The estate agency was in a side-street of heavy grey Victorian buildings: small shops, three other estate agencies and a couple of building society branches, with accountants and second-rate solicitors in the offices above. Revolving carousels of inner-city terraces and semis in the suburbs blocked off the agency interior from the street outside. I pushed open the plate-glass door and came up against a girl with blonde big hair, sitting behind a desk and rifling through a filing cabinet.

I asked for Miles, and listlessly she agreed he was in. Even more listlessly, she drifted to the back of the office and called through a half-open door. Miles bustled out looking incongruously energetic, like the disco-freak Phil had accused him of being.

He seemed surprised I'd bothered to come, but he was affable enough – shades of the unctuous servility I recalled from when Nick and I had been potential Keylocks customers. He showed me into his office, asked Lisa to bring coffee, sat behind his desk, clasped his hands and gave me a professional, red-cheeked smile.

'Good news, or more questions?'

'Neither, I'm afraid.' I explained the engineers' position, and watched Miles' smile fade. He reminded of Tory residents who think they've opened the door to a friend, and twig only slowly that it's not even Avon calling, but Labour canvassing.

'It's incompetence,' he said. 'They obviously haven't done a proper evaluation.'

'That's why it's not incompetence,' I said steadily, 'because as I just told you, the investigation isn't over yet. I appreciate you're disappointed, but I'd have hoped you'd be more realistic than those residents who think we should have had the tunnels surveyed and filled in yesterday. You're a pro, you know what's involved, and of course you appreciate it can't be done overnight.'

My modest attempt at flattery drew no visible response. Miles said belligerently, 'I know exactly what's what, thank you. I told you on the phone that I'm not prepared to wait for the tunnels to be filled in. I want to go home, and I'm willing to take the minuscule risk of another collapse. I'll put that in writing.'

'It won't help,' I said. 'It's a question of other residents who aren't in a position to weigh the risks, and of keeping the road closed, too. We can't make you an exception.'

Miles scowled. 'If you can't help me I'll have to get onto someone who can.'

'Feel free to ask for a second opinion. You've a Tory ward councillor, Rex Canning: try him.' I gave him my sweetest, if insincere, smile. Lisa was just coming in with the coffee, and I wished I'd thought to refuse it. I wouldn't gain anything from prolonging the encounter, but now I'd have to make some sort of conversation while I sipped away.

'I shall,' Miles said bluntly. 'And if he doesn't produce results, I'll go to Dilys Drake. She's always interested to hear about incompetence at City Hall.'

It was too feeble a threat to stir my anger. 'Dilys might buy this as incompetence,' I said, 'but nobody else will, Miles. The Argus certainly won't. There's a lot of public sympathy for the engineers, because they're still suffering from Bill Baxter's loss. Sheila Brennan's very competent, and things are happening, but you can't press too hard in the circumstances.'

'It's a big department. One man's death can't make that much difference.'

His callousness left me breathless. 'Death always makes a difference,' I said coldly, 'and Bill's has made a big difference to an awful lot of people. Professionally he had expertise that's hard to replace, but that's the least of it. Strangely enough, people are shocked when a friend and colleague is murdered. I'd even have thought you might be a little shocked. You knew the man, after all.'

Miles' face was inexpressive as a puppet's. 'I don't know where you got that idea,' he said. 'I never met him.'

'Oh, come on,' I said. 'Of course you met him. I saw you together, on Flint Hill.'

He froze, hand half-outstretched to take his coffee cup. Then, slowly, he drew it back and clasped it with his other one, on the desktop. His eyes had narrowed into black currants in his bun-face. 'Can't say I recall,' he said.

'By the barrier, the day of the collapse. You had an argument with him.' And they hadn't been strangers, I felt sure.

'Oh. Yeah. I just about remember talking to some bloke then. I was upset, though. I didn't take it in that he was the one who was killed.'

Liar, I thought. It must have showed, because Miles forced a smile, and added, 'May seem weird to you, but you have to see it from my viewpoint. You meet so many people in our line of business. Council staff are, well, council staff. Like the milkman, you know his face but you don't know his name.'

I knew my milkman's name. No matter. I said, 'The structures section isn't particularly large, actually. Bill Baxter was our chalk mine expert, and as I said, his experience isn't easily replaced. But you may like to remember the name of his successor, Sheila Brennan. If you want to be updated on the situation, she's the person to contact.'

'Er... right.' Miles smiled again, uncomfortably. 'Look,' he said, 'I must sound really hard to you, but it's not like that, honest. I've got to push, because it's my house, isn't it? I've got to get back into it. Okay, they've got problems in City Hall, I can see that, and I am sorry this bloke's dead. But I can't just sit back and wait, I've got to get things moving. No hard feelings, right? I'm just, like, looking after my own interests.'

I could see that, even if I didn't like the way he was doing it. I said so, and Miles sat back as if he was confident he'd won me round.

'I remember you,' he offered. 'You came in once, didn't you – house on Denver Close. I'm selective, know what I mean? Policemen all look the same, but I always remember clients.'

'That's a handy knack.' I drained my coffee. It was good coffee, too. I stood. 'I did my best for you,' I said.

Miles stood. I topped him by six inches, but he shook my hand with Napoleonic confidence. 'Yeah, I believe you, but I'll keep on at it myself.'

'And there's one thing you could do for me.'

'Business? Any time.'

'Not exactly business. There was a map of Flint Hill and the tunnels in the Argus. I wondered, was it you who gave it to them?'

There was a flicker in Miles' currant-eyes. 'What d'ya mean?'

'There's no hidden meaning, I just wanted to know how the press got hold of the information.'

Miles shrugged. 'Can't have been difficult, people get to know these things.'

'Not many people knew the tunnel layout before the map was printed. Did you?'

He'd moved to the door, and was holding it in a time's-up manner. 'It's my business to learn things,' he said.

'And your business to tell other people?'

I'd angered him, and I thought he'd refuse to answer. But he paused only momentarily before saying challengingly, 'They deserved to know. It's a free country.'

'So it was you who passed the information onto the press?'

'Wasn't a crime, was it?'

'No,' I agreed. 'Thanks for telling me, Miles.'

'If I need you again I'll phone you, right?'

'Any time.' I felt sure he wouldn't.

23

TUESDAY morning Ted did ring. Cool and businesslike, he told me a couple of detectives had gone over to the City Engineer's Department to search through Bill's papers, but both had drawn a blank. His team had considered what to do next, and had decided that if I was willing I should go in myself, to see if I could spot anything with a personal significance that the detectives might have missed.

Ted clearly wasn't keen – I guessed he'd dissented from the team decision – and he told me I could opt out if I felt nervous. I was nervous – didn't tell him so – but I thought it could be useful, so I said I'd do it.

Evidently he'd expected me to acquiesce, since he went on to tell me that he'd already cleared it with David North. The police had no official power to send me in, but it would have been difficult for North to refuse a councillor, even if he'd been inclined to. (I didn't ask if he had.) North had however been adamant that I shouldn't disrupt his staff, who were already behind with their work schedule, so he and Ted had settled that I'd go at half past six the next morning. It was an hour before the office normally opened, but no matter – the security guards would unlock the place for us.

'Half past six!' I exclaimed unwarily.

'You're to meet North at the door, and he'll show you everything. Okay? You haven't another appointment tomorrow, I hope?'

At six-thirty my appointment was with my pillow, but I didn't like to tell him that, so I had to agree I'd make it. 'Come into the police station when you've finished,' Ted added. 'I should be there most of the morning.'

Now that was almost worth braving David North at six-thirty for.

I MADE it at twenty-five to seven, showered, dressed and heavy-lidded. David North was already there, but the security man was only just ambling up, so it wasn't simply me who had made him wait.

Even so, he was irritable – and convinced it was a waste of time. He and his staff had looked for anything that might be useful, the police had looked, and what could Bill's work have to do with his death anyway? So he said, at some length, as we headed up to his department and he switched on a battalion of lights. He went straight past the reception desk to a door labelled 'Conference Room'.

'I had Sheila Brennan leave the file on Flint Hill here yesterday,' he said curtly. 'I've booked the room for the whole of today, so you can take as long as you need with it.'

'David...' I said quickly, as he seemed on the verge of leaving me.

'What is it?'

'I'm sorry, but this isn't what I want. I don't even know that it's Flint Hill I'm interested in. I'd like to see where Bill worked, what papers he left...'

My voice trailed off, because North was looking at me as if I'd asked him to do a striptease.

'We don't normally allow strangers beyond the barrier.'

'I'm not a stranger, I'm a councillor,' I said sharply.

North frowned. 'Oh, if you must...'

The barrier he'd mentioned was a wooden flip-over one by the end of the reception desk, closing off the rest of the open-plan office. He flipped it, and led the way through a forest of partitions to a corner area with a couple of adjustable drawing boards set at angles, a variety of chairs, and a narrow plank-type desk fixed onto the partition, with a shelf full of books and binders above.

'Sheila Brennan generally works in this area. Bill used to work over there, with Gary Temperley next to him. That's the layout table. These shelves hold mostly manuals. The plans of Flint Hill are in the plan chest – do you need me to unlock it?'

'Yes please.' I was looking round in dismay. It was years since I'd worked in an office, but I'd assumed this place would be much like those I remembered. It wasn't. Where was I to start?

'I'll have to look for the key.' North chugged off, propelled by the steam of his anger.

I didn't follow, but put the Flint Hill file I'd picked up in the conference room on the layout table, slung my bag across the back of what had been Bill's chair, and sat down in it. He'd had the place nearest the window. We were three floors up. Some of the buildings around were taller, but I could see the castle, framed in concrete.

I hadn't expected to be left alone, and it was a little eerie in the deserted office. But in a sense I was lucky – I'd have hesitated to snoop in front of an audience, but now I had a chance to nose wherever I chose. Sheila and Gary would arrive before nine, perhaps well before, so I couldn't afford to waste the time till North returned.

There were some plastic containers, more like tubs than drawers, slung on rollers under the desk. I pulled out the nearest one and peered at its contents. On top was a sheaf of blank forms in a broken paper wrapper; beneath that, a larger, scruffier sheaf of the same forms filled in. I peeled off one and read it. It was a survey about subsidence: name, address, type of subsoil, details of cracks and other damage, all completed in spidery writing.

I flicked through the rest of the forms. Some – perhaps six or eight out of a hundred – had red biro stars on the top, but I couldn't see why. Nothing else caught my eye, except for the odd familiar name. *'Mr and Mrs A Denton':* that was Allen Denton, a friend of Nick's who belonged to the squash club, and his wife Sara. I pulled their form out of the sheaf.

A big box was headed *'Reason for Request'. 'Estate agent advised,'* the spidery hand had written. Below was a question, *'Known chalk mine area?'* The *'No'* box was crossed. On the line beneath, *'Known bomb damage?'* also had the *'No'* box crossed.

The Dentons had a red star.

I searched for another red-star form, and read about Mr and Mrs J Wilson. Again, their estate agent had advised. I assumed that meant they wanted to sell their house, and an agent had told them it might be subsiding – much as had happened to Nick and me, although we'd never thought to consult the engineers.

Without that kind of prod, who'd notice a tiny crack in a side wall? The Wilsons' house too was not in a known chalk mine area and had no known bomb damage.

I looked at a couple more. It seemed all the red-star forms were not in known chalk mine areas and had no known bomb damage, but there were other forms with *'no'* and *'no'* checked which didn't have red stars. It'd be a waste of my time to puzzle out the rationale, when Sheila or Gary could explain it in a minute.

Even if this was Bill's work – and I wasn't sure it was – I couldn't see anything here that he'd have wanted to pass by me, let alone anything that would justify murder.

I turned to a filing cabinet just along from the plastic box. It was full of suspension files, each label written in the same spidery handwriting as had appeared on the forms: names of engineering consultants, press cuttings, negatives. I took the 'negatives' folder out and was holding up to the light a strip of negs of chalk mine interiors when David North reappeared.

'Oh, you've started,' he said without heat. 'I'm sorry, but I can't find the key, so you'll have to wait till Sheila comes in.'

I told him I'd get on with what I could find. I thought he'd stay, but I wasn't pressing him to, and in fact he retreated, saying I should be careful not to get anything out of order, and I'd find him in his office if I needed him.

I didn't know where his office was, and didn't ask. I put the negatives back, and ran my finger down the row of plastic file-labels, searching for a trigger.

Nothing. I took out two more files at random. One contained technical letters from, and carbons to, a man working for Nottinghamshire County Council; the other, specifications of methods for testing ground conditions.

It was five to seven, and my spirits were sinking. I could have used a black coffee to waken me: we'd passed a hot drinks machine, but it hadn't been switched on. There was a mountain of material here, far too much for me to read through, even if I could have understood it. As for finding a clue, making a connection, duplicating a discovery which Bill might have been murdered for... Hell, I was more likely to die of boredom than because of my dangerous knowledge.

I couldn't see how I could even begin unless Bill had left me a pointer; but if he had, then Gary, Sheila, North or the police should have found it.

Serendipity? Blank my mind? No, I told myself sternly: be logical, concentrate. You're looking for something that might point to illegal activity.

I went through the file labels again, but nothing connected. I ran my eyes along the shelf: it held half a dozen copies of the preliminary mine study I'd already read, and several sheaves of computer printout in blue plastic folders.

I could definitely have used a black coffee. Was it worth going to the machine and figuring out how to switch it on? The place was so empty, so quiet – what time did people start to come in?

I reckoned I could keep looking for a while after they did, but I would be more constrained. I wouldn't be able to look over Gary or Sheila's personal —

Do it now.

I didn't think North would come back in a hurry, and if anyone else arrived I'd hear the creak of the swing door from the stair lobby. I'd be hidden behind the petition, and would have a minute's warning to get back to the filing cabinet.

Sheila's chair – at least, I thought it was hers – felt cool after the one I'd warmed. There was a plastic tub nearby, under the strip-desk: I pulled it out. It was jam-packed with papers, a bottle of handcream, a packet of paper tissues, a hole punch and a stapler. Praying she didn't have a system I hadn't noticed, I heaved the lot onto the desktop, then put back the handcream, the stapler, an internal phone directory and a blank lined pad, and started to work through her papers.

It's strange how immaculately-groomed people can be such scruffs in other directions. She bent corners over, she doodled. Her writing looped and scrawled. I returned to the tub a fast-growing pile of staff memos, Nalgo circulars, a half-written letter, pages of notes and calculations: no time to puzzle over them, one glance had to do. There was a transcript of an answerphone message from the Chair of Environmental Health, and another from Rex, asking a long list of questions about Flint Hill. I paged through the double-spaced, much annotated draft of a report to Planning Committee.

Her desk diary was halfway down the pile. Serviceable, brown-vinyl-covered, it was the page-a-day variety, and sparsely written-in, I saw at a flick. She hadn't marked many forward meetings, and there was barely an entry a day through January and February.

Bill had died on February 28th: I turned to that page. She'd had an appointment with City Works at 10 am, and there was another entry which she had crossed out. It looked as if she'd scribbled across it, but found this didn't erase firmly enough, so she had taken a black marker pen and drawn several heavy lines across entry and scribbles alike.

I held the page up to the light, but I couldn't read what was written underneath the marker pen. Was it important? I didn't know it wasn't. I rested the diary on my knee and carefully tore the page out. It came cleanly, leaving a tiny nubbly edge down the spine. Sheila would notice if she looked back, but why would she? I scuttled across to Bill's chair and shoved the page, folded, into my bag.

Nothing clicked in the rest of the entries. It was past seven, and staff would be arriving before long. On impulse I shoved the rest of the papers back, turned over the pile to put it in roughly its original order, and crossed to the stretch of desk I hadn't yet investigated.

I assumed the next tub would be Gary's, and this was confirmed by a neat folder containing a record of his working hours and expenses claims, going back just over a year. He'd gone to a conference in January, but otherwise it was minor stuff: three, five, six miles of travel at a time. Beneath was an address book. I looked up B: Bill's home number was down, but Sheila's was not. T: no other Temperleys, this was strictly business. There were numbers for professional bodies, in-house extensions for the Planning Department, and several numbers for surveyors and estate agents. They'd be useful to a structural engineer, I supposed. I looked up K, and found Keylock listed: not only the agency office, but also Miles and Fred's home numbers. Was this how Miles had got hold of the information for the map of the mine?

Jack Wells, the Tory leader, was down too – one number only.

Under the address book was a fat folder labelled 'house surveys.' I could ask to look at that later. I worked down past a couple more folders, to the dozen or so loose sheets at the bottom of the tub. A handwritten draft of a letter. An invitation to a party, printed by computer: I recognised the name, it was a girl who worked in Personnel. At the very bottom were four pages of A4, typed sideways and stapled together. A typed heading, *'Miscellaneous Subsidence Reports'* was followed by three typed columns of information: *'Ref. number'*, *'Name'*, and *'Address'*. Three more columns had been ruled by hand. One was headed, *'Surv'r'*, one *'Agent'*, and the third *'Checked?'*

I glanced down the names, saw Mr and Mrs A Denton, slid down to Mr and Mrs J Wilson, and decided this was some sort of index to the forms I'd found earlier. I didn't think the names of surveyors and estate agents had featured on those, though. Presumably Gary had been given the job of adding them.

No: Bill had done it. At least, it had been done in the same spidery hand as had completed the forms – and that wasn't the writing in Gary's address book. Mr Spider had filled in the three extra entries for most of the first page of names and addresses, but for only a sprinkling on the next three pages.

Some of the *'Checked'* entries were a simple tick, but the Wilsons had a tick followed by, *'By Tony Underwood. No damage found',* and there were several similar entries.

I'd got this far when I heard the clunk of the swing doors and a woman's voice. I slipped the papers back, the files on top of them, slid the tub back under the desk and, bending my knees and hunching my shoulders, scuttled back to Bill's old chair.

I was peering into the filing cabinet, a sheet of paper in my hand, when a head popped round the edge of the partition and a cheerful voice said, 'You're in early, She — Oh.'

'No, I'm not Sheila,' I said into the silence which ensued.

The woman took a step forwards and frowned at me. She was older than Sheila Brennan – in her forties, I guessed – with blonde-to-grey hair and a navy coatdress.

'Police?' she asked.

'Not exactly.' I stood up, held out a hand, introduced myself, and told her I was there at the police's request, and that David North had shown me in. She stared at me, and didn't take the hand.

'Can I ask who you are?' I added.

'Oh, sorry. Kate Vernon, from the Roads Group. I just... I thought the police had already been over everything.'

'They have. This is an extra check.'

'Well... I'd better let you get on.'

'Before you go, when does the coffee machine get turned on? I'm dying for one.'

'I'll see what I can do. How d'you have it?'

'Black without. Thanks a lot.'

Ms Vernon went off. I didn't think she was suspiciously antagonistic, just protective of Sheila and the rest. I hoped she'd linger when she came back with the coffee, and give me a chance to chat. When she reappeared, though, it was with Sheila, who was camel-wool-coated and taut with annoyance. Kate Vernon handed over a plastic cup and retreated fast.

'David didn't tell me you were coming in,' Sheila said accusingly.

'Didn't he?' Ted's instructions, or his own lack of consideration? 'I hope you're not too busy this morning,' I added. 'I've been trying to make some sense of all this myself, but I've come to the conclusion I need some help.'

'Obviously I'm busy, extremely busy. Maybe you don't care if Flint Hill never opens again, but I do. I've got to finish setting up the full inspection, and if you've messed up any of the files —'

'That makes two of us,' I said quite mildly – I didn't blame her for being rattled. 'Being busy, I mean. I've got a mountain of work on at home, and I wanted this bloody search about as much as a double puncture, but the police didn't give me any choice. They seem to think it could help them find Bill's killer, and who am I to argue with that? D'you want to get a coffee and sit down?'

Bright spots of colour had appeared in Sheila's cheeks. 'The police sent you?'

'Detective Inspector Zahler. Phone him if you want to check.'

For maybe ten seconds Sheila glared so hard I thought she would; then her eyes went blank. She let the coat fall open and slip off her shoulders. Under it she was wearing a maroon bouclé suit over a navy vest. She hung the coat on the stand in the corner, and came over to me. Close up, her face looked almost grey. I could see faint lines around her eyes, and even – more faintly – on her cheekbones. It was a good suit, but slightly rumpled. I'd known, of course, that she'd taken Bill's death hard. However, I couldn't let on that I knew why.

'I'm sorry,' I said. 'This must be a real shit for you. What happened to Bill, and getting dumped with two people's work, and now endless people rummaging through the files. Tell you what, bring your chair over and I'll get the coffee. How d'you take it?'

I half-expected her to protest, but she didn't. 'White, no sugar. You know where...?'

'I passed the machine earlier, so I dare say I'll find it.'

I did. I also found David North, who emerged from his office to ask if all was going well; and by the time I'd got rid of him and to the coffee machine, Gary Temperley. It was past eight o'clock, and a dozen people had arrived in the office. As Gary and I walked back to Sheila, I filled him in on why I was there.

Gary was less angry than Sheila, but he seemed equally unimpressed. 'All right, the police've got to try everything,' he grumbled, 'but they've already cut us up and sieved the bits. Anyway, it's not as if Bill's work had anything to do with what happened to him. Know what I think? It was a nutter. Bill went over to check on the collapse before that meeting, and ran into some psychopath who did him in.'

It sounded cold-hearted, but it was a piece with his normal manner. What else was he to imagine – that David North had done it in a fit of jealousy over Sheila? I said 'Could be' noncommittally, and assured him I wouldn't disturb his work more than I had to.

He seemed to take this as permission to ignore me: as soon as we reached the structures section he went to the plan chest – presumably Sheila had unlocked it – and got to work.

I gave Sheila a minute to drink her coffee, and took a gulp of the lukewarm brown ink I'd been given. Then I fished the survey forms out of Bill's tub – I didn't want to admit I'd looked in Gary's – and asked her what they were about.

She seemed more composed now, and there was more than a touch of her usual crispness as she gave the forms a very cursory glance. 'This is self-explanatory, I'd have thought: just a summary of the subsidence queries we've received.'

'What's the point of that?'

Sheila shrugged. 'It's something Bill wanted to do. He had an idea that if we plotted every enquiry we might home in on undiscovered mines, but it didn't work because the data's too unreliable. People in the most ridiculous places phone up worried about subsidence – and half the time the bloody surveyors encourage them. It's self-insurance gone mad: no surveyor dare carry out a survey in Costhorpe without adding some caveat about a subsidence risk.'

'So you don't think there's much correlation between the people who enquire and the places where mines are?'

'None. Anyway, most structural damage is the result of wartime bombs – mines are a strictly secondary cause. Even Bill admitted it was hopeless. He plotted all this on a map, and you can see from that.'

'May I?'

She shrugged again. 'If you must.' When I didn't answer, she went to the plan chest, withdrew a large sheet and spread it across the layout table. I saw it was a standard street plan of Costhorpe, marked with hatchings and crosses in three different colours. 'Blue's for chalk workings,' she explained, as I leaned with her over it. 'Red's for bomb damage, and green's other causes: leaking drains, steep slopes, whatever. Then there are a few cases where people came to us after an outline survey or a warning from an estate agent, and went on to have a full structural survey which confirmed the first man was talking nonsense. I couldn't see any point putting them on, but Bill wanted to, so those are the little outlined-green squares.'

'There aren't very many.' I supposed there were twenty or thirty in all, compared with three or four times as many of the crosses.

'We don't always get feedback. Bill had this idea of chasing up, going back on all our enquiries a year later, but it'd be terribly time-consuming and David refused to authorize it.'

'So that's all the work Bill did.'

'That was more than enough.' Sheila glanced at the survey sheets, which I was still holding. 'Was the summary with those? An index listing the names and addresses?'

'No,' I said innocently.

Nor was it in the map folder. Sheila searched the filing cabinet, but not surprisingly she didn't find it. She asked Gary if he'd seen it – and more surprisingly, Gary said he hadn't. Prompted, he did a grouchy search through his tub, but he failed to turn it up.

Now that was interesting. Gary's tub had been comparatively tidy, and I couldn't see how he could 'lose' four sheets of paper. This was worth telling Ted, I thought. I didn't mean to make that apparent to Sheila or Gary.

I turned to my next question. 'How about these red asterisks? What do they mean?'

I could see past Sheila to Gary, and I saw his hand freeze over his calculator.

Sheila didn't know. She looked through the sheaf, read several sheets and checked the plan again. All the asterisks corresponded to outlined green squares on the map, but not all the green squares were matched with asterisks. She asked Gary, and he said he didn't know either. Gary said it deadpan, though, and Sheila said it irritably. I had the impression she couldn't understand why there should be anything about Bill's work she didn't know.

It didn't seem so odd to me. It looked as if Bill had done a lot of work on these stray enquiries, maybe more than David North had authorized. It also looked as if Sheila had thought it a waste of time. Affair or no affair, why should he have chosen to keep her genned-up?

But if he hadn't told her...

This was something else I meant to tell Ted. I thought of taking the survey forms, but I had no authority to do that, and I reckoned that rather than ask North myself, I'd do better to leave it to the police. I thanked Sheila for her help, thanked Gary for his – although he didn't know he'd given me any – and retreated to City Hall, where I could hope to grab a decent strong cup of coffee before moving on to the police station.

24

It's not often I walk into the Members' Room on a Wednesday morning and have the lousy luck to run into Rex Canning and Jack Wells. Rex, grey-suited, grey-shirted, fair hair elegantly ruffled, was leaning against the photocopier; Jack, also grey-suited but looking portly and disgruntled, was standing by the window.

They appeared no more delighted to see me than I was to see them. There were no committee meetings that morning, so presumably they had met specially to discuss something. The Members' Room isn't designed for confidential discussions, though, and I wasn't in the mood to vacate it for their convenience. 'Excuse me,' I said, and went to pour myself a coffee from the jug on the hotplate.

'I'll phone you tonight,' Wells said to Rex.

'Okay. And I'll do as we agreed.'

'I'm not saying I agree to —' Wells gave me a bitter glance. 'Watch your step, that's all.' He left the room.

I supposed there were worse times for re-establishing a polite-but-distant relationship with Rex, so rather than scuttle nervously after Wells I claimed a place on the lumpy green sofa and settled down to my first good fix of the morning. I was conscious of Rex watching me.

'You have a meeting this morning?' he enquired.

'I've been talking to the engineers.' There was no point making a secret of it, when the whole department knew I'd been there.

'About Flint Hill?'

I shrugged noncommittally.

'I wanted a word with you about Flint Hill. I thought we agreed the suggestion I made to you about the Dunburys was strictly off the record.'

'So we did,' I said. 'It wasn't such a stroke of genius that the cops couldn't have worked it out for themselves – and you did want them to, didn't you?'

Rex frowned. 'Arguably. I suppose you know the Dunburys are

now regarded as prime suspects for Baxter's murder?'

'I'm not that surprised.'

'Erica! It's utterly incredible, and you know it.'

'Why?'

'Because... damn it. All right, it's obvious now that there's not much of a case against your Rasta friends, but that doesn't mean it has to be Dunbury. I may as well tell you, Jack and I are investigating other options. If the police won't —'

'Estate agents?'

Rex paused in his tirade. I earned his best Sexton-Blake look. 'Am I to take it you're investigating too?'

I took some time considering what to reply. Getting into a full-scale row with Rex hadn't been my intention, and since he was in such a choleric mood, I might only avoid one by wrapping up the conversation quickly. But I wanted to know what he was up to, and walking away wasn't going to tell me. Polite but distant, I reminded myself.

'I think you're wrong about the police, Rex. My impression is that they're making enquiries in all sorts of directions. I've been helping them as far as I can, which is why I went to see the engineers – the police asked me to. I don't know that they've got far, though, so if Wells wants to use his contacts...'

'He doesn't,' Rex said curtly. 'Even to chat up Fred Keylock's too much to ask, apparently.'

'I'd have thought you could chase Fred yourself. Or Miles, at least – hasn't he been on to you about Flint Hill?'

'How did you know that?'

'Yesterday, wasn't it? He tried Mike and me as well.'

Rex slapped his thigh, hard. 'The little shit. I spent ages checking with Sheila Brennan, and when I asked for advice from him in return, what did I get? Miles is no expert, anyway: Fred's the one we need. Jack goes on about delicate relations, but I went into public life to get things done, not to drink sherry and shake hands and get put up for the North Anglia Club.'

'Good for you, Rex.'

He was too agitated to pick up on my irony. 'That's what we were arguing about when you came in. Whatever I suggest, Jack has some damn reason not to do it. Of course, he's not the one who gets the Dunburys ringing him every bloody day.'

What had Rex said just after I came in? 'I'll do as we agreed.' Only Jack Wells hadn't agreed, it was evident. And Rex was... hovering, I guessed, on the edge of doing it. I liked the idea of dividing the Tory Group.

'What will you do then, Rex?' I asked innocently.

Too innocently – Rex wasn't completely self-absorbed, and he noticed. I watched with interest as he reacted by bringing his temper down into first gear. Neutral; parked. He went to get a coffee, good delaying tactic. Then he turned, and considered me across the room.

'What I intend,' he said, accountant-style, 'is to go to Flint Hill. I mean to take a gander at number thirty-three. The police seem to be fixed on the idea that Baxter went through the Dunburys' cellar, but there is the alternative of the mineshaft.'

'The police won't like it if you go into the evacuated zone.'

'I shall be checking on the problems the road closure's causing, a perfectly proper activity for a councillor. As you will confirm.'

'Will I?'

'If we're asked. You'll come with me, Erica, because you're nosey. You want to know what I'll find out. And I'll take you with me because I also want to keep an eye on you.'

'Thank you for telling me.'

'So far I've told you everything – and in return you've been rather less co-operative than Keylock. I don't see why. I believe you're trying to help the police, so why don't you believe I'm trying to help them?'

I thought about that question. 'I do,' I said.

'Well then. Are you free now?'

Drawbacks? The Labour Group might – no, how could they learn of it? Nobody else would be in Flint Hill's evacuated zone on a Wednesday morning. Rex and I might – no, we wouldn't. I wouldn't. I'd got Ted Zahler, or the hope of him, to act as my shield.

'I could manage half an hour's time.'

'What can you possibly need to do in the next half-hour?'

There was real Rex sarcasm in that question. To hell with being co-operative. 'I've arranged to see a friend,' I said coldly.

'I almost believe you. I'll see you by my car at eleven.'

I DID think of telling Ted Zahler what we were planning, but he was so angry about the diary page that I didn't dare. Evidence or not, apparently it was utterly unacceptable for me to have whipped it. When I handed it over he looked at it with such disdain that I half-expected him to order me to take it back.

He didn't, however. 'We may as well take a look,' he said grudgingly.

'And you'll chase up the subsidence report?'

'Yes. That's interesting – you've done a good job there, Erica. I'll ask North to get hold of it when Temperley and Brennan go home.'

He wasn't saying any more. Evidently I'd done my bit, and now I was to be filed back under 'potential help'. If he'd been more forthcoming I might have thought twice about going with Rex, but he wasn't.

I did feel a little uneasy about Rex's plan, but I told myself there was no real reason. Costhorpe's a pretty safe place, I'm a sensible person and not inclined to run risks around deep holes, and so was Rex, I reckoned. We weren't going to endanger our lives, only to do a little gentle investigation.

When I got to City Hall car-park Rex, black-cashmere-overcoated, was leaning against the wing of his Audi. I hadn't got my car, so I couldn't protest at going in his. We drove in a fairly companionable silence over to Flint Hill, he found a parking space on a side road, and we walked, also in silence, to the road barrier. No one was in sight, so we both slipped past.

'You know the Buntings?' Rex asked as we were approaching number thirty-three. 'Have you been in the house?'

'I didn't know them before the collapse. I've seen the outside of the house, but that's all.'

'Pity. We need to look for things that have changed. Anything that's out of place, or...'

'I have a brain of my own, thank you, Inspector Alleyn.'

I earned a quelling look for that. Too bad, I hadn't gone into public life to ingratiate myself with Tories. Ignoring him as best I could, I tried to think back to the morning of the collapse.

More than three weeks had passed. It had been rainy and cold that day; now it was cloudy but dry, and the daffodils were out. The Buntings' gate had been open then, and so it was now. Rex slipped rapidly through it; but it stopped me.

'Come on,' he hissed. 'We don't want anyone to see us.'

'Just a minute. There was a thingy fixed to the gate – an octopus.'

'A what?'

'You know, one of those springy luggage fasteners you use to fix everything onto the roofrack. It was wound round the gate. I suppose Mandy used it when Ben played out the front. The latch is useless, so she'd have pulled the octopus tight round the gatepost to stop him from getting out.'

'When did you last see it?'

'I only remember noticing it when I first came. I'll try to remember. We might as well go on.'

We did. The front door and windows were boarded over, and we could tell at a glance that there was no way to see inside, so we made for the side alley and the barrier that blocked off the hole. I led the way to the barrier, and stopped when I reached it. It hadn't rained for a week or more, and the hole looked a little less muddy than before.

'Did you come down here on the morning of the collapse?' Rex asked, low-voiced.

'No,' I said. 'That afternoon I looked at the hole, but I went through Phil's garden – number thirty-five – and in at the far end of this one. And I came over again when Bill went down the mine, but then I went through the garden on the other side. The only time I came down this alley, before or after they put up the barricade, was when I came with you.' I added, wanting to keep the confessions in balance, 'How about you?'

'I came here on the afternoon of the 28th.'

His voice was neutral, but the words dynamited me. 'The day Bill was killed? What time?'

Rex didn't react to my shrillness. 'About five o'clock,' he said calmly. 'I left work early so it wouldn't be too dark, because I wanted to look everything over before the meeting. I'd asked Baxter to come with me, but he said he was busy, and I didn't push him since I assumed he'd be at the meeting.'

What time had Bill been killed? The police presumably knew, but I didn't. Did Rex know?

If he did, it couldn't have been at five o'clock, because the man wasn't half-witted, and yet he still seemed perfectly unconcerned. He went on, 'I walked down the road, had a look at the Dunburys' house to make sure everything was in order – they'd been onto me about security – and went as far as the newsagent at the bottom of the hill to buy an Argus. Then I came back up the hill, up this passage and had a look at the hole just as we're doing now.'

'Did you see anyone?'

'Not really. A couple of kids were in the back garden, but they ran off as soon as they saw me. And I bumped into Jack as I was going.'

'Jack Wells?'

'Obviously. He was doing much the same – I'd asked him to talk at the meeting, and he'd come to check out the situation first.'

'This was at five o'clock?'

'Nearer five-thirty, I suppose, because it was shortly before I left.'

'Did you tell the police this, Rex?'

Rex turned on me a condescending look. 'Be sensible, Erica. Well over a hundred people came to the meeting just up the road that evening. People walk up and down, in spite of the barriers; people go to the newsagent and the bank – and the fish and chip shop, although one wonders why. Why would the police want an inventory of everyone I'd seen?'

'You said the place was deserted,' I pointed out.

'Not entirely deserted, since Jack and I were here; and Jack told me he'd just been talking to the Keylocks, as well as to the newsagent. Erica, even you can hardly point a finger at Jack. There's no more respectable man alive.'

Leader of the Conservative Group on the Council, and an estate agent – thus a member of two professions with dubious reputations. I wasn't ruling out Wells from suspicion. Nor was I looking to antagonize Rex unnecessarily, though, so I silently filed the information for Ted, and said, 'I'm just edgy – it's a long way down the hole. Do we need to climb the barrier?'

'Let me think first. The rope... no, it can't have been here that day, or I'd have noticed it. When we came on Saturday morning I noticed it straight away.'

'So someone put it there between Friday afternoon and Saturday morning.'

'That's the logical conclusion. Now we should climb over. Can you manage?'

I should have changed, I'd got my red and grey jersey outfit on. It was too late now. I clambered over as carefully as I could, and paused on the other side to get my breath.

'I didn't go into the house on the Friday,' Rex said, 'but I want to look now. Can you get there if I hold your hand?'

'I should think I can manage without.' I edged along the barrier to the house wall, following Rex. He paused at the place where the yellow rope had been tied to the scaffolding, drew a pair of leather gloves out of his coat pocket, and put them on. 'Wait here,' he said, and reached for the scaffolding. Hands on one horizontal pole, feet on another, he paced sideways to the point where the wall ended, then took a big step onto the remnants of the kitchen floor.

'Do you have gloves with you?' he asked.

Why would I? Winter was done with, and I hadn't come prepared for housebreaking. I told him so, and he threw me his. They fitted loosely, adding to my nervousness. Gritting my teeth, I copied Rex's strut along the scaffolding. I needed his hand to help me into the kitchen, but I managed the rest unaided.

The door from the kitchen to the rest of the house had been boarded up, but no attempt had been made to secure the kitchen. Evidently we weren't the first to have clambered in. The worksurfaces which had been crammed on the day of the collapse had been cleared of all but a few crumbs and black circles, and the pattern of the cushionflooring was almost obscured by endless muddy footprints.

Rex tried the boarding across the door, but it was firmly fixed. 'I won't resort to criminal damage,' he said. 'We'll stay here and I'll hypothesise. Say, Baxter came here Friday afternoon. Perhaps he'd remembered something he wanted to check out, or perhaps he'd made an appointment with someone who wanted to look over the collapse.'

He paused, and I said, 'Go on.'

'At least, someone met him here, either by accident or design. Possibly it was more than one man. Either there was a quarrel, or the man or men might have lured him here with the deliberate intention of killing him.'

'Or he surprised a tramp,' I suggested.

'That's possible too.' Rex was looking around as he spoke. 'I can't believe Baxter would have taken anyone down the mine without equipment, so we'll assume he was at least knocked out up here. Using what?'

'I can't see anything.'

'Nor can I. Maybe there was blood. There are no stains visible, so if there was, the killer must have cleaned the place up. Presumably he had the sense to wipe away any fingerprints too, although I'd like to be reassured that the police have checked the scaffolding for them.'

He paused again, and I waited for him to go on. The picture was all too clear in my mind. Bill and a stranger in this room...

In my annoyance at Ted, I hadn't bothered to tell anyone where I was going.

'Then he had to dispose of the body,' Rex continued. 'He had a rope, a yellow climbing rope, so he used that to lower the body down the mine. Afterwards he went down himself, and carted the body a short way along the tunnel.'

'That'd be difficult for one man.' I listened to my own voice: it sounded quite steady.

'So it would. I think it more likely there were two. They lugged the body between them, and dropped it in a place where there was a large chunk of flint in the tunnel roof. They arranged the body to look as if it had fallen naturally, and levered out the flint, causing a small-scale roof collapse. They must have had a tool to do this, so maybe it was the same tool that they'd used to hit Baxter.'

A crowbar or something similar.

'All agreed?' Rex enquired.

'It makes sense,' I confirmed.

Silence. Rex scanned the painted cupboards, the mucky rear window, the row of cupboards which had been hacked to a halt at the edge of the hole, and the flooring which stopped jaggedly, several feet short of where the wall had once been. I scanned both them and him. He had made no move I could interpret as threatening, hadn't tried to walk behind me. What was I thinking of, getting nervous of Rex Canning? He might threaten a kiss, but he'd hardly do me in.

Jack Wells had known Rex meant to come here, I thought uneasily. Maybe not when, but he'd known in outline. He couldn't have known that I would come too.

'It's hardly the obvious place for a discussion,' Rex said. 'Unless one was discussing the collapse, of course – which increases the odds that the motive for Baxter's killing was related to that.'

'You're assuming the killer met him here,' I pointed out. 'That's not necessarily true. Maybe they met somewhere else, and Bill was knocked out somewhere else. Everyone in Costhorpe knew there were tunnels here, and that Bill was investigating them. The killer might have been miles away, and thought, Christ, what do I do now? Then he remembered the tunnels.'

'I appreciate I'm merely hypothesising,' Rex said tartly. 'Making assumptions, if you know what those are. My assumption, unproven admittedly but credible I think, is that Baxter met a Flint Hill resident here. You know as well as I that many of them were extremely worked-up about the mine. They had a natural motive.'

Not much of one, I thought. I'd felt more confident that I was on the right track in the engineers' office. Of course, Rex knew little or nothing about Bill's obsession. He continued, 'The Uttings... the Duchênes... I only know the residents who've contacted me. I suppose a different lot have contacted you.'

'I suspect most of them have contacted both of us.'

Rex didn't appear to listen. 'The only ones who weren't worked up,' he went on, 'were those to whom it hadn't come as a surprise. James Dunbury, for instance: he knew his house was safe.'

I thought it was a thin argument, but I wasn't going to dispute it with Rex, who in any case had moved on. 'There's another thing – I wonder if Baxter had a key? Or if he didn't, maybe the killer had a key? The Buntings still have one, I suppose.'

'Remember all this is a hypothesis.' Rex swung his head and gave me a disapproving look, and I added, 'They might have argued in the garden.'

'That's hardly the place one would choose to commit murder.'

'If we're talking about probabilities, I'd remind you this house is unsafe. Bill was a cautious bloke. Would he really have agreed to meet someone inside it?'

'Let's check out the garden.'

That suited me: the house seemed creepy, and I was glad to get out of it. Rex managed, with some shoving, to open the back window, and I was able to climb over the sink and out, which saved me from having to brave the scaffolding again. He followed.

Keep calm; remember. The crane had gone, but the mess was little changed – not only the heaps of chalk and earth, but rusty bikes, old tyres, a half-buried sheet of plastic. A new season's nettles were beginning to grow up, and a couple of wan narcissi dropped their heads in what had once been a flowerbed.

'It's overlooked,' Rex said. 'From the windows of all the houses over there. I can't take this seriously as a murder scene, but there might conceivably be evidence among all this junk. Mind your legs.'

If by that he meant, follow me across the nettles, he was destined to be disappointed. I stayed on the patio, and watched him pace deliberately over the debris. He went up to the far fence, turned, and began to pace back a yard or so farther over.

Halfway, he stopped and bent. He took the gloves I'd returned to him out of his pocket, put them on, picked something up and straightened with it in his hand.

It was the octopus.

'Is this the thing from the gate?' he asked, when he'd reached me again.

'It looks like it,' I agreed.

'If one had to lower a corpse down a mine, being careful not to mark it in ways that couldn't be explained by a roof fall...'

I saw his drift. 'That's ingenious. There's a sheet of plastic over there, like those Royal Mail bags for broken parcels.'

'Where?'

I pointed it out. Rex deposited the octopus on the patio and went over to the plastic sheet. He grabbed the end and yanked it out from under the rubble, glancing down at his coat hem and suit trousers and making a face. It was a large sheet, maybe eight feet square. He folded it carefully, still wearing his gloves, came back to me, picked up the octopus and said, 'Time to go to the police station, I think.'

25

WE squabbled in the car going back to the police station. Rex was determined to have me come in with him to deliver the octopus and plastic sheet, and I was equally determined not to. I didn't want Ted Zahler to learn what I'd been doing. Even if we asked for a different officer, the murder squad couldn't be so very large, and he'd get to know.

Also, the Labour Group might get to know.

Perhaps I should say, almost equally determined – Rex won. After all, as he pointed out, even if I didn't come in he would tell the police I'd been with him.

If Ted was going to know anyway, I decided I'd rather tell him face to face. I told Rex I'd ask for him, and after another short argument Rex agreed. I did so, and we hung around in the front office for ten minutes before Ted appeared.

'Officer,' Rex said promptly, standing up with octopus in one hand and plastic sheet in the other. He was several inches taller than Ted. 'You may think this is very interfering of us, but we've brought you some possible evidence. Would you like us to give you a statement?'

Ted gave me a glance which I didn't quite return, and frowned at Rex and his burden. 'Are there fingerprints on these?' he asked expressionlessly.

'I'm assuming it's possible. Not ours, though, since neither of us have touched them with bare hands.'

Ted had the desk sergeant call down an officer who relieved Rex of both octopus and sheet. Then he asked Rex to follow him, and told me to wait in the front office. I did, for some time; then they both reappeared, Rex said 'Bye, Erica', and Ted told me to come with him.

I was expecting to be taken to an interview room – his manner wasn't friendly – but those are on the ground floor, and he headed for the stairs. 'The social club bar's open,' he informed me. 'I'll buy you a drink there.'

I followed him up several flights, along a dingy corridor, and through a swing door into a large, comfortably furnished room. A scattering of mostly uniformed officers were sitting at pub tables, and a couple were playing snooker. I specified an orange juice, and Ted bought two and led us to a table by the window, which had an even better view than the canteen's of City Hall car-park. I could see Rex walking back to his Audi.

We sat on a red velvet bench. Ted stared straight ahead. 'I blame myself,' he said, with audible difficulty, 'for sending you in to Baxter's office. But I did hope you'd have more sense than to turn it into a game of amateur detectives.'

I thought that was less than straight of him, since I was sure he'd dissented from a group decision to send me in. I also thought it ungrateful, considering how much information I'd provided that morning. It occurred to me too that I wasn't the only one who found it hard to make rational judgements when sex came into the frame.

'Okay,' I said. 'I'm not a pro. I don't pretend to be, and I don't want to be. You seem to think that's a weakness, but I'm not sure I agree. It gives me a different perspective from yours. I think that's a plus.'

'No. It means you don't follow the rules. In no way is that a plus, it's a minus and a very dangerous minus.'

I was having to work to keep my temper. Maybe I could rationalise his hostility, but I still reacted to it. I took some deep breaths and a couple of gulps of orange, then said, 'Danger and rule-breaking aren't synonymous, and I don't believe I've run a real risk at any time this morning. What you mean is, I shouldn't have taken the page out of Sheila's diary. Point taken, it was a little bit naughty – a very little bit, which I think you're exaggerating for your own private reasons. It's worth remembering a man was murdered. If it takes a few thefts of paperclips to find the killer, then I'm not too sanctimonious to nick them.'

'The rules are there for a good reason.'

'So are the informers,' I said. 'You also think I shouldn't have gone into the evacuated zone, I suppose. In terms of crimes, I can't see that even rates a caution.'

'Are you really so dumb that you don't remember there's a murderer out there?'

'No. Are you really so hung-up that you have to act like your ninety-niner's been beat when I find out things you didn't find out?'

He jerked round to me, and I glared back at him. Intense emotion gulped at us for an instant; then Ted was back in control.

'If it looks like that to you, I'm sorry. You and your friend have given us some interesting leads. I'll follow them up, I promise you, but I want you to stop it there.'

'Why?'

He had to think, to find a good answer. 'I'll give you an analogy,' he said. 'I'm an archaeologist, and you're a lad with a metal detector. It's a powerful tool. It goes beep-beep and away you dig, and up comes a piece of buried treasure. Beginner's luck; no, not only beginner's luck, because powerful tools give powerful results. What you don't notice is all the more subtle evidence that you destroy in the process.'

'Some of my best friends are archaeologists. Yes, they curse at the bandits, but they actually use the members of detector clubs.'

I could tell he was still on the edge of anger. 'All right, you're clever, and I can't afford to patronise you. My analogy still holds. You've been useful, you've come up with the goods, now it's time for the painstaking work. Sifting the deposits. That's for the pros. We say thanks to the amateurs and rope off the site and keep them away. I appreciate I'm doing a bad job of saying thanks.'

Deep breaths, Erica. 'Yes you are,' I agreed. 'I'll try to take it as read. By the way, there are some other things I meant to tell you, but maybe you don't want to hear them.'

Obviously he didn't. The timing was all wrong, I was all wrong, he wanted to go off and hammer a punchbag or whatever he did to let off excess pressure. But he was professional enough to restrain the temptation, drain his drink and fetch another one for us both, and say, 'I would like to hear whatever you feel you want to tell me.'

And unruly amateur that I was, I gave it all to him, as coherently and honestly as I could. Rex and Jack Wells and their plans to investigate. Miles Keylock and his refusal to play. Rex's hypothesis in full, in case Rex himself had edited any of it. Rex and Jack and their visit to Flint Hill on the afternoon of Bill Baxter's death.

'Five to five-thirty,' Ted echoed.

'So Rex said. He was very insouciant, but he's not normally dense. I wondered if he knew that Bill had been killed earlier, so it wouldn't make him a suspect?'

'Not from me he doesn't, nor from the press, because we haven't released that information.'

I said carefully, 'Since I am a blundering idiot, you may think it's worth warning me if it does make him a suspect.'

Ted considered for a while, then said, 'I may. I hope I can trust you not to share this conversation with Canning. Baxter was killed after one, when he was last seen, and probably before five. And if you swallowed Canning's whole hypothesis you might like to think about when the rope was there and when it wasn't. No; don't think. I mean, keep out, but for what it's worth, the answer's not that simple.'

'I thought it was quite a baroque hypothesis,' I said mildly.

He made no reply; then a minute later he asked me, 'What can you tell me about Wells?'

'Not much,' I said. 'He's been on the Council maybe fifteen years, and he was Lord Mayor three or four years back. He's an estate agent – Wells and Durrant as used to be, till they were bought out in the eighties boom. The rumour is that it made him rich, because he sold at just the right time. I think he still works for the firm, maybe as a consultant, but I can't tell you in detail what he does. He's a Tory, we don't sit on the same committees – I hardly ever talk to him.'

'Is he friendly with Keylock?'

'Fred, you mean? I don't know any more than I've already told you. I don't move in those circles.'

'And what's his relationship with Canning like?'

I gave that question a lot of thought. Then, 'They're not close,' I said. 'Not in any non-political sense. They both belong to the Tory Group, and there's only five in it, but I doubt if they see each other socially. To be honest, I think Rex rather despises Jack Wells. Rex is the pushy new school of Tory, demand efficiency, cut down public services, all that – and Jack's the bumbling old-fashioned kind who joined the Conservative Club because he thought he'd meet a good class of person. Jack's installed as leader, and he's not an effective one. I think it chafes Rex to be under him.'

'But Canning would be loyal?'

'Protect Jack from you? I guess so. More loyal than he'd be to the Dunburys, and you've seen what he's done for them.'

'So I have,' Ted agreed. 'Thanks for your honesty. Are you ready to go?'

'Am I allowed to ask you one question?'

He didn't like that. But he said only, 'I won't promise to answer.'

'Did you get anything from Sheila's diary?'

I watched him frown, and thought he'd refuse. But he didn't. 'The word Bill,' he said. 'In capital letters. Crossed out.'

'Oh.' I wished I hadn't asked.

I ARRIVED home in time to do a couple of hours of work, which were followed by an evening I'd rather have passed up on. I had my councillor's surgery first, an hour of grumbles about Flint Hill and council houses, then I went on to a meeting of the Costhorpe Preservation Trust. We'd pushed a couple of old houses over to them recently, and they wanted a bigger grant to help restore them. I can never understand why nice middle-aged Tories like those on the Preservation Trust don't comprehend that if they vote for cutting public spending, it means no grants when they want them. I tried to explain, and they didn't like it.

I could have used a drink after, but the vibes weren't right for suggesting it to any of the Management Board, so I went home alone at a quarter to ten and opened a bottle of Phil's Koonunga Hill. I know it's dangerous to drink alone, but I wanted a glass and I had nobody else to drink with.

My answering machine tape was half-full of messages. My sister, inviting me over. Rex – saying he wanted to talk, giving no explanation. Ted, sounding cool and distant: phone me please, I'm at home, here's the number. Sheila Brennan, saying can you call me in a small voice. Steve Black, louder, almost aggressive: I've something to tell you.

Why hadn't any of them given me more indication what they wanted? And how was I supposed to bow out of the Baxter case when all the world was onto me about it?

I phoned Steve back first. The number he'd given was Eddy and Clara's, and I had to wait some time before he came to the phone. He sounded strung-up. 'Hey,' he said without preamble, 'that yellow rope.'

'Yes?'

'I've been asking around like you said I should, and I've found out whose it was. Some mates of mine go potholing, and they meant to have a look down the mine. They got the rope fixed, then the fuzz came crawling around and they had to scarper. They went to the pub and came back an hour or so later, and some bastard had nicked it.'

'Nicked it?'

'Yeah. Gone. Disparu. Honest Injun.'

'When was this, Steve?'

'Friday lunchtime.'

'You're sure of that?'

'Course I'm sure. They waited till Friday because the engineers went in Thursday and made the shaft safe, at least safe enough, and it was lunchtime because they went to the pub.'

If so, why was the rope... no point mulling it over while I was on the phone. 'Have they told the police this?' I asked instead.

'That's why I phoned you.'

'What's why?' I sensed that something I wouldn't like was coming.

'They won't, will they? I mean, an exhibit in a f...ing murder case, they saw what the cops did to me and Raze, why the f... should they get mixed up in that?'

'They'd get the rope back,' I offered hopefully.

'In ten f...ing years' time. Look, don't ask, they won't do it. What they said is, they'll talk to you. They'll phone you and tell you, and you can tell the cops.'

'They could phone the police direct,' I said. 'They wouldn't have to give their names, they could just ring and give the message. Steve, I honestly —'

'Look, I'm not arguing. That's what you said you'd do, and now you've gotta do it. You in tomorrow morning? They'll ring you then.'

'Steve, I don't know why you think I —' I was talking to a dialling tone. I hung up and cursed out loud.

Mao-mao moseyed up and hopped into my lap, digging her claws into my thigh. She walked in a couple of tight circles and settled down heavily. I drank some wine, sighed, and heaved her off.

I felt too uptight to phone Rex or Ted, and calling Sheila wasn't likely to be a bundle of fun either. I drew the curtains, turned up the heating, and put highlights from Figaro on the stereo. Then I stretched out on the sofa, eyes closed, Mao-mao reinstalled, listening to *Voi Che Sapete* sung by Frederica von Stade.

That helped.

Once the aria had finished I apologised to Mao-mao, turned down Figaro, got Sheila's number from the pad by the answering machine and rang her.

None of the likely reasons for her to call had struck me as appealing, but the actual one was the worst. As soon as I'd given my name she said, 'You stole a page from my diary.'

I was too tired to fence. 'Yes I did,' I told her.

She hadn't expected me to admit it. It took her a moment to get back on target; then she fired. 'The nerve of it! How dare you! That's my private diary. What bloody right have you got to —'

'Shut up, Sheila,' I said so sharply that at least momentarily, she did. I went on fast before she could resume her tirade. 'You want to know why, I'll tell you. The police sent me in to find anything at all that might give them a lead on Bill's murder. I looked through your papers, and I looked through Bill's papers, and I looked through Gary's papers. Looking for anything, anything that might help. What did I find? An entry you'd scrubbed out on the day of Bill's death. Maybe it was boring, maybe it was irrelevant, but maybe not. It was worth finding out. And maybe I should have asked you what it was, but I'm not the cop, I'm just the messenger boy. So I took it to show the police and shut up, because if I'd told you I'd been through your papers you wouldn't have helped me afterwards.'

'It had nothing to do with his death. Nothing at all.'

'You're probably right.' Even exhausted, I could see it wouldn't be wise to admit I knew what it said. 'If you are, the police will ignore it.'

'You thought I might have done it?'

Her voice was thin. It occurred to me I ought to be sympathetic, but I was clean out of sympathy. 'No,' I said, 'but then I've never knowingly met a murderer, so I'm no judge. Did you do it?'

'No!'

'All right, who did?'

'You think I know?'

She sounded almost hysterical. It maybe wasn't kind to persist, but I had a sense I was getting somewhere. 'You might,' I said. 'Might guess, at least. Did Gary do it?'

There ensued a silence long enough to make me worried. Sheila whispered, 'Is that what you think?'

'No,' I said wearily. 'I can't imagine why he would. But I'd like to talk to you about it.'

'Now?'

It was my turn to be surprised.

'No, Sheila,' I said. 'Thanks for the offer, but I'm dog-tired and in a lousy temper, and I don't suppose you're feeling much better. Could you make the morning? Say, nine o'clock? I know you ought to be working, but this is more important.'

'I'd rather you came now.'

But it was ten o'clock, there were two calls I hadn't yet returned, and I needed wine and Mozart an awful lot more than I needed Sheila Brennan's true confessions. I told her to try to relax, and arranged to meet her at City Hall at nine in the morning.

I WAS alert now; I asked myself why Rex had called, and the answer was obvious. He knew what he'd told me, and had realised what I might be thinking. He'd be aiming to provide a reason – or several reasons – why neither he nor Jack Wells could have killed Bill Baxter.

I was willing to tell him I didn't think he'd done it, and I'd also have liked to hear why he thought it wasn't Wells, but I doubted he'd give me much more than Tory propaganda.

I had a think, and decided it would be sensible to call Ted before I spoke to Rex. I'd feel more comfortable if someone knew about every conversation I was having, even if it was a disapproving someone. Ted might even tell me not to call Rex back. I might even take his advice.

I drained my wineglass and turned the cd player back to *Porgi, Amor*. Three minutes thirty-nine seconds of the Countess yearning was about three minutes more than was needed to tell me I should have chosen a cheerier number. Yearning and policemen are an uncomfortable combination.

Ah well – he'd be businesslike. I dialled fast and he answered fast, and businesslike he was. 'That list you told me about, the one Temperley had.'

'Yes...?'

'North claimed it wasn't there.'

'It was,' I said. 'I saw it, Ted.'

'It's possible North missed it. Can you get over now?'

'Over where?'

'To the City Engineer's office. North's on standby to let us in.'

'Ted, it's past ten.'

'I know, but this is a murder investigation. You're not in bed yet. Can you make it in ten minutes?'

I told him I guessed I could.

I PARKED at City Hall, and got to the City Engineer's office at ten-twenty-five. North was there, looking bad-tempered, and so was Ted, in a blue parka. The security man with the keys was not. I couldn't talk to Ted in front of North, and North didn't seem inclined to talk to either of us, so we stood stamping our cold feet in the dark.

Ten minutes later North said he'd go to find the security man. I waited till he'd gone, then told Ted rapidly about the rope and about Sheila Brennan. 'I didn't ask for any of this,' I added. 'They phoned me, I didn't phone them.'

Ted didn't waste time on criticising me. 'You have an answering machine, don't you? If these potholing jokers ring you in the morning, tape them. Get definite times for when they first went with the rope, when they left it and when they came back. And ask them to ring me. You can tell them they've nothing to fear: we'll be grateful for their statements, and if all they did was trespass we won't charge them.'

'Okay.'

'I don't want you to talk to Sheila. You may think you can handle her more sensitively than my people could, but it won't do, Erica. If she wants to discuss Baxter or her work, you must bring her over to us.'

'She might not,' I said.

'But if she does, I want to hear it. Don't say anything to North.'

North was approaching again, with a security man and a bunch of keys, and I hadn't needed telling to shut up. We were let in, the security man disappeared, and North switched on the lights and succumbed to the remonstrance he'd not bothered with earlier. How did I know there was a list? He wouldn't have left me that morning if he'd known I'd search beyond Bill's papers. Anyway, if there was one – and he wasn't admitting it existed – it wasn't in the office. As if we couldn't trust him to look...

Actually I wouldn't have trusted him to look. I doubted he was a hands-on manager of the structures section; most likely, I thought, he wouldn't recognize the index if he saw it. But I couldn't blame him for not having found it, because he was right – it wasn't there.

I searched all through Gary's tub, the shelf above it, Sheila's tub and Bill's tub. I searched the filing cabinet too. The survey sheets were where I'd left them, but not the index.

'Is all the information on these sheets?' Ted asked, flicking through the stack.

North didn't answer, so I said, 'Not quite, but I guess you could reconstruct what's missing.'

'We'll take them.'

'All those?' North protested. 'That's valuable information. We need it here.'

'We'll return it, sir, or give you photocopies.'

26

I'D ARRANGED to meet Sheila Brennan in the reception area at City Hall, and with a heroic effort I got there at eight-fifty. Sheila wasn't there, and I settled down on a leather-covered backless bench to wait for her.

I waited till nine-fifteen. Patty Fowler came by, and gave me a look-over but didn't approach. Sheila didn't appear. Had she thought better of talking to me, or was there some other reason for her not turning up? Maybe I should have let it be, but I felt like I was sitting on a drawing pin. I went up to the Members' Room, rang the City Engineer's Department Reception and asked if she was at work.

'Just a minute,' the receptionist said. I waited two, and David North's flat Mancunian voice came onto the line.

'Councillor, I have to protest. I need my staff, those I have left, and I can't have them interrupted every five minutes. If you want something from Mrs Brennan, the request should come through me.'

'If it was straightforward Council business it would have done. Is she there, David?'

'This isn't amusing, councillor.'

Could she be there? No, she couldn't be there. He was annoyed because she wasn't there? How was I to know? 'Can you tell me where she is?'

'No I cannot.' I didn't have to wait for the dialling tone: I heard the sound of the receiver being slammed down.

Was this a normal reaction? I'd felt I'd lost all sense of what was to be expected. Maybe it was reasonable for North to be short-tempered after the police had crawled all over the office and his staff, sent a councillor in to nose around, and walked off with his files; but for heaven's sake, a man was dead. Why weren't his colleagues willingly co-operating? Why didn't they want to find out who killed him?

Because they were scared of the answer?

I was pretty nervous about the answer myself, but my immediate concern was with Sheila Brennan. Did she know the answer? Did the killer believe she did?

Her home phone number was in the book, so I rang it. There was no reply, not even an answering machine. The address was in the book too: seventy-one Kimberley Avenue. That was to the west of the city, only a ten minutes' bike-ride away. I wouldn't find out what was going on if I sat by a phone that didn't answer, so I left City Hall and biked over there.

Seventy-one Kimberley Avenue proved to be a narrow sixties townhouse fronted by a boring square of lawn and a border of wallflowers. The curtains were drawn across, upstairs and down. It was twenty to ten. I couldn't believe the nervous woman I'd spoken to the night before would still be asleep.

I rang, then I knocked, then I rang again. I had the feeling I was getting nowhere even before the woman next door poked her head out and said, 'Can't you tell? There's no one in.'

'Did you see Mrs Brennan go out?'

'You think I watch her door all day long?'

'Is there a way round the back?'

'No,' she said shortly, and shut the door; only to open it again and add, 'And if I see you prowling around, I'll phone the police.'

That mightn't have been a bad idea, I thought wryly. I waited a minute to see if her lace curtains twitched – they didn't – then I went on the prowl.

In Costhorpe there's almost always a way round the back, but it looked as if Sheila's terrace was an exception. Twenty houses along I admitted defeat. I went to the callbox on the corner and phoned Ted – he had wanted to talk to her too. And he'd told me to bring her in to him that morning, so I wasn't pleased to learn he wasn't available. Instead I was put onto DC Sunley, who was at least polite and interested. I gave him a quick run-down, and he promised to come over.

He arrived, with DC Allen, twelve minutes later; not bad. They rang, they knocked, then they broke down the door. They told me not to follow them in, so I only learned what they'd found from Allen's white face when she emerged. Sheila had been in bed, with an empty bottle of sleeping pills on the carpet next to her.

Foul play? No; I was jumping at shadows. Her lover dies, her workmates are under suspicion – who could blame her for deciding she'd had enough? Allen told me in the ambulance that this sort of thing is usually a cry for help, especially when the person doesn't leave a note. I wasn't so sure. I can smell despair as well as the next woman. If I'd been Sheila, I wouldn't have depended on someone I barely knew to haul me back from the brink; and perhaps she hadn't troubled with a note because she hadn't felt there was anyone to write it for.

I waited at the hospital until I was told, first that she'd live, and second that I wouldn't be allowed to see her that day. Then I trailed back to Kimberley Avenue to retrieve my bike, and rode it to City Hall.

Damn Ted; what was he doing? Nothing that I could interrupt, I guessed. I set off for the City Engineer's Department, meaning to say something cutting to David North, but half-way there I changed my mind. The news would cut more than deep enough without my leaning on the knife.

I couldn't imagine telling it direct to North, though; and even less to Gary Temperley. I asked at the reception desk for Kate Vernon, who had seemed a pleasant woman, and reasonably friendly with Sheila. The receptionist looked dubious when I gave my name, but she phoned through, held a whispered conversation I couldn't quite hear, and told me Kate would be with me shortly.

Apparently she meant, shortly as in half an hour. I paced the little reception area, inspected the map of Costhorpe on the wall and asked myself why I was bothering. Then North's office door opened, and he came out with Rex Canning.

Their feet and voices stopped simultaneously – and fast. North recovered first.

'Councillor, unless you have a good reason to —'

I'd had enough. 'Actually,' I said in a voice which I could hear was too loud, 'I came to tell you Sheila Brennan tried to kill herself, but it seems no one round here's interested. Are you coming, Rex?' I cut past his back to the swing doors and the stairs down.

No sooner was I through the doors than I could have cursed myself for my last remark. I hadn't wanted in the least to talk to Rex, I'd simply been ratted to have seen him all buddy with North. I quickened from a fast walk to a trot going down the stairs, but it wouldn't have done to break into a run, and I knew that if Rex wanted to catch me he would.

Evidently he did. His hand grabbed my arm when I was on the last flight down, and we skewed to a halt at the same time, one step up from street level.

'That was some performance,' Rex said.

'So was North's,' I retorted. 'One of his staff is dead, another tries to kill herself, and he blames me for wanting to know what's going on? I'd like to know why it's my fault. The list of suspects may be almost endless, but as far as I know I still don't figure on it.'

'You're about the only bloody one who doesn't,' Rex spat back. 'We can't talk here. Come on.' He still had my arm in a firm grip, and he reinforced this remark by tugging me, not at all gently, towards the outer door.

'Rex, I have nothing at all to say —'

'But I have plenty to say to you. In here.' He propelled me firmly down the street and into a hamburger bar a couple of doors along, to the back of it, and onto a bench-seat, sitting outside me so I was thoroughly trapped.

'You're supposed to wait till —' a weary-looking waitress came up to protest.

'Two coffees, please,' Rex interrupted her. He turned back to me, waited till the waitress had drifted off, and said, 'The police took Jack Wells in for questioning this morning. His wife phoned to tell me, and when I rang around to see what was going on, I found out from North that you'd been spinning the police some crazy tale about surveys and estate agents. What's more, they've taken Temperley in too, and now you tell us you've pushed Mrs Brennan to the brink of suicide.'

I jumped at the information about Gary; knew Rex had felt my reaction, and jerked my arm free of his. 'I didn't push Sheila, the whole situation pushed her,' I told him hotly. 'As for taking in Jack and Gary, I thought you wanted the police to wrap up this investigation.'

'Wrap it up? Christ! First you nudge them towards the Dunburys, then when you realise that won't stick you pick up a remark which I made to you in all innocence and pretend you think Jack Wells is involved.'

'I like the pretend!' I shot back. 'What's to say he isn't?'

Rex's face turned purple, and I suspect only the clatter of the coffee cups which the waitress banged onto the table saved me from physical violence. The little interruption served to bring us at least partly to our senses. I lowered my voice to a near-whisper and went on, ‘For heaven’s sake, Rex, they’re investigating, that’s all. They haven’t charged anyone, they’re only asking questions. What’s such a big deal about that? You’ve been questioned and I’ve been questioned, so surely you don’t have to blow a fuse because Jack Wells is being questioned. It’s not an affront to the Tory Party, it’s a logical next step.’

‘Like it was logical for you to rummage through people’s drawers when David had trusted you to look through a file alone?’

‘Sure it was, if it was the only way to get vital information. What it comes down to, Rex, is that we have to find out who killed Bill Baxter.’

‘Oh, I mean to, don’t worry. But I’m not having you and your pretty little inspector frame up Jack as the culprit.’ With which remark, hissed into my face at short range, Rex got up and strode out of the café.

It was as well I didn’t want to follow him, since one of us had to pay for the coffee. Clearly that would be me, so I reckoned I might as well drink at least one of the cups. I took a sip and tried to calm down and think about what I’d learned.

That the police had nabbed Gary didn’t surprise me at all. How else were they to investigate the subsidence survey? As for hauling in Jack Wells...

I totted up what I knew, or thought I knew. Bill’s hint about his obsession. Gary’s purloining the index to the subsidence survey. Dark mutters from Alex Yelland about a scam involving property and chalk mines.

Wells was an estate agent.

Wells had been at Flint Hill on the afternoon when Bill had been murdered.

Also there were the octopus and the plastic sheet, which might have had fingerprints on them – Ted would know if they had by now, but I didn’t. And there was the rope, and the mystery of why it had disappeared then reappeared; and the wider question of when and how Bill had been dumped in the chalk mine. I hadn’t been home when Steve’s friends should have rung so I’d not done too well with the rope enquiry.

Of course there was also Sheila, and the network of overheated emotions surrounding her. There was James Dunbury with his dubious antique deals and transparent lies. There was Miles Keylock, another estate agent. For completeness maybe I should add back in Raze and Steve, too.

Say there had been a scam, I thought, and Bill had uncovered evidence of it. Someone else – maybe someone in his office – had realised what he knew. Either the discoverer was in the scam, or they had let onto someone who was. The conspirators realized Bill had to be silenced, and...

The hamburger bar wasn't cold, but I was shivering.

Now Rex, convinced that Wells was an innocent bystander, was going to nose around to see if he could prove...

I shivered again.

What exactly was Rex planning to do? And what would happen if he beat Ted Zahler and his colleagues to the answer?

27

It wasn't that I thought Rex would do anything illegal to protect Jack Wells: what worried me was that he'd blunder in, asking questions, trusting people I wouldn't have trusted to post a letter, too convinced it wasn't Wells to see the dangers in time if it proved that it was.

Now he knew about the subsidence survey, he'd obviously set out to follow that trail. The police were following it too, and they had Gary and the survey sheets. But if Gary didn't know anything, and Rex chose to ask someone who did...

I couldn't sit tight and trust Ted to find the answers first. It was too much of a risk. Too many people who would talk to Rex wouldn't talk to the cops. Some of them might talk to me. I didn't understand exactly what had happened, but I reckoned I understood more than Rex. I'd ask better questions than his; or choose better people to ask.

Where to begin? Dubious deals, I thought to myself, as I started on the second cup of lukewarm khaki-coloured liquid. Corruption. Backhanders to people who get an inkling: the City Engineers, maybe even the Planning Committee. That's what we were talking about.

I like my politics clean. I value my tiny slice of power, but I don't like the thought of others hustling me because of it. I hadn't gone into the game with the aim of making dirty money, and as far as I knew, neither had my colleagues. Okay, people hinted to me sometimes that they weren't all chalk-white, but it was words, that was all. Standard modern cynicism. I'd never heard any specific allegations, let alone discovered proof of any.

Not wanting this kind of thing to happen didn't mean it didn't happen, though. Maybe the reason I hadn't seen was that I'd chosen not to look.

The way it worked, if you looked, if you saw (if there was anything to see), you got sucked in. You were compromised, just as Raze had tried to compromise me by offering dope. Ask anyone in that position what was going on, and I'd be treading on a brown-paper floor.

What I wanted was someone who knew, but who hadn't been sucked in; someone with secrets of their own, perhaps, who had traded silence for silence. Someone with the kind of ferret's nose which twitches in, and the kind of misfit personality which gets twitched out again.

I knew only one person who fitted that blueprint: Alex Yelland. When he'd made his allegations at Eddy and Clara's party I'd taken them for standard modern cynicism, but there was a chance they were something more.

He was the sort of man who might know plenty, and not take it to the police. Would he tell me what he knew, though? I thought it conceivable. He'd hinted at it already, so maybe he was just waiting for someone to ask him.

I wasn't crazy at the idea of going to Yelland, but I couldn't think of a better way forward, so I rode home again and hunted out the card he'd given me at Eddy and Clara's. I rang the number on it, and got a woman who announced 'Yelland Enterprises'. I asked for Alex, and was treated to a longish silence followed by a polite enquiry what exactly I wanted. Advice about property development, I said. This led to another lengthy wait, then to the abrupt offer of a two o'clock appointment.

It was then eleven-forty. Maybe Yelland had a lunch date, maybe he only wanted me to think he did. Why was I doubting it? He had an office and a secretary, so why shouldn't he have a lunch date? I agreed to two, trying to sound as if I felt honoured. I did half an hour's exercises and spent half an hour flat on my back, curtains drawn, listening to Beethoven's Pastoral.

I was still feeling far from calm, and I reckoned it was because I had good reason to be nervous. It struck me that I ought to tell someone where I was going; also that I couldn't tell Ted, because he'd probably tell me not to go there. Nor could I tell anyone who would feel obliged to mother me, or Rex, or anyone connected with the Council.

Who was left? I drove over to the university and found Allie, long-navy-skirted, alone in her book-crammed office, which was lucky at ten to one.

'Do you know anything about a man called Alex Yelland?' I asked her.

'Not a thing. Should I?'

Maybe not. Phil hadn't known him before they'd met at Eddy and

Clara's. 'He's a property developer.'

'That sounds posh.'

'There are synonyms for it which aren't. Allie, I'm going to talk to him.'

Allie gave me something dangerously close to her mother-hen look. 'You're telling me that,' she said, 'as if you know you shouldn't.'

'I know I should, only I don't relish it. I don't want you to stop me, just to know where I've gone.'

Allie sat back, skirts rustling, dangling earrings tinkling, eyes narrowed. She said slowly, 'Do you want me to come with you?'

'I wish you could, but he's not the man to talk to a committee.'

'Could he be Bill Baxter's murderer?'

I reckoned I could hold her at arms' length without fibbing. 'In theory anyone could,' I acknowledged, 'but I'm pretty sure this man isn't. I just want some information from him.'

'What'll the police think of this?'

She was asking more questions than I'd bargained for. I suspected she could see my nervousness like an aura. Yelland would see it too, I thought gloomily. I said, 'I shouldn't think I'll be falling over cops at Yelland's office, and anything I find out I'll take straight to them. That's a promise, Allie.'

Allie stretched out a silence, then shook her head. 'You're a big girl, Erica. It's not my job to tell you you're being an idiot. Let's have all the details.'

I gave her them, and added the number of the police station and Ted Zahler's name. I felt better afterwards. I walked over with Allie to a campus snack-bar, and managed to eat a bacon sandwich without throwing up. Then I biked to City Hall, locked up, and walked over to the address on Yelland's card.

I hadn't realised previously how close his office was to Keylocks Estate Agency. Not only was it in the same row of grey Victorian houses-turned-offices, it was a scant four doors away. I had to pass Keylocks to get to it. I paused outside and looked between the carousels for Miles, but although I could see the big-haired blonde, there was no sign of him.

I hadn't paid enough attention to Miles, I thought uneasily. I'd spent ages working out that he was the one who had given Patty Fowler a map of the mine, but I hadn't asked myself... for instance, what he had been arguing about with Bill Baxter on the afternoon of the mine collapse.

Of course I hadn't needed to focus on him, because I'd known for ages that he wasn't a suspect. Ted had told me the Keylocks both had alibis for Friday afternoon. They had been – I couldn't remember where, but well out of Costhorpe.

Only, hadn't Rex said something about Jack Wells seeing them in Flint Hill?

As I watched, Fred Keylock emerged from a door at the back of the office, his hand full of papers, and feeling suddenly exposed, I took a step back.

Brokering houses for sale. Working for the vendors. Advising them what to do, if their house was subsiding, for instance. Keylocks always mentioned subsidence. Self-insurance, Sheila had called it. It seemed – more than ironic, that subsidence-obsessed Miles should have bought a house on Flint Hill.

Hadn't there been a clue? The slope of the land, the fifty-foot contour, the remains of an old quarry, nothing at all? Nothing to make it a poor professional choice?

All this needed more thinking through, but I couldn't do that standing outside Keylocks' office pretending to be interested in the revolving carousels. Anyway it was already two o'clock. I headed on up the street and found Yelland Enterprises without difficulty. There was no shop below, just the barely-altered house front. The door was up a short flight of steps, and surrounded by a jumble of business plates and entryphones.

I gave my name to an entryphone, waited for the click, and pushed the door open to reveal a small hall and a flight of uncarpeted stairs. Come up, the secretary had said, to the second floor.

The place wasn't scruffy, it just wasn't smart; until I went through the frosted-glass door of Yelland Enterprises. On the other side there was thick red carpet and sleek black furniture, and another big-haired blonde sitting behind a desk.

I was given the whole rigmarole: taking my jacket, hanging it in a black cupboard, buzzing Mr Yelland to tell him I'd arrived. She asked me to wait, and asked if I wanted coffee. I said yes please, but she made no attempt to produce any. After ten minutes Yelland buzzed her and told her to send me through. He didn't rise as I closed the door of his office behind me.

The office was at the front of the building, but double-glazed and purringly quiet. Yelland's desk was a bare expanse of mahogany. He looked small behind it, except for his eyes, which were magnified by the red-rimmed glasses I remembered.

'Sit down, Councillor Massen,' he said in his whiney voice.

'Erica.' I wasn't there as a councillor, and I didn't want him making out that I was. The carpet was even thicker than in the reception area, and it gave under my feet as I stepped across to a chair.

'You're looking for advice?'

'I —' I paused, because there was a knock on the door. It was the secretary with coffee, and it smelled real. I waited till she'd served it up and left us, then said, 'Yes Alex, I am. There were some things you said at Eddy and Clara's...'

He let my voice die before saying, 'Were there?'

'About chalk mines. About a...' – he was looking at me so warily that I couldn't bring myself to say scam – 'about ways in which they distort the property market.'

Yelland was twiddling a silver pen between his fingers, and he didn't reply. His glasses might have been thick but the eyes behind them were sharp. His manner was crisper, his voice less slurred, than when I'd met him before. I'd wondered at Eddy's if he was drunk, and now I felt sure he had been.

I said very carefully, 'I got the impression those distortions made things tough.'

'Did I say that?'

That didn't justify a reply, so I took a sip of coffee.

'Nah,' he said suddenly. He swung his chair round to the window, turning profile-on to me. He leaned back, his vee of beard sticking out, and said to the window, 'Don't know nothing about that.'

But he'd told me to come over. 'Let's say,' I said, 'that somebody wanted to mess up the market. Let's say they had an idea how it could make them a profit.'

It was so quiet. The room hummed with silence. The coffee smelled overpoweringly strong. Yelland still wasn't giving. 'I'm not saying it happened,' I said, 'only that it could. There could be a scam, but I can't see how it would work.'

'Dumb of you,' Yelland said, without turning to me.

'I can be very dumb,' I agreed.

'If I told you, what would you do?'

'Tell the police,' I said promptly. 'Naming no names; I'd just like to give them a lead to follow.'

‘So. Let’s say there was a scam, and I ain’t saying there is. Let’s say I let you onto it. Let’s say the police follow the trail, and let’s say the man at the end of the trail turns round and follows it back to me.’

If I was right, the man at the end of the trail would have more immediate concerns than taking revenge on Alex Yelland. I didn’t think it would be wise to say so. ‘Alex,’ I said, ‘I won’t need much from you. Let me tell you what I’ve got, then you’ll maybe see that. It’s to do with subsidence, and the price at which houses that are subsiding are sold. Maybe it’s to do with people being told their houses are subsiding, when really they’re not. You told me at Eddy’s that the scam involved people pretending there are chalk mines where there aren’t.’

Silence. A long silence. I drank some more coffee. Yelland said, ‘So.’

‘So can you tell me the rest?’

‘There ain’t no rest.’

It felt to me like there was. ‘If I hit the answer,’ I said, ‘it’ll save Raze and Steve a heap of trouble.’

‘They ain’t in no trouble now that I noticed.’

I bit my lip. I wouldn’t bluff him quite so easily. ‘All I need’s a clue,’ I said. ‘Something I might have hit on by myself. There’ll be no reason for anyone to trace it back to you.’

Yelland turned, and fixed his pale enlarged eyes on me. ‘I got an application coming up this month. Denning Road. Five-bedroom house I want to turn into bedsits.’

Councillor.

‘Two storey?’

‘Yeah.’

‘You’re not likely to get permission.’

His expression didn’t change a millimetre. He stared at me, and I stared back. If this was the price, I wasn’t paying it.

It couldn’t be much. But damn it, whatever it was, I didn’t have it. I took a deep breath. ‘When you don’t have friends on Planning, it must be tough suspecting others do.’

I still didn’t see him move, but he must have done, because the light from the window now hit his glasses, and I couldn’t see his eyes any more. ‘I don’t suspect it,’ he said. ‘I know it. Now get out.’

28

IT'S NOT often I leave a cup of coffee unfinished.

I know it, I know it, I repeated to myself as I walked briskly back to City Hall. I wanted to put plenty of space between me and Alex Yelland.

He'd used it in the wrong context, but maybe it was the right phrase. Maybe I knew the answer, or should have done. Maybe I genuinely was being dumb. Maybe, like all the rest, I didn't want to see too clearly what was in front of my eyes. It was time I started looking harder.

Jack Wells?

No, what Yelland had said didn't point to him, because Wells didn't sit on the Planning Committee. I'd been surprised at that when I'd first joined the Council, but as Nick had pointed out to me, it made sense. Wells was involved in so many of the property deals in Costhorpe that he'd have had to declare an interest and withdraw during half the items we discussed.

Nor could I think of any Planning Committee member I'd seriously suspect of dirty dealing: not ours, not the Lib-Dems, not the Tories.

I biked home without going into City Hall, phoned Allie and told her all was well, and sat down with a sheet of paper.

There had to be another approach.

First, try the obvious. *'Subsidence survey,'* I wrote. Then I wrote *'Sara and Allen Denton'*. I tried to think of other names I'd read on the survey sheets, but I couldn't recall any of them.

Bill had apparently checked out Sara and Allen, so maybe I should do the same. I looked up their number and phoned it. There was no answer.

Think, Erica, I told myself. Allen must be at work, while Sara...

Is fetching the kids from school. I made a cup of peppermint tea, and phoned again ten minutes later. This time I got her. Long time no see, Erica. Oh yes, we saw Nick and Jenny a few weeks ago. All okay with you? Fine, fine. Yes, we're fine too: we went to my parents for half term and got back Sunday.

It took five minutes of chat and two interruptions from Sara's kids before I got us onto subsidence. She remembered Allen phoning the City Engineer's Department. It had stuck in her mind, she told me, because one of the engineers had called round as she was packing to go away.

As she was...

On Friday afternoon, just before half term – Friday February the 28th. Bill Baxter had called round at about two o'clock.

I couldn't believe what she had just said. Did she really mean two o'clock on Friday afternoon?

She did. She was sure it had been around two, because she had gone to collect the children just after three, and immediately afterwards they had set off for Newcastle. Apparently she had told Bill it wouldn't be at all convenient, but he had claimed it was urgent; although she hadn't been able to see how it could be urgent then, almost a year after they had moved from the house Allen had called the engineers about.

She had been away ever since, so she hadn't known about Bill's murder, or the importance of the information she possessed.

'Sara,' I said, 'when did he make the appointment?'

'What's all this about, Erica?'

'I can't explain right now, but it's important. When did he fix it?'

'That morning, I think – no, lunchtime, twelveish. Otherwise I'd have got him to come some other time. He phoned me up and we had a weird conversation. He wanted to know what estate agent we'd used, then he said he had to know more, and could he call round. It was desperately urgent, etcetera. He took ages too, went all through when I'd contacted the agents and what they'd said to me and what I'd —'

'Which agent was it, Sara?'

I'd been rude, I could tell from the quality of her silence, but she decided to overlook it. 'We used two lots, actually. First I went to Keylocks, and it was the man from them who went on about subsidence. Allen thought it was a load of rot. He rang up the City Engineers, and they said we weren't in an area where there was much subsidence, so we went to Langhams for a second opinion, and they said it was a load of rot too – which it was, because our buyers had a survey which said the house was perfectly sound. Apparently it's standard practice with some Costhorpe agents to mention subsidence, because they like to cover themselves in case there's an undiscovered mine; but I thought it was rather sharp practice. The man even suggested we might have to sell to a developer who specialised in underpinning. I mean, it'd have lost us thousands!'

'I'm sure it would.' While somebody else would have gained the thousands. 'Sara, can you describe the man from Keylocks?'

'Erica, it's a year ago! First Mr Baxter, now you. He was young, that's about all I can remember – young and eager.'

'Dark haired? Reddish cheeks?'

'I honestly can't remember. I racked my brains for Mr Baxter, and...'

And Mr Baxter had discovered this. Mr Baxter had been so anxious to find out more that he'd passed up on his appointment with me; and what Mr Baxter had discovered had...

Somehow I managed to thank Sara and agree that I'd love to come over to supper soon. Then I rang off and fell back in my chair.

Keylocks. It couldn't be a coincidence.

I should have seen it so much earlier. Miles Keylock had done the same to me and Nick.

Yelland was right, I'd had all the pieces of the puzzle – I just hadn't put them together.

The Dentons had contacted the engineers. Nick and I hadn't done that, but we too had gone to another agent. But if we hadn't obtained a second opinion – if we'd believed young Miles when he told us what a problem we faced – if we had sighed with relief when he told us how we could get out of it...

We would have been in the same position as Harry and Molly South. They'd told me about it at the Hillside Labour Party Branch meeting; and keyed up with the excitement of the Flint Hill collapse, I'd barely listened to them.

I phoned them next. Harry's retired, and they were both at home. They remembered every detail. Yes, they had used Keylocks. They had dealt with Mr Fred Keylock and his son, that nice young Mr Miles, and how helpful they had both been! The Souths had only had to worry for a week or so before a builder had called round, checked over the place, and offered to take it off their hands. He'd made them a reasonable offer, only ten thousand less than they had originally hoped to sell for.

Only ten thousand. Play that game two or three times a month, and...

I knew Ted would need a step-by-step proof. I got Harry to give me the builder's name, which he did, Grendon Builders: to my relief, it meant nothing to me. I asked if he had contacted the City Engineers, but he hadn't. Why should he have? He'd had everything nicely sorted out without them. I asked if he'd noticed building work going on at the house after it had been sold, and he told me he'd driven past occasionally, but he couldn't say he had. He'd noticed it was occupied again, but had never spoken to the new owners, and didn't even know their name.

I checked the address with him, and thanked him profusely. Then I biked over to the house, which was at the top end of Hillside ward, part of a handsome Victorian terrace. This was flat land, well out of the river valley, and I could see no sign of chalk workings. I could visualise Bill checking *'no'* and *'no'* on his survey form.

The door was opened by a harassed woman with a couple of toddlers clinging to her skirts. I told her I was her ward councillor, and was doing a survey of residents – it seemed less alarming than telling her the truth. She asked for proof of my identity – no fool her – then answered me readily enough. She and her family had moved in about eighteen months before, four months after the Souths had sold. No, there had been no building work done before they moved in, and nor had any been needed. She was certain of that because she and her husband had known about the chalk problem in Costhorpe, and had commissioned a full survey.

Keylocks had been the selling agents. They had recommended a surveyor, and very good he had been.

Yes, Keylocks would know their surveyors. Keylocks would know all kinds of things about their surveyors.

I thanked her, and took her name so I could pass it on to the police. Then I unlocked my bike from the nearest lamp post, feeling sick. At two o'clock on a Friday afternoon Bill Baxter had got as far as I'd got now; and not long afterwards he had been dead down a chalk mine.

It was wearing onto the evening rush hour, so it was just as well I had my bike and could freewheel past the inner-ring-road jam of cars. By a quarter to five I was at Costhorpe Central Police Station; but Ted Zahler wasn't. Detective Constable Sunley came down to the front office and told me Ted had been working all night, and had gone home an hour before.

I didn't want to tell Sunley. Assuming nobody else had yet reached the point I'd reached, I wanted Ted to know first. He'd understand most readily; and I wanted him to get the credit. Even if he'd gone to bed, he surely wouldn't mind being woken to be told something as vital as this.

I'd phone him from City Hall, I decided. It was only a few yards away, so that wouldn't cost much time. I hared round two corners, up the flight of steps at the front of City Hall, up again to the Members' Room, and fumbled the digital lock on the door.

It swung open to reveal Rex Canning sitting by the phone, coat off, grey-suited, a cup of tea by his elbow. I cursed to myself as I fell breathlessly against the inside.

'Such drama,' Rex said. 'Late again, Erica? Very late, I assume, because I've been here ten minutes, and I haven't seen anyone waiting impatiently for you.'

'Maybe I was running to meet you,' I said tartly.

'Why would you do that?'

He said this in his most irritating faux-naive manner, and I scowled. I'd been too keyed-up to watch my words, but this wasn't the time for silly flirtations. I said, 'You told me you were going to nose around the Bill Baxter case – and that worried me, Rex.'

'Relax, I haven't discovered much yet.'

That was a relief. I thought of telling him I'd cracked the scam myself, but I knew I couldn't afford such an indulgence. The police would still have to prove a connection between the subsidence racket and Bill's death; and for all I knew there were others – maybe Council insiders, Tories or otherwise – involved along with the Keylocks.

I'd got my breath back, so I went over to the kettle and checked to see if Rex had left enough water for another cup of tea. He hadn't. I thought about going along the corridor to refill it, and decided to empty the coffee pot instead. It yielded me an inch and a half of smelly black mud. 'I'd like to make a phonecall,' I said as casually as I could.

'Feel free.'

'In private.'

'I should be gone within ten minutes.'

'Waiting for someone?'

'Yes, Fred Keylock.'

I nearly dropped my coffee cup.

'I said relax,' Rex said drily.

'I know you did, thank you. Why are you waiting for Keylock?'

'He's going to enlighten me about subsidence and related topics. I spent the afternoon reading up Baxter's chalk mine survey, and now I've some questions I want answered.'

'By Fred?'

'Exactly. Jack'll damn me for it, but I reckoned he was the best choice. He's got the connection with Flint Hill, and a lifetime's professional knowledge.'

'Rex,' I said as steadily as I could, 'please don't.'

'I'm aware you'd rather I left it all to nice Inspector Zahler, but I'm not prepared to do that, Erica. Not until the police let Jack off the hook.'

'I... think they will.'

'I'll make sure they do,' Rex coolly corrected me. 'You've gone white, Erica.'

'Rex, this is important. You mustn't talk to Keylock. It could be dangerous. Please believe me.'

'I'm flattered you should be so concerned for my safety, but there's absolutely no need. Even if Fred and I solve the whole mystery over a drink, the murderer's hardly likely to walk up to us in The Dove. Anything I discover I'll tell your friend, so there's nothing to get worked up about.'

'I'm serious, Rex. You'll be messing up police enquiries if you talk to Fred.'

'You'll have to do better than that, Erica. I know perfectly well the police have already interviewed him.'

'I'm begging you, and I wouldn't do that unless —'

I stopped at this point, because there was a knock at the door. 'That's probably him,' Rex said with a glance at his watch. 'Deeply punctual, unlike some of us.' He strode over and opened the door to Fred Keylock's portly figure and red face. 'Evening, Fred; good of you to come over. You know Councillor Massen?'

A glance at Keylock, and I'd had to look down at my cup. I could hear it rattling on the saucer, and I put it carefully next to the kettle as Keylock said gruffly, 'More or less.'

'You could join us, Erica,' Rex said lightly. 'Allay your worries, broaden your mind. I'll buy you a g and t – unrepeatable offer.'

'I... have to make a phone call.'

'She's worried about the Labour Whip,' Rex said to Keylock. 'Apparently he gets suspicious if any of his troops show signs of believing us Tories are human. Well, far be it from us to compromise your political integrity. I'll see you anon.'

With which stroke of deathless wit, he and a probable murderer walked out together for a cosy drink.

Galloping gorillas. What would Rex say to Keylock? Tell me, Fred, can you imagine why Bill Baxter had a growing obsession with miscellaneous cases of unproven subsidence? And what would Fred say? Let's go for a walk in a dark alley, Councillor Canning, and I'll tell you all about it?

I could hardly still my hand enough to turn the pages in my Council diary, find Ted's number which I'd written in and punch it out on the phone. It rang first time, and I stood listening to it, urging Ted to wake up and answer, trying to breathe deeply so I'd be in a state to tell him all when he did.

He answered on the eleventh ring. I won't say I was calm, but I managed to put across my story. Ted asked a question or two, then said, 'It fits. It's not proof of murder yet, but it's enough to justify bringing those two in. Is it just Fred who's with Canning?'

'Unless they're meeting Miles, and Rex didn't say they were.'

'I'll get over there as soon as I can. Now go home, love, and I'll call you later.'

Go home? Leaving Rex and Keylock head to head? The Dove was a hundred yards down the road, and although I didn't know where Ted lived, I assumed it was a lot farther away than that. Nor did I trust him to ring the station immediately and send someone over; at least, if they did, it would be an idiot like Sunley.

I knew he'd be furious if he arrived at The Dove to find me installed, but I couldn't jeopardise Rex Canning's safety for the sake of my romantic prospects. No, I was needed at The Dove, right away.

I would have run, but I didn't want to arrive breathless and have Keylock wonder why. So I walked fast, although not fast enough to keep the hundred yards from feeling like ten miles.

I knew The Dove, although I'd only rarely been inside: it's a smallish pub, and had recently been done up in a romanticised public bar style with a polished wood floor, no-nonsense tables, framed adverts on the walls and lots of dark green paint. I saw Rex and Keylock as soon as I came in. They were sitting a couple of tables from the door, part-drunk gin-and-tonics in front of them, like any couple of businessmen enjoying a drink after work.

Rex was facing me, but he was leaning over to talk to Keylock, and I had to come right up to them before he noticed me.

'Oh, Erica,' he said limply, and rose to his feet.

I forced a smile. 'Do you mind if I take you up on your offer, Rex?'

'An unexpected pleasure, but you're welcome, naturally. What'll you have?'

'Bitter'll do.'

'Ah, a beer-drinking woman,' Fred Keylock said. I couldn't bring myself to sit next to him, so I took the empty chair next to the one Rex had vacated to go to the bar. 'That's the rule among socialists, is it?'

'We believe in free choice, Fred. We just have different ideas to the Tories about how to achieve it.' I was prepared to block between him and Rex, but not to charm him. Nor, in spite of the florid bonhomie, did he seem at all pleased that I'd joined them.

'So you're... on the Planning Committee?' he asked.

'That's right.' This conversation was limping, and we were both glancing over to see how Rex was faring at the bar.

Fortunately there was no queue, and a moment later he returned with my drink. He reclaimed his seat and said briskly, 'You'll forgive me if I don't go back over the territory we've just covered, Erica – you've a fair idea what I'm getting at, anyway. Fred, I know you say there isn't, but let's assume there is another source of information on the chalk mines. Maybe someone has an old map which tells them exactly where the mines are.'

This sounded safely off-target, so I breathed a little easier as Keylock said, 'All right, they'd know where to avoid – but it isn't on, Rex. First of all, there ain't no map. I should know, I've lived in Costhorpe all my life, and I've investigated the mines as much as anyone has. And if there was...'

'How'd you gain out of it?' Rex said. 'Good question. Let's say... this is an idea to get us started... you go to someone whose house is on the route of the mine, and tell them you're thinking of showing the map to the Argus.

'Blackmail?' I put in.

'Yes. As a hypothesis. It'd work, wouldn't it? Come to that, if there wasn't a map you could fake one.'

Obviously Rex had an unsuspected talent for shady dealing. I liked it. It was wrong, but I liked it.

Keylock evidently didn't, to judge by his frown. Why had he come? I wondered. He must have known what sort of questions Rex would ask. Maybe he hadn't dared refuse.

'Okay,' he said, 'it's logical, but it's wrong, mate. There's no one in Costhorpe who'd do anything like that. Rex, you know most of the property agents in Costhorpe. Come on, you can't tell me you think Percy Grey or Phil Barringer's going to go around with some faked-up map like Robinson Crusoe.'

'Captain Hook,' I said.

Keylock and Rex both ignored me. 'Now Rex,' Keylock went on, 'if you want a motive for bumping off that poor engineer, you're on a hiding to nothing looking at estate agents. You ask me, the police already know those druggies did it. Maybe they haven't got the evidence yet, but they know it, you mark my words.'

The door opened, and in came Ted. I saw Rex look up, so I said quickly, 'Ah, it's a friend of mine. D'you mind if I have him join us?' I stood up to greet Ted, and took the opportunity to kick Rex hard under the table.

I was expecting surprise and/or anger, but Ted was too well trained to show them. I saw a flicker in his eyes, no more. And Rex, to do him justice, read my message and produced nothing more telling than a faint frown as I introduced Ted by his first name only.

I could have done without the frown; and I thought Ted could have dredged up a bit of enthusiasm in greeting Rex. Assuming he wasn't going to bring out the handcuffs until we got Keylock alone, he'd have to pretend for a while that this was a matey drink after work.

Why couldn't they both act more friendly, I wondered, irritated? Rex wasn't pretending not to have recognised Ted, he was simply behaving as if he didn't like the man. In fact, now I thought about it, he'd behaved that way ever since I'd first introduced them at the police station. Your pretty little inspector, etcetera – heavens, was Rex jealous?

Conceivable, I had to admit. I'd almost forgotten about Rex kissing me, but maybe he hadn't. Maybe he'd even had ideas of doing it again, until he'd realised my interest had waned?

It was a ridiculous time to be thinking this. Concentrate, Erica. I turned to Keylock, wondering if he too recognised Ted, but there was no indication of it on the estate agent's red face. And why would he? Ted hadn't been at the public meeting, and Fred would have been questioned at the police station by a constable, not an inspector.

Rex offered, rather grumpily, to buy Ted a drink, and Ted calmly said he'd have a tonic water, thanks. He sat down next to Keylock and gave me a long level look.

No, there wasn't strong anger lurking in it. Reassurance, mostly; at least that's what I read. I felt, in good old-fashioned style, that now the policeman had arrived I had nothing to worry about.

There seemed no danger any more in sitting with Fred Keylock, gossiping about wicked deeds. Instead it was... promising. The police still had to bridge the gap between scam and murder, so why not try to do that now? I began to play with the idea of nudging Keylock towards a confession.

Real Sexton Blake stuff, but what was there to lose? Nothing that I could see, although I suspected Ted might disagree. I told him lightly that Rex, Fred and I had been dreaming up nefarious schemes involving estate agents. 'Really?' he said.

The response was neutral enough for me to take it as permission to push on. Rex had had one amazing idea, I continued, and I'd just thought up one almost as good. I turned to Fred and gave him a smile.

He produced a chortle rather like a washing machine draining. 'Are you and Rex going to make me listen to every property wheeze you can think up? Tell you what, for every story you tell against estate agents, I'll tell you a joke about politicians. Want to bet who'll run out first, ha ha?'

'Ha ha,' I said. 'Fair enough, so long as I get first turn.' I paused, because Rex was returning with Ted's drink, which he plonked down roughly on the table. Don't wreck it, Rex, I wished under my breath. 'How about this? Someone wants to sell a house, and they go to an agent for a valuation. They wouldn't normally have a complete survey done, would they?'

'Not normally, the buyer does that. My turn. What did Bill Clinton say to John Smith? I envy you, you've a safe pair of hands. And what does Smith say? Want a tip – borrow my barber.'

Rex said, 'Erica, what are you...?'

He'd sat down again, and I risked a second kick. 'Jolly good,' I said to Keylock. I barely glanced at Ted before turning to Rex. 'It's just an idea I had, Rex – a variation on yours. Fred, isn't it true, though, that the agent gives the seller some general advice? How much the place is likely to fetch, how to go about selling, all that kind of thing?'

Keylock's eyes swivelled from me to Rex to Ted, sitting silently next to him. Back to me. I could see his flabby face stiffening, but he manoeuvered it into a smile. 'That's the idea, love. We're the pros, we know the market, but that's not a survey. How about this one?

Knock knock, who's there? Karl. Karl Marx? No, Karl up and die, the revolution's over.'

Ted gave a polite snort of laughter.

Maybe I could do it. I could feel my adrenalin building up. Mustn't let it sprint away with me. Must concentrate, must look casual. Must smile at Keylock's appalling joke.

'You'll have to save them up, Fred,' I said, 'or you'll run out before I do. Give me a chance to sketch this scheme out to you. Okay, the agent gives an opinion. Let's say he says, you've got a dodgy one here. This here's a chalk mine area, and that means trouble. Any lender's going to demand a full survey, and chances are it'll say, uh-oh, subsidence risk.'

'They don't always,' Keylock said. 'You politicians overrate this chalk mine business. People buy houses in Costhorpe every day. Now Rex, you'll like this one: a woman socialist goes to a pawnbroker and says, what'll you give me for this here? He says, what is it, love? And she says, it's new, unused – hey, get this – it's Labour's ban the bomb policy.'

'What would you give for that?' Ted said to me. 'Two thousand cases of leukaemia? Ten Chernobyls?'

'What're you, another bloody socialist?'

I'd annoyed Keylock. Glee bubbled inside me. I smiled back at Ted, and said lightly, 'All the best men are. No, seriously, Fred, let's assume this agent does say that.'

Rex was looking at me oddly, but Keylock seemed to have regained his self-control. He even produced a facsimile of a smile. 'So what's wrong with that?' he asked. 'If there's a risk we have to mention it, because we need to cover ourselves. We like to sell houses too, mind, so we try and find a happy medium. Now there's a story about John Smith and a parrot, I'm just trying to remember —'

I leaned farther across the table. 'But this agent, this imaginary agent, ignores the happy medium. He's not so bothered about selling, his aim is to build up the risk. He gets the sellers worried, and no wonder: maybe they want to sell fast, they're moving to a different city, and they can see it's not going to happen. Even if they find a potential buyer they're likely to have the sale fall through. Maybe they'll have to get a survey done themselves, and it'll cost them hundreds. Maybe they'll have to underpin the house. That'll mean months of delay, bridging loans, insurance won't cover all the costs, and buyers are wary about underpinned properties, so even afterwards it won't be so easy to sell.'

My eyes were on Keylock: I didn't dare look at Rex or Ted. Fred still had an affable look, but it was growing decidedly strained. 'What is this?' he asked.

'It's an idea, Fred, that's all. I'm doing the same as Rex was doing, trying to work out a scam involving chalk mines. I'm getting there, if you'll just be patient. I'll laugh at your Smith joke afterwards. So far we've got a seller who wants to sell, and an agent who wants the seller to sell, because how else will he get his commission, but who's going to buy? The agent has the answer. There's this friend of his – no, don't let's say friend, that might sound fishy, let's say, acquaintance – who specializes in buying up subsiding houses. He buys them cheap, of course, then he does whatever work needs doing and sells them on at a profit.'

I paused. Ted and Rex were silent, their eyes – like mine – on Keylock. The chatter from the other pub tables was a dull murmur through the filter of my concentration. Keylock's face was growing redder.

'There's nothing wrong with that,' he said. 'Fixing people up: that's a part of business life.'

'Setting people up,' Rex murmured.

I kicked him again. 'So the buyer buys cheap,' I said, 'and the seller moves away. The buyer waits a while; but he doesn't do the underpinning, because he knows it doesn't need doing. He simply puts the house on the market again, at full price; and it'll sell, because it'll have a clean survey. He doesn't just pocket the builder's profit, he pockets the whole difference between the reduced price and the full price – minus a little cut here and there.'

I could see the sweat working through onto Fred's forehead. 'It's neat,' he said, after a strained silence. 'Never heard of it happening, mind, but I suppose it could. Hey, I remembered the punch line.'

It was an act of kindness to make him save his joke, because none of us were about to laugh. 'It's almost foolproof, isn't it?' I said. 'Even if a seller finds out, what'll they think? They'll curse themselves for not getting a second opinion, not paying out for a proper survey. They might suspect they were done, but how can they prove it? The builder hit lucky, that's what they'll say to themselves. What they can't know is, the builder hits lucky every time.'

'You want to watch it love, you'll put ideas in my head.'

I went on fast. 'But what if this happens? The sellers don't want to waste good money on a survey, but they do want a second opinion, so they phone the City Engineer and ask if there's any evidence of chalk mines in their area. The structures man in the Engineer's Department says no, not around that street; it's odd for anyone to have suggested there might be. Maybe the sellers will get a survey done then; maybe they'll just move to a different agent. The scam won't go through, but the engineer will know that an estate agent gave a strange piece of advice.

'Now imagine time passing – two years, three? The engineer comes across quite a few cases where people have been given strange advice. He gets curious. He starts to go back and ask who gave the strange advice – and what a surprise, it was almost always the same agent. He starts to ask himself, is that agent really such a lousy judge of subsidence risks, or could there be another reason? Then he starts to discover an answer.'

Keylock said hoarsely, 'Even if it happened – which it didn't, not in Costhorpe – that wouldn't be illegal.'

Ted said, 'Show a sustained pattern, and a jury would see it as evidence of fraud.'

'And even if they didn't,' I added, 'it'd be enough to destroy the estate agent. It'd finish his business, wreck his reputation, get him drummed out of the Rotary Club.'

The table hummed with tension. Keylock broke it. He put back his shoulders and said, 'It's an interesting theory you got there, love. Not a thing to do with the Flint Hill business, but worth thinking about. Rex, you ready for another drink?'

I glanced at Rex, and Rex looked back at me. 'Wait till I've finished,' I said. I turned back to Keylock.

He'd stood, but he couldn't leave the table, because Ted was sitting outside him. I said, 'There's a couple called Harry and Molly South, good friends of mine who used to live at forty-two Ranmoor Villas. They went to an agent who told them their house was subsiding, and on his advice they sold it to Grendon Builders for sixty-five thousand. Grendon sold on to the Drinkwaters four months later for seventy-four nine fifty, and in between they didn't drill a hole or lift a spade. I know Allen and Sara Denton pretty well, too. When the same agent told them their house was subsiding, they checked with Bill Baxter. More than a few people did that. Bill drew up a list of them, then he started to check out the cases on the list more carefully.'

Rex said, ‘So that’s the paper the police took from the Engineer’s Department.’

‘Not quite.’ It was Ted who answered him. ‘That’s the paper Gary Temperley hid. We’ve asked him about it, and he’s given us some interesting answers.’

‘What the —’ Keylock started; and stopped.

‘Detective Inspector Zahler of North Anglia CID,’ Ted calmly went on. ‘Of course that’s only the motive, then there’s the opportunity. There’s Jack Wells’ evidence about running into you and your son at the bottom of Flint Hill on Friday afternoon. It’s strange that you both told us you were in Cromer that afternoon. There’s also the forensic evidence: the plastic sheet, the suitcase fastener, the rope which you bought in Hallams on —’

‘I never bought that rope! That was there already, we just – ‘

I was last on my feet, after Ted, after Rex. Unlike Rex, I didn’t cut round to the far side of the pub table: no need, when he and Ted were already blocking Fred Keylock’s way.

‘Maybe,’ said Ted, ‘we should continue this interview at the police station.’

29

I WAS euphoric until Rex and I left Ted and Keylock at the police station. It was only as we stood watching them disappear through the glass double doors that I thought: that man is a murderer. That I remembered Bill Baxter, the anguish on his wife's face at his funeral, Sheila in hospital and all the rest.

It had grown dark and was starting to drizzle. There were demons in the shadows, and tremors in my legs.

'I'll buy you a brandy,' Rex said brusquely. 'Then I'll take you home.'

It was Ted I needed, but I wasn't ungrateful. For a moment I thought of letting him do just that. But I'd got my bike; and tomorrow we would be rivals again.

So I said thanks but no thanks, and rode home alone. I made myself a cup of cocoa and played Cosi Fan Tutti. I thought of phoning Allie, thought of phoning my mum. But everyone could wait.

As did I, for almost a day – till three the following afternoon. He didn't phone, he came round in person, bringing roses and the smile that made my heart turn over. For a while we both forgot Bill Baxter, the Keylocks, Flint Hill and everything except each other.

Later, over coffee in my living room, he told me all the things I hadn't known. I wanted to believe it had been an awful accident, not that I'd drunk in The Dove with a psychopath, and Ted said, to my relief, that that was how he thought it had been. Both Keylocks had claimed they hadn't intended to kill Bill, and his death had carried all the marks of an unpremeditated crime.

I learned that Bill had not only spoken to Sara Denton, he'd contacted at least two more of the people on his list that fatal Friday afternoon. One of his contacts, an elderly woman, had phoned Fred Keylock to ask what was going on, and Fred had got Miles to ask Bill to come and talk to him at home.

Bill had presumably realised what the Keylocks wanted to talk about – although they had used the Flint Hill situation as an excuse, and asked him to Miles' house even though it was in the exclusion zone – but he had been excited, anxious to confront them, and hardly expecting violence in Costhorpe on a quiet Friday afternoon.

So he had gone to number four Flint Hill; and being the man he was, had refused the Keylocks' invitation to accept a rake-off. What had happened next we'd maybe never know, except that it had ended with Bill falling and knocking his head on the marble fire surround in Miles Keylock's grey-painted front room.

Ted told me that Fred had claimed Miles had struck the blow, Miles claimed it was Fred. However it had happened, both had left the body at number four and gone to the public meeting, hoping that together with their fictitious trip to Cromer it would provide them with an alibi.

They had obviously had an informative but disturbing evening, since they had discovered that the search for the doors would lead to Miles' house being investigated, perhaps the very next morning. They had panicked, knowing that at all costs they must remove the body that night. So they had hidden up in Miles' house after the meeting, and at two am, when the exclusion zone was dark and silent, they had lugged the corpse across to number thirty-three.

Oh yes, a policeman had been on duty – two, in fact, Ted told me grimly. But I knew for myself how difficult it could be to find a policeman in an area that was supposedly 'crawling' with them. It hadn't been difficult for the Keylocks to wait until the two had made a rendezvous at the top of the hill.

Steve's friends hadn't phoned the police – yet – or left a message on my answering machine, but it seemed their story was true. Miles had been to investigate the hole that lunchtime, purely out of curiosity, and had found the rope tied to the scaffolding. He had decided it was dangerous to leave it there, so he had untied it and taken it home. When he and Fred were arguing how to dispose of the body, they had thought of the rope – and how its discovery would lead the police along the wrong trail.

As would putting the corpse down the mine, when everyone was thinking about the doors and their owners; as might the roof fall – at least, it would make it harder to identify the fatal blow. They had tied the body up just as Rex and I had guessed, Miles had gone down the shaft, and Fred had lowered it to him. Then Fred had followed him down – Fred had sweated buckets recalling this, Ted said – and they had carried the corpse to a suitable spot. A heave with a car-wrench – of course Miles possessed one, as so many men do – had brought down the roof, and they had cleared off fast.

'So it was just the two of them,' I said.

Ted shrugged. 'Most likely no one else was involved in Bill's death, but several people must have known about the scam. The builder was in the thick of it; in fact, I think we'll find there were several firms of builders involved. Gary Temperley also knew what was going on, at least in outline. The Keylocks became nervous when Baxter started his chalk mine research, and they got Temperley to keep an eye on him.'

'I don't understand why a young man like that would...'

'It's easy, love. Start with a drink, work up to a lunch, a free holiday... it doesn't take a villain. Men turn with no trouble if you're patient and they're greedy. Maybe Temperley wasn't even consciously greedy; just eager for contacts and influence, and flattered that they were taking an interest in him. I doubt he did much, until after the murder. I have a suspicion he was the one who burgled your house, although we may not be able to prove it. And when you came into the office and started asking questions about the chalk mine survey, he panicked and took the summary sheets. He didn't dare to steal the rest.'

'By then,' I said slowly, 'he must have known the Keylocks were the killers.'

'He must have suspected; that's all we'll be able to prove. It's easy to say he should have told us, love; but people often don't in his situation. He knew he'd lose his job if it all came out, and that's a powerful reason for staying silent. Gary'll suffer out of this. He didn't strike a blow, probably didn't gain very much, but there's enough against him to see that he never works in local government again.'

'How about the rest of the department?' And how about the councillors, I added to myself? It made me even more queasy to think that some of us might have been involved.

Ted said, 'I doubt if David North knew a thing. Both the Keylocks and Temperley are adamant that he wasn't involved. He didn't keep much of an eye on the structures section, but that's a management issue, not a crime; and he discouraged Baxter from pursuing his research, but I can't see a sinister motive behind that. It seems all Bill's colleagues thought he was potty for putting in so much effort on the subsidence survey.'

Hadn't known, or hadn't wanted to know, I wondered? Maybe it had been a combination of both. It takes a special kind of person to look in directions which might uncover corrupt dealings.

Ted went on, 'I have a feeling Wells knew more than he's letting on, but I doubt it goes as far as direct involvement in the scam. Much the same's true of Yelland. There's work to do still on tying up the ends, but at this stage I don't expect us to charge either of them; and Sheila Brennan's also in the clear so far.'

'I rang the hospital today.'

'You've seen her?'

I shook my head. 'The nursing staff said it would be okay for me to speak to her, but she refused to come to the phone. She barely knows me, Ted, and she's the kind to lick her wounds alone. Maybe in time...'

'You want her to cry to you?'

'Wouldn't you, in my place?'

He didn't reply. But he was a man who understood what it was to care about others, and I reckoned the unspoken answer was yes.

I THOUGHT of having a word with Patty Fowler, and asking her to make sure the Argus didn't mention my name. But I didn't do it, and when I picked up the paper at Allie and Phil's that evening I found I needn't have worried: neither Rex nor I featured in *'Two Men Charged with Chalk Mine Murder'*.

Maybe that was Rex's doing; at least, at the next Planning Committee Patty and Rex sat side by side again. They exchanged a lot of glances and a couple of very private smiles, and I decided that although Rex might briefly have been miffed at me, he sure hadn't been heartbroken. Nick grumbled at the thought of his getting even cosier with Patty, but I didn't care much: there's more to life than a paragraph in the Costhorpe Argus, as Ted and I were busily proving.

Most of the things we do as councillors never get a mention anyway; but some people are grateful, and not always the predictable ones. When the Buntings moved into a three-bedroom terrace on Blenheim Way I got a thank-you card from Mandy and Graham, with a scrawl by Ben on the cover. Ted was pleased with the Buntings, too: Graham had come clean about the antiques he and James Dunbury had hauled out of the chalk mine in the two days following the collapse.

Where they'd gone, though, Graham couldn't say; and with no proof, Ted wouldn't have a hope of making a charge stick. Nor could he do much with lying in the course of a police investigation or staying overnight in an exclusion zone – as the Dunburys must have done, since no other explanation fitted. I wished James wouldn't walk away untouched, but it's men like James Dunbury who always do.

Ted was philosophical about it. He'd got his murderers, and some information that could prove useful in future; he said he'd seen cases turn out worse.

Waking to a yellow morning, sitting up in bed and watching him sleeping, it occurred to me that I hadn't done too badly either.